After leading a pretty staid and frankly boring life Drusilla Montgomery lands the job of her dreams . . . working as an assistant to her all time forever favorite romance writer, Gabrielle George. Gabrielle's assistant, Justin Hunt, is also a slice of Dru's dreams — tall, dark, handsome and with a nice set of pecs and buns. Night after night they work side by side, answering fan mail, proofreading manuscripts and keeping up the famed author's social media sites.

For Dru this is more than a job. With the death of her strict and controlling mother — a woman very much like the starchy housekeeper in a dark gothic — Dru finally has a chance to pursue the life of her own dreams. Traveling from the sleepy cities of Marin County, California over the Golden Gate bridge to Gabrielle's Victorian seems like entering an entire new world. Like the fog lifting over San Francisco bay, Dru's life takes on new color. Even when her mother reaches out from the grave in the guise of her attorney who threatens to take her home from her, Dru remains undaunted.

As she gets deeper into the job, however, questions are raised about her oh so handsome co-worker — Justin. He is never seen in daylight, he doesn't eat and there are no mirrors in the elegant Victorian they work in. Is she working with a vampire or just a guy with a quirky personality? And . . . if he is a vampire, is Dru ready to say bite me?

The Secret
Copyright © 2020 Regan Taylor
ISBN: 978-1-4874-2892-1
Cover art by Martine Jardin

Published by eXtasy Books Inc or
Devine Destinies, an imprint of eXtasy Books Inc

Look for us online at:
www.eXtasybooks.com or www.devinedestinies.com

THE SECRET

BY

REGAN TAYLOR

DEDICATION

To Vanessa — there will never be a way to truly thank you for the best job of my life.

PROLOGUE

Have you ever wanted to change your life? Not just the paint on the walls or change the color of your hair, but your entire life?

To become someone entirely new and different?

Drusilla Montgomery wanted to.

Desperately.

More than any other dream, she wanted not only to simply change her life but to become someone entirely new and different, like a butterfly breaking free of its cocoon. In her humdrum life on an oak shaded street in a small town in Marin County, California, it wasn't likely to happen . . . but in the pages of her books, the tomes she snuck into the house on Clark Lane, she became whoever she wanted, whenever she wanted. With the turn of each page, she became someone new and exciting who lived far away from Clark Lane.

She wanted to wake up one morning and find herself with a whole new life.

Then one night, her life did change.

Maybe.

CHAPTER ONE

Dashing out of work promptly at 5 p.m., Drusilla Montgomery hurried to her car, her very practical gray Honda Civic with a simple AM radio. It was the car her mother, Martha, chose for her and never one to dispute, at least outwardly, what Martha wanted or suggested, Dru complied. Martha would have flipped if she knew where her otherwise obedient daughter was off to tonight.

But Martha could no longer object to or interfere with anything her daughter wanted. This was now Dru's life and only Dru's.

Carefully turning on her turn signal, Dru pulled out of the Midland Savings & Loan parking lot and headed toward the 101 freeway. With glee she pushed down on the gas pedal and let the car hit its cruising speed in seconds. She drew in a deep breath, closed her eyes for a moment and gave into the spark of imagination that it wasn't a dark, hard plastic steering wheel in her hands but the throttle of a spaceship taking her to another world, another life. One where all her dreams would come true.

It would darken soon on this crisp, late fall night, but before then the sky would be painted in the vivid violets and blues she so loved. Tonight the green of the hills of Marin melded with that pallet of color, creating an array of color any artist would envy.

Fog, like a thick, downy, white comforter, greeted her as she approached the Golden Gate Bridge. When she pulled out of the Waldo Tunnel, now known as the Robin Williams

Tunnel, Dru laughed to herself, "Well the old saying certainly is true ... Don't like the weather? Wait five minutes. It'll change. Well I'll take that as an omen. My life is going to change tonight. It is definitely going to change. I just know it."

Racing across the Golden Gate Bridge, she drank in the sight of the fog as it sat like a silent sentinel over the ocean with its fairy-like tendrils reaching into the avenues. Letting that bit of her imagination out, the part she kept hidden from her mother for so long, Dru wondered if somehow, beyond the fog, something wonderful awaited.

Off the coast, beneath the rocky cliffs of San Francisco's Seaside neighborhood, Mile Rocks appeared to hang in the clouds, miles above the earth, rather than being an offshore beacon meant to warn ships of danger as they passed under the Golden Gate on their journey into the Bay. Looking out over the railing of the bridge, she likened the fog to the fabric that is San Francisco. Like magic, its damp grayness cast a spell over all that enter the City by the Bay. By land, sea or air, it greeted each visitor, wrapped them in its damp caress before its tentacles dug in and held on long after you have moved on. Like the detectives of old, the fictional Sam Spade and those of his ilk, anyone who has walked the City's streets when the fog is low to the ground, threading itself around their ankles, it entrances them with its promise. No one can deny its pull.

Then, in the blink of an eye, it dissipates, leaving all in the stark light of day, only to return when it is ready. Then, and only then — when it is ready — does it come again. Like a living thing, the fog becomes one with those who venture into its fold.

San Francisco's fog can be bone-chilling cold. The kind of cold that you never quite warm up from. Not quite the cold sterility of death. No, something else, something more, yet at the same time, indefinable. It is part icy blast that chills to the very marrow of your soul and part safe cocoon.

The fog does that. The fog and the silent toll of the bell at a lighthouse. Sterile, cold, like an ice tomb. Yet at the same time, there is a security to its depths. A feeling of safety in the anonymity its gray embrace can give you.

Her heart beating a tad faster in anticipation of what was to come, Dru headed along Park Presidio toward Golden Gate Park and into the Haight where Gabrielle George's Victorian sat. A full moon rose above the clouds casting a mystical glow to the ground below. It cast the park in a surreal aspect and she half expected to see a vampire or werewolf peek out from the trees flanking the street. The lights from the Asian Art Museum filtered through, giving the area an alien-like landscape. Rather than scare Dru, it mesmerized her. The tendrils of fog surrounding her car were akin to bathing it and marking her for something new and exciting.

"Okay, Drusilla Montgomery, time to reign in that imagination of yours and get your clear-thinking head in place because you really want this job."

A few minutes later she pulled in front of the rather imposing Victorian owned by her most favorite author of all time, Gabrielle George. *Wow, plenty of parking out front here. How odd is that?* Not wanting to look a gift horse . . . or parking space . . . in the mouth, she parked right in front of Gabrielle George's Painted Lady. Moonlight winked in and out between the trees as Dru exited the car. A chilled breeze came up and traveled up her legs, caressing them. "Definitely the makings of a scary gothic romance," she muttered to herself.

She double-checked the address and walked along the knee-high, black, wrought iron fence to the gate leading into the yard. As she pushed it open, it squeaked as if no one had passed through it for many years. Without warning, the moon disappeared behind a wall of fog creating a scene that only

San Franciscans can appreciate — dense fog on one side of the street; blue-gray moonlight on the other.

A dry, dead leaf bounced along the walk momentarily startling her. It scraped on the pavement, unnaturally loud, in the otherwise quiet evening. She glanced up and down the street, surprised that not another soul was out and about. No cars drove by, no birds chirped in nearby trees. It was as if time had stopped the moment she crossed the boundary past the creaking gate.

She paused at the foot of the Victorian's dark wooden steps, painted to a gloss so high you could see each rung despite the darkness, and gazed up at the front door. Dim light filtered out of the entry hallway inside the house. Framing either side were stained glass mosaics of purple and blue flowers nestled among dark green leaves. At the inner corners were the likenesses of fluffy black cats with orange eyes. Potted plants sat on either side of the door, just inside the frame created by the stained glass.

Above the door was another breathtaking piece of stained glass. This one depicted a full moon looming over yet another black cat.

Dru jumped at a scraping sound skittering up the pathway. Relieved to see it was only another leaf traveling on its way, she released the breath she didn't know she'd been holding. Oddly, still no cars traversed the street. Aside from the leaf's scraping and the slight whistle of wind, not a sound was to be heard.

She tilted her head back to take in the entire form of the Victorian with its Gingerbread trim. In the dim light she saw a woman sitting at an upper window, gazing out. Was that Gabrielle George? Gazing out the garret window waiting for her interviewee's arrival?

She stepped back to take a better look and in that instant, the woman in the window disappeared, like a ghost, leaving

Dru to doubt if she'd seen her at all. Well, she'd be meeting the famed author soon.

Drawing in a deep breath, she started up the stairs and reached for the bell.

Before she could even touch it, the heavy wooden door creaked partway open and revealed a dark, gaping hallway.

She peered in. "Hello?"

Silence.

"Hello? Is anyone there?"

CHAPTER TWO

A surreal feeling of the past, present and future whirling around her as she stood in the open entry, caused Dru to pause. She gasped in recognition of what brought her here to this place, this moment in time . . . her hopes, her dreams — the things she wanted for herself that had been denied to her until she'd picked up the phone a mere two days ago and made that call. She had a sense that the moment she walked through the portal before her, everything she wanted for herself, rather than what was demanded of her, would finally come into being. What drove her to finally seek what would make her happy was here. Now. In a distant part of her mind, despite the passage of years, so many years, she could hear that voice, her mother's shrill screech, "I wanted a little girl! Is that too much to ask?"

If she crossed the threshold, would it be to another life? A happier life? Or would her mother's words that she was a failure, that she was lacking, said so many times, prove true?

As if watching someone else's story unfold, in her mind's eye, the memory of herself as a vulnerable five-year-old froze her in place and kept her from walking through the door . . .

Underneath the faded blue car, five-year-old Dru looked over at her dad and smiled. It wasn't the first time she and her father shared a private oh so quiet chuckle, at her mother's proclamations. Martha couldn't help it. She was, after all, a product of her times. At least that's what Dru's dad told her time and again. Even at the tender age of five, Dru'd heard her mother lament more times than she could count how she always wanted a little girl. No faux paint splattered rompers for little Drusilla. Oh no. Even as a tiny tot she was dressed in frilly dresses and pristine white sox with delicate lace around the tops. If Martha dressed her in leggings they were a soft pink, pale green or other feminine looking pastel. And every chance Dru got, she toddled off to whatever her father was up to. What daddy did was far more interesting than anything her mother had in mind.

Her Father, Frank Montgomery, was a mechanic. A bus mechanic and as such he came home with grease beneath his fingernails – he washed up before he left work and showered again at home, but it was the nature of his job. To hear him tell it, he enjoyed what he did. Despite the seemingly mundane life of fixing bus engines, working on the brakes, changing tires, he always had a funny story to tell each night when he got home.

Martha was never interested in hearing Frank's stories.

Dru, on the other hand, loved to sit by her dad listening to the details of his day.

So there they were on a bright Easter Sunday and her dad wanted to check the brakes on her mom's car. Never one to miss out on time with her dad, Dru climbed right under the car with him. He was in the middle of explaining how a certain part connected to another when Martha found them.

"What the hell are you doing?" Martha yelled loud enough for the neighbors four doors down to hear. "I swear, you aren't normal. Drusilla Montgomery, get out from under there. Now! Frank, what do you think you are doing making a grease monkey out of my daughter?"

"Dru climbed under and . . ." he wearily tried to explain.

"Of course she did. Why can't you do these things when she's not around? Or tell her no? I swear you do this to me on purpose. My pressure! My blood pressure! All I ever wanted was a little girl."

Dru smiled at her dad once again. Her mother always ranted about her blood pressure, whatever that was.

He winked back at her, and she slid out from under the car.

"Drusilla, look at you. Just look at you. Your dress is ruined. Just ruined." Martha swatted at the skirt of her dress.

Dru looked down. There was a small grease spot on the hem — nothing that wouldn't come out in the laundry. Whatever was her mother's problem? Why couldn't she be a little girl and learn something practical at the same time?

As she grew up, school was a challenge for her. Not because she didn't enjoy learning. In fact she maintained a straight A average without having to work too hard at it. It was because of the rules dictated by her mother and having to squelch her dreams into a secret place in her mind.

In junior high and high school, sports were fun . . . but her mother signed her up for girlie sewing. Although . . . with a little help from her dad . . . she managed to sneak onto the T-ball team.

As she grew older, despite Martha's best attempts to girl-ify her, Dru found more exciting things to do like horseback riding and skating. Oh there was girlie type figure skating and then there was speed skating. Even better, she took her allowance and with her dad's blessing and assistance, she joined the horseback riding club. When the club prepared to name her horsewoman of the year, Dru declined — her mother would never have understood. The drama at home would have gone on for days and it just wasn't worth it.

But it was in her books, her stories, the world shifted for Dru. While Martha, a devotee of whatever religion caught her attention, bought up whatever book the church of the week touted, Dru discovered the Empress of Romance, Gabrielle George. It was Gabrielle George's heroines who showed Dru there was more to life than the mundane, gray streaked world her mother built for them and her never-ending laments about wanting a little girl. In those romances there was love and light and romance just waiting outside the fog — if Dru were only brave enough to step through its magical portal. She'd waited a lifetime for that magical portal to find her.

CHAPTER THREE

"In here." A deliciously rich, deep masculine voice that sent tingles down Dru's spine called out from somewhere down the hall.

The kind of voice she'd dreamed of hearing.

The kind of voice Gabrielle George's heroes had.

The kind of voice no one at Midland Savings & Loan had. Ottila Millan, her micro-managing supervisor and close friend of her mother's, had a bit of a lisp and hired only women, generally older women desperate for a job. Then she played favorites with the ones who were most like her. Policies at MS&L meant squat, especially to Ottila. If one behaved with total devotion and adoration, Ottila treated them with a modicum of fairness. If you spoke up about things that weren't fair or were unethical, she'd go after you with a vengeance. Being Martha's daughter saved Dru from Ottila's tantrums on more than one occasion. Unfortunately each . . . save . . . put Dru deeper and deeper under Martha's wing.

Not that she could have flirted with any male employees, if there were any, with her mother or micromanager extraordinaire Ottila standing there on the side, watching every move she made. Between the two of them, Ottila and her mother, Dru depended more and more on the escape her books, those scrumptious romances she snuck into the house and devoured under the covers with the dim glow of a flashlight at night, provided. At times she felt like a secondary limb of her mother's—that she wasn't and would never be her own person with her own feelings and thoughts. If it weren't for her books Dru had no doubt she would have lost her mind big time.

And then she saw the ad; she knew she'd arrived.

Maybe.

She couldn't believe the ad when she'd seen it . . .

San Francisco-based multi-published historical romance author looking for competent assistant. Must have experience with all current computer programs. Confidentiality a must. Ask for Madeline Yellen. Non-readers need not apply.

With her mother dead and buried, this was her chance. Working for Gabrielle George would be a dream come true. Gabrielle George introduced her to love and romance and a world beyond the black and white mendacity of her mother's control.

As soon as she saw the ad, she quickly put together a resume and emailed it. Yesterday, a mere two days later, a woman, the Madeline in the ad, called saying she had a few questions for a pre-interview. Was that a good time? Dru didn't hesitate. "Yes, it's perfect." Murmuring low and keeping an eye on Ottila across the floor of the bank, Dru answered Madeline's questions.

After those well-chosen questions and her careful answers, Madeline confirmed what Dru was already so certain of — the position would be in San Francisco working for Gabrielle George.

She couldn't believe it. Gabrielle George's assistant! In one fell swoop Dru hit the big time. Maybe.

First she had to get the job. If anyone knows Gabrielle George's writing it's me! Me! Me!

To prepare for the interview, she looked over each of the author's books, made note of her favorites and which ones Gabrielle George said were her favorites. Talk about a dream come true.

When her best friend, Haley, told her that there were probably hundreds of applicants and chances are they were just being nice, Dru didn't let it deflate her. "That's the kind of thing my mother would say, Haley." And darn if it didn't feel good to stand up for herself.

"Well it's true," Haley murmured in response.

"And it's also true they called me almost as soon as they got my resume, so give up on trying to burst my bubble. Some best friend you are."

"I'm sorry, Dru. I'm just trying to be realistic. I don't want you to get your hopes up and then be crushed."

"You mean like my mother always did? Like when I'd want to do something and she'd say 'we'll see. I have to think about it' and then every time she'd say no? Like that?"

"Well . . ."

Shoving aside Haley's negative comments and memories of her mother's interference, Dru stepped through the Victorian's doorway, fanciful with the thought that she was crossing into another time. Perhaps even into a century gone by.

Thick, eggshell-colored candles adorned wall sconces every few feet, separated by paintings in heavy gilt frames that lined the long, wood paneled passage. Aubusson runners showed the way to the inner rooms. It was a very Victorian entryway.

"Hello? Ms. George?" Dru called.

"In here." That luscious male voice called out once again from further down the hall. "I'm on the phone. Give me a minute."

She followed the sound of his voice, past what a quick glimpse sure looked like a true Victorian living room, to a room so familiar she was certain someone plucked it from her dreams. Floor to ceiling bookcases lined every wall save the one directly across from the doorway. That wall held a brick fireplace large enough for Dru and several close friends to stand in and not even begin to bump their heads. The bronze-colored fender surrounding it held plush blue velvet-covered cushioned seats wide enough for two people to sit side by side at either end. The crackle of a warm and welcoming fire greeted her as she entered the room. Of course, the room felt so familiar since she'd read every one of Gabrielle's books, especially the ones that took place in Victorian mansions just like this one, over and over. No doubt this room was an inspiration for many of Gabrielle's drawing room scenes.

The wall spaces not covered with books held framed photographs and paintings. A large silver candelabra sat on a side board, the dozen or so tapers in it were lit, cast a soft glow in the room. On one side of the table was a bowl of fresh fruit and a silver tea or coffee service on the other. A plate of croissants sat near the silver service pots. In lieu of lamps, thick, stocky beeswax candles burned brightly on several end tables. A massive desk sat caddy corner to the fireplace. Incongruous to the rest of the room, on top of the desk sat a flat screen monitor, laser jet printer and several other pieces of modern office equipment. Across the room was a smaller desk that also held a computer, printer and telephone.

Take out the computers and their accouterments and the room existed in another century.

" . . . that's right. The end of May . . . no I'm not joking . . . look, Madeline, I need the break. Okay? We've been turning out six a year for the past five years. And we're not talking those 250-300 pagers. We're talking the full-length, 400-500 page books. I need some time for me and I'm going to take it between the end of May and June . . . no, I don't know where I'm going to go or even if I am going to leave town. Maybe I'll just stay home and enjoy my house and all its idiosyncratic issues."

For a moment Dru felt like an interloper. Who was this man and why was he in Gabrielle George's office? Or maybe it wasn't her office but he was the assistant who'd supposedly retired. That was all the agent, Madeline, told her—that the

former assistant had retired and Gabrielle George was looking for a new one. Although, looking at this guy with his back
to her with his shoulder length dark hair, broad shoulders,
pale blue cambric shirt and stone-washed jeans that showed
off an amazing ass, he certainly didn't *appear* near retirement
age.

He was probably ugly as sin.

Then again, given how creepy the neighborhood felt before
she entered the house . . . a slither of chills ran down her spine
at where those thoughts were going. A man who was old
enough to retire but didn't look it? Maybe this was a for real,
living Dorian Gray. Or a vampire who needed to take a time
out and come back under another name?

Or maybe she had read one too many paranormal or gothic
romances.

"Look, someone is here. I'm not negotiating this. It's not
like I'm not giving you plenty of notice. End of May, through
June, I'm off duty . . . I will. I'll talk to you soon . . . Yes, I
promise."

The man turned to her.

He wasn't quite ugly as sin.

The more accurate definition would be sin incarnate.

Dark brows over rich chocolaty brown eyes, straight nose
and lips that a woman could kiss for hours and never need
draw another breath, looked her over. From where she cow-
ered . . . yes it would seem she was cowering because the man
was the epitome of every deliciously scandalously handsome
hero in every romance she'd ever read. His shoulders looked
a mile wide and his shirt did nothing to hide a set of pecs no
cover model could match.

That's it! She mentally snapped her fingers! He had to be
Gabrielle George's inspiration. He was certainly inspiring
her. Had she seen him on the cover of one of Gabrielle's
books?

"And you are?" He finished looking her up and down as he asked the question.

"Ex-excuse me?

"Well you didn't answer to hello so I thought I'd skip to the chase and ask, you are?" He assessed her with a quick look up and down her frame.

He'd said hello to her? "Dru-Dru-Drusilla Montgomery. Ms. George's new assistant." She muttered, "I hope," under her breath.

Mr. Sin-saltional frowned at her.

"Maybe I'd misread the ad," she muttered while beginning to turn away thinking maybe she didn't understand what the agent told her on the phone. Maybe her assistant hadn't retired and she'd only been fanciful, seeing what she wanted to see. After all, Martha imagined things all the time. Why not Dru? Could be a family trait. Or maybe it was a joke someone planted on the online job search list along with a bogus phone call with fake interview questions. *If my mother were still alive it was exactly the kind of mind game she'd play.*

She backed toward the door only to find it closed behind her. Thing was, she didn't remember closing it. The howling sound of the wind on the otherwise still evening didn't help too much at that point either. Across the room a candlestick toppled over.

"*My* new assistant?"

"N-no. Ms. George's. Look, I'm sorry. Clearly I've made a mistake. You see I saw the ad, on the internet list — which of course I should have checked on the Scope or Snope-list to be sure, that she was really looking for a new assistant. Her old one, well not exactly old because I don't know how old she was, so I guess the former one is a better word, retired. I had, I have an appointment but um, I think, that I, uh . . ." Rather than babble any more than she already had, Dru reached for the door handle behind her and tried to quickly and quietly twist it so she could leave the room and flee down that chilling walkway, back into her car and to her safe and secure, albeit boring, bank teller job. With luck, she'd wake in the morning to find out the whole embarrassing situation was only a dream. Although, if she was dreaming about guys like that . . . well he could certainly appear in another dream.

The metal door-knob was cold enough to freeze her hand. And the knob wouldn't move. Her stomach twisted in panic. Across the room, far from either of them, a glass figurine tumbled not far from the candlestick. This time the man glanced over ever so briefly and unfazed by its untimely and unexplained fall, returned his gaze to Dru.

She gazed up into implacable, dark brown eyes of the man who had suddenly appeared next to her at the door and she hadn't seen him move. One second he was at the desk and the next, he stood beside her opening the door. It was the sensation of something slithering between her legs, however, that made her shriek and try to grasp the door handle away from him in a desperate effort to run from the room.

"Vincent, leave the lady alone," the man ordered, albeit with a smile in his voice.

A throaty meow sounded between her legs and a furry black head peered out beneath her knee-length skirt. The room started to spin.

CHAPTER FOUR

"Miss? Are you all right? Miss?"

Dru looked up into those luscious brown eyes and fought the urge to plant a big, fat, wet kiss on those totally sensuous lips. Clearly she'd died and gone to her just rewards. Either that or failing to stop for dinner before coming to the city caused her blood sugar to dive and she was hallucinating big time.

"Miss?"

A longhaired black cat jumped up on her stomach, surprisingly light and gentle given his size. She realized as he . . . or she . . . sat there looking down at her with demon yellow eyes, the cat was mainly fur and actually quite light. She couldn't resist the urge to reach up and pet the silky fur. For longer than she could remember Dru wanted a cat and made a mental note to adopt one of her own as soon as time permitted.

And then mentally shook her head at herself for letting her mind wander.

She looked around, and it appeared the man or someone had placed her on the settee.

Dru cleared her throat. "I'm fine. I'm sorry. That was . . . odd for me. I don't faint at the drop of a hat."

"No worries." He smiled a smile that did funny things to her tummy. Not so much ha ha funny, but that kind of funny the heroines in her books talked about having when they met the man they were destined for. "So, how about we start at the beginning? I'm Justin Hunt and you are?"

"Drusilla Montgomery."

"Good to meet you, Drusilla Montgomery. And you are here for . . ."

"The job. But it looks like I may have made a mistake."

"Job? Oh, oh man, I'm sorry. With everything going on I completely forgot. We're on a deadline and things have been hectic at best." He rose and walked over to the desk, and after fumbling with some papers, located what appeared to be a calendar.

Confused, Dru wondered why he would have told a total, unseen stranger to come on in. But then he did tell the woman on the phone that someone was there, but didn't mention it was an interviewee.

Justin broke into her thoughts and told her, "Yes. You're right. I do have an appointment with you today. For the assistant job." He smiled. "Clearly I need one."

She felt suddenly deflated. Of course Gabrielle George wouldn't hire her own assistant. And with an inspiration like Justin Hunt hanging around her halls, she certainly didn't need Ms. Plainer Jane typing up her books and such.

"Yes. Well I did. But of course I can see . . ."

He cut her off. "How fast can you type?"

"Um, my last test was eighty-five words a minute, with no errors."

"And you know Word and Excel and the other standard office programs?" He glanced down at her resume looking for her keyboarding skills.

"Yes, including the most recent releases of them."

"Great. Have you read any of my . . . Gabrielle George's books?"

"Of course! Who hasn't? I mean, what fan of romance, especially historical romance, hasn't? At least twice."

"Good. Then you know her style, her voice. Excellent."

"But, well, I don't understand. The woman on the phone said her assistant retired. You don't look old enough to retire.

I mean, that is . . ." She lifted her hand as if reaching out to take hold of her thoughts and then let it drop.

"I see." Justin thought for a moment. "Well it's actually for a second assistant. They got confused on the retirement part. I have my hands rather full with wri . . . what I do and need help with some of the more mundane aspects of the job. For the secretarial aspects so I can focus on, well the non-secretarial ones."

She considered what he said. At this point anything was better than the bank if for no other reason than she didn't want to follow in her mother's footsteps. Not if there was a way out.

"Sounds exactly what I'm looking for," she told him.

"Good."

"So what can I tell you?"

"You already did."

"I did?"

"Yes. You can type and it sounds like you know your way around an office. If we offer you the job, when can you start?"

"Start?" The moment the word left her mouth she wished she could recall it. "I mean, I can any time . . ."

A gust of wind silenced her, which was definitely to her favor. She was single handedly bungling the interview. With a howl the wind rattled the windows and it seemed to roar through the room, causing the flames in the fireplace to flicker and several of the stout candles to go out. But with the windows closed and the door to the hallway firmly shut, where could the breeze have come from?

A clock chimed nine times in another part of the house. She'd been there over two hours yet it felt like she'd only just arrived. *Was I unconscious for that long? Or did time simply fly looking at this living piece of eye candy?*

"Great. I . . . we have a few more people to interview so we'll let you know in a few days."

"Um. Okay."

"You seem a bit distracted. Are you sure you're okay?"

Dru sat up straighter. "Yes. Sure. I, uh, don't you want to ask me any other questions?"

"Like what?"

"I don't know. Office type questions." She was so seriously blowing this. The guy knew she could type and knew all the latest programs. She confirmed she knew all of the famed author's books. So why couldn't she keep her mouth shut and just leave it at that? *Maybe because this Justin is the best looking man I've ever laid eyes on and I really, really, really want him . . . I mean this job.*

Justin pondered her question. "Hmm, I'm not sure what else to ask."

"I kinda came to that conclusion myself. I mean if someone, like me, knows what she's doing in an office, which I do . . ."

"Exactly. So like I said, I'll let you know in a couple of days. We'll figure out salary and all that. Oh, um, I will ask you to keep the address confidential. It's Gabrielle George's house and even though she loves her fans, having them line up outside isn't conducive to getting a lot of work done. Plus she's very reclusive and while she'd never want to be rude, her privacy is very important to her."

"Sure, I understand. Sounds good." Dru started to rise from where she sat on the couch.

"Oh yeah. Where are you coming from? Your address says Marin. Are you still living there?"

"Uh huh."

"Would that be a problem? Getting here?"

"No. Not at all. I've got a car that runs pretty well. I mean, I haven't had any problems with it and it looks like parking out there is pretty easy." And clearly she was babbling again. Justin Hunt didn't need to know anything about her car now, did he? No.

Justin looked out a window that faced the side yard. "Yes. Parking. We have space behind the house where you can park. By the garage. You can park there if things work out." He studied her neck for a long moment. "Ms. Montgomery, after your fright with Vincent, are you sure you are well enough to drive tonight?"

"Of course. Like I said, I don't pass out. That was a first for me."

"Yeah. Vincent kind of sneaks up on people. He thinks it's fun to see what people will do."

Dru looked over at the cat that now sat at the other end of the settee watching her. "Glad I could make your night, Vincent."

The cat closed his eyes and opened them again to continue to stare at her.

"Well, if that's that I guess I'll be going then. Unless you have any other questions?"

"Nope."

She picked up her purse, which Justin had apparently placed beside her on the couch. "Then I'll be off. Thank you for seeing me. Vincent, nice to meet you too."

The cat looked over at her, raised a paw and proceeded to groom himself. At least Vincent was relaxed about the whole job thing.

Justin walked Dru down the hallway, past the living room and to the front door. He paused as he opened it and told her to drive home safely. She was aware of him standing at the open door while she walked down the steps, through the gate and on to the sidewalk. The gate's creak sounded inordinately loud in the otherwise still night. A black bird flew by, low to the ground. Dru could have sworn she saw it glare at her and fancifully wondered if the bird saw her as dinner or an annoyance for disturbing the otherwise quiet night.

And there it was again. That preternatural quiet. What neighborhood in San Francisco was that soundless at nine o'clock on a weekday night? She glanced up at the other houses on the street only to see dim lights behind the tightly drawn curtains. Only Gabrielle George's painted lady emanated any true light and that was from the flickering candles behind the curtains. Unable to help herself, Dru's gaze was drawn to the third floor of the stately Victorian, to the window in that tower room. Except for a tiny pinpoint of light, it was dark now. The famed author probably turned in early. Aware that she wasn't alone, Dru lowered her gaze to see Justin standing in the doorway watching her. She raised a tentative hand to wave goodnight to him, turned and headed to her car.

Suddenly nervous, she entered quickly, locked the car door and belted herself in. *He's just a guy. Just a guy standing in the doorway of a house. Just a house. Just a house on a street. Just a regular old street. In San Francisco for goodness sake. What's there to be nervous about?*

After checking her rear view mirror, Dru pulled out of the parking space, surprised there was no car waiting to pull into the space behind her. There was always another car ready to pull into an empty space in the city. So why wasn't there one tonight?

With a shrug, she drove down the street, headed through the park and toward the bridge. Not surprisingly the fog had settled in over the bridge. Thick and dense, it surrounded her in its gray glimmer. Finally a pair of taillights showed in front of her. She released a sigh. At least there was another person out and about tonight.

Once on the bridge's approach traffic thickened, Dru slowed and gave her thoughts free reign. *I'm being fanciful thinking that the rest of the world stopped while I was in Gabrielle George's house. It's just a house and Justin was . . . is . . . just a guy. Okay, he could easily be the man of my dreams but man . . .*

By time she reached the Waldo Grade, the fog had dissipated and traffic flow was normal. So normal she wondered if perhaps she'd dreamt the whole interview with Justin

Hunt. Her thoughts turned to what had brought her to this point in time. What brought Gabrielle George into her life . . .

"She's at it again," Dru told Haley, one afternoon out on the playground when they were about thirteen.

"Who? And what's it?" Ultra-girly, blonde-haired Haley asked her dark-haired friend.

"My mother, who else." Dru leaned back on the worn wooden stadium bench with a sigh.

"Your mom? What is she doing?"

Haley often thought, or at least had said, Martha was the be all and end all of mothers. For whatever reason Haley thought the sun rose and set with Dru's mom – and it wasn't like she didn't have a mother of her own. Maybe it was because Martha fawned all over Haley like she was the queen of Sheba or some such.

"Another church."

"Dru, your mom is very religious."

"No. She's not religious. She just goes from church to church like a bee on a honey hunt. Seriously, think about it."

"She's on a trip . . . a quest. You know like Don Quixote."

"My mother is so not on a Don Quixote quest. Or she might be on a quest, but it's all about her. This is like her fifth church in four years."

"What's wrong with that?"

"Hale . . . how many churches have you gone to in the past four years?"

"Well . . ."

"I've watched her do this, over and over. You've seen her in action. She is so desperate for attention and admiration that she goes to one of those cult churches and they all fawn all over her like she's something special. She gives them a ton of money – money my dad says we don't really have – and they act like she's god's gift. They fuss all over her and hug her and say all these gushy things about her."

"So?" Haley drew circles in the dirt with her foot. "It makes her happy."

"When someone new comes along, the church people start to fuss

23

over that person and my mom becomes just another member of the church. She can't handle that, so she looks around for another one that will make a big deal over her. I swear she doesn't believe half the stuff she spouts. She talks about all these plat-plat . . . what's that word?"

"Platitudes?"

"Yeah. Platitudes but I don't think she believes any of it."

Haley leaned back and let the sun warm her cheeks. "Does it really matter?"

"No. I don't suppose so. If anything it keeps her busy so I can," Dru reached into her backpack and pulled out a worn paperback, "read this."

Haley snatched the book out of Dru's hands and studied the cover. "Oh my god! He's naked!"

"No. He's not naked. Well maybe half-naked. Isn't he gorgeous?"

Together the friends studied the buff cover model, leaning over a woman with long, flowing hair in suggestive dishabille underneath the name Gabrielle George.

"I'm going to marry a guy that looks just like him some day," Dru sighed while she traced the model's chest with her finger.

"Your mom would never go for it."

"Well of course she'd never go for a half-naked guy."

"I don't think she'd go for a guy that looks like him or does that for a living."

"You mean is a pirate on the high seas on a clipper ship?"

The pair shrieked with delight at the image of Dru coming home to a pirate, complete with cutlass on his hip.

With lunch break over, they headed back into their classroom. Dru carefully tucked the book back into her pack, making certain to cover it with her other possessions. Outside the classroom door, Haley whispered, "You aren't really reading that, are you?"

Dru nodded. "I am. I have. I've read it four times already and I'm going to read it again. Gabrielle George is a great writer."

CHAPTER FIVE

Justin stood behind the closed front door and peered out the side windows as the woman slowly drove away. "Vincent, I think she may be exactly what we are looking for."

The cat meowed and threaded his way through Justin's legs. When Dru's taillights disappeared down the street, Justin turned and headed back toward the office. He sat down at the desk and pulled out a file folder holding the names and resumes of the top applicants. They'd received over two hundred resumes in three days. Most had letters gushing about how exciting it would be to work with an author. Most didn't even refer to the fact that it was a famous author. Many of the letters talked about how the applicant aspired to be a writer him or herself. A few sent writing samples. Some talked about how they could provide tips and plot lines for the unnamed author to read. Most seemed to know it was Gabrielle George, although that didn't seem to matter to the ones who spent most of their cover letter talking about themselves and their writing aspirations.

There were very few resumes like Drusilla's. "I like her name, Vincent. Drusilla. Doesn't that sound like a marvelous name for a put-upon heroine? Drusilla."

The cat looked up at him expectantly.

Justin fanned the pages of the file that contained the best candidates, which included Dru's. "And more than her name, she seems the most professional of all of them. She is direct and to the point. She's applying for the job and tells us about her skills. Nothing about how she would love to help design covers and meet the models or recommendations for plot lines. Just straight to the point, there are her skills."

Clearly bored with Justin's assessment of the woman who had just left their house, Vincent turned and headed back to the couch. He groomed himself a few moments before turning, intent on a nap.

Justin sat in his leather desk chair and again reviewed Dru's resume. He smiled, looking at the short, sweet and to-the-point job history — aside from working at a bank there was nothing. She'd worked there part time in high school and then went full time. There was every indication of practicality and loyalty.

"She's got a story, Vincent," he told the sleeping cat. "Shy, a bit nervous and one job so far . . . she's got a story. I bet we can tell it."

Once again he fanned the pages in the file of potential applicants. "And she's cute. There's just something very appealing about Miss Drusilla Montgomery."

With a glance at the computer clock, Justin picked up the phone and dialed. Madeline would have been long gone and they wouldn't talk until tomorrow evening, but she could take care of business during the day tomorrow. When her voicemail picked up, he told her, "I think I found the right person, Drusilla Montgomery. Let's start her at the top step we talked about plus benefits. Call the others on the list and tell them . . . tell them we need to reschedule and will call in a few days." There was no reason to interview the others if Drusilla took the job. And if she didn't? If she changed her mind? Well, he'd deal with that if the time came to do so.

Yes, Drusilla Montgomery was the perfect choice for what he had in mind.

CHAPTER SIX

"I could hardly sleep last night," Dru told Haley over the phone during her morning break. She'd taken her cell — one of the few things she bought following her mother's death and walked outside of the bank. There was no way she wanted Ottila or her minions to hear her conversation. Haley, however, worked at a local doctor's office where they didn't mind if she took an occasional personal call.

"You went? You seriously went?"

"I sure did. Haley, I have to tell you about it. *All* about it. From Gabrielle George's ultra hot assistant to this house she lives in. It's like something out of a gothic romance."

Haley laughed. "Only you would think something like that."

"Well what can I say? Can you meet for lunch?"

"Sure. I'll meet you at Turbo's at noon?"

"See you then."

For a change, the morning flew by and before she knew it, it was time for lunch. Dru raced over to Turbo's and snagged a table near the window. When Haley arrived a few minutes later, Dru waved her over to the table.

"You're absolutely glowing," Haley told her. "I haven't seen you look that happy since you got accepted to college.

"I was pretty excited then and yeah, it feels kind of like that, only better and not just because my mother can't stop me this time. This could totally be my dream job and unlike college, my mother won't be able to interfere. This is one dream that's going to come true."

"I hope so, Dru. I really do. And I'm sorry for being a downer about it when you told me about the interview."

"It's okay, Hales. I understand."

The waitress came and took their orders — the Turbo special burgers with extra pickles. Dru decided to indulge herself and ordered an extra thick chocolate shake to go with hers.

When the waitress left, Haley gestured in a come-on move, "So what would you be doing?"

"Um, well, office type things."

"Dru, you said it was your dream job. What do you do at a dream job?"

Dru huffed out a breath. "Well let's see. Justin, her main assistant, he's the total manifestation of my dream guy, he did the interview. It was a preliminary one."

The waitress returned with their burgers and drinks.

Dru smiled. "Thanks."

"So you said the interview was preliminary?" Haley shook a hefty dose of catsup on her burger and took a bite.

"Uh huh." Dru swallowed her mouthful of her own burger . . . well done, not almost rare like her mother would have ordered for her.

"I thought it was for the job itself."

"I did too. The woman who called me at first is apparently in New York. She's Gabrielle George's editor, did an initial screening for candidates. Then Justin . . . Haley, this guy is so gorgeous, unbelievably gorgeous, is her assistant here in the bay area. He was doing another screening and we talked for a while last night."

"So when will you know?"

"In a few days." Dru took another bite, chewed and swallowed before continuing, "It was kind of weird. All he did was ask if I knew the latest computer programs, and I told him yes and that was sort of it. Maybe my resume is better than I thought."

"Maybe. I thought it was kind of sparse, but then again just having one job in your whole life is pretty stable. Employers like stable."

"That's true."

"So did you meet Gabrielle George?"

Dru looked out the window at the cars and people passing by for a moment.

"Dru?"

"Huh?"

"Did you meet Gabrielle George?"

She frowned before answering, "No."

"Something is on your mind," Haley told her. "What?"

"Yeah. Last night. It was kind of weird. The house. It's like it exists in two times—the turn of the 19th century and our time."

"Uh huh."

"And, Hales, there wasn't another car on the street. Not one and there was a parking space right out front. I mean *right* out front. It was kind of eerie the way no one was out and no cars or anything."

"Maybe cause it was dinner hour?"

"I guess but when I left there weren't any either and that was a couple of hours later. It's like time stopped in the house and on that street."

Haley shook her head. "So what's her house like?"

"Hmmm, on the outside it's your basic Queen Anne. Inside, it's definitely got that Gothic thing going."

"Really?"

"Yeah. Well, actually, all I saw was the hallway, a glimpse of what might have been the living room and what seemed to be the office. The outside is a typical Victorian, you know, all gingerbread and just cute. When I went in I didn't have a lot of time to look around, but what I did see looked like a living room with everything looking period perfect. You know, a fainting couch, heavy tables, chairs, old-fashioned lamps. At least from what I could see. They work in one of the downstairs rooms, which is totally an office setting. It's got computers, a fax, and printer . . . things like that, but it blends in with period pieces They use candles. Lots of candles, all over. In fact, the only really modern things were the two computers and some office equipment. Otherwise, it was like a Victorian drawing room. Well not chock full of stuff and all crowded, but that kind of elegance you see in pictures from back then. I figure she has the house set up like that for inspiration. And Justin, well he could be on the covers of Gabrielle's books."

Haley picked up a fry and twisted it through her catsup. "You mentioned that about him. So what do you think your mother would say about it?"

"Haley. She'd hate it. She would absolutely hate it." Dru couldn't hold back the laugh that bubbled up just thinking about her mother and her reactions to men in general. No one was ever good enough for Martha Montgomery.

"Will you take it if they offer you the job?"

Dru smiled. "Absolutely."

"Really? You'd give up the security at the bank? Just cause her assistant is hot?"

"Security? It's not worth it. Not if I have to put up with the likes of Millan the rest of my life. And I don't want the job just because Justin will give me something juicy to think about at night when I'm going to sleep."

"I can just imagine what your mother would say . . . but it does sound like it will be an interesting job."

"Haley. She's dead. Martha is dead and gone and she can't tell me what to do anymore. If they offer me the job, I'm going to take it and it will be the best job ever. I know it. I just know it."

"So you'll take the job?" Justin asked her two days later.

"Yes! Yes!" Dru did her own personal happy dance behind her teller station at work while trying to act as cool as possible on the phone. "Um, not to blow my chances, but won't Ms. George want to meet me first?"

"Ms. George?"

"Yes. If I'm going to be working for her, won't she want to meet me before I start and all?"

"Ah. Well, um, you'll actually ah be working for me. I, uh work for her and the job is actually working for me."

"Was there a mistake in the ad? Not that I'm turning you down. I do want the job. I'm just curious, you know?" With the phone cord entwined in her fingers, she twisted around to make sure no one was within hearing distance.

"Right. Ah, yeah. I understand. Completely. And I know that online job list has had some problems but um, well, the job, this position is, um, working for me. I get my instructions from Gabrielle you see and then my assistant, you know, gets them from me."

Something suddenly didn't feel so right. "Mr. Hunt, is there really a job?"

"Ah, yes, of course there's a job. Sorry if this sounds, um, I don't know . . . odd? I haven't had my own assistant before so I'm not sure I'm explaining . . . you heard the conversation I had with my publicist, I mean Gabrielle's publicist, right? They want Gabrielle to churn out six books a year—most authors turn out three or four. Hers are longer, more complex and have intricate story lines. I need help so she can continue at that pace."

"So the job is only for a few months?"

"No, no, sorry I'm not explaining very well. It's a permanent job and we will pay for benefits and a retirement. When I take my break, I'll still need someone to run the office and make sure things are taken care of."

"What about public appearances?"

"Public appearances?"

"Yes. Book signings and things like that?"

"Oh, Gabrielle stopped making them years ago. If you're a fan, you know she's quite reclusive."

She saw Ottila looking over her way so she turned and lowered her voice a bit more. The dictatorial micro-manager had a hard and fast rule about personal calls inside the bank even though Ottila, herself, spent a good part of the day talking to her daughter and friends. Everyone pretty much knew what she paid for her car, her mattress and the problems her daughter had at school. "Yes. They mention it in many of the news articles about her. So won't I be meeting her?"

"Not for a while. Not till we know how things will work out. Are you still interested?"

"Definitely."

"Great! When can you start?"

"I need to give two weeks' notice at my current job, so two weeks from tomorrow? Would that work?"

"That would be perfect. Gabrielle will be thrilled. I'll get a confirming letter off to you this afternoon."

"I can't wait. Mr. Hunt, thank you, thank you so much for this opportunity." She squeezed the phone cord, trying to keep her voice down and at the same time express her enthusiasm about the job. This was it! Her big break, her chance to have at least part of the life she wanted . . . if she wanted.

"Thank *you*, Drusilla. This is going to work out wonderfully for both . . . all of us. And please, call me Justin. If you have any questions, just give me a call."

"I will. Oh! While I think of it, what will my hours be and is there a dress code?"

"Wear whatever is comfortable. And hours . . . I'll let you know in a few days. I need to check with Gabrielle when it will be best."

"Sounds good. And thanks again for the opportunity."

Dru hung up and looked at the phone for a moment, oblivious to the sounds and people around her. Her dream was finally coming true. In a short two weeks she'd be working for her favorite author. Well, her assistant. Her very hot and handsome assistant. Could life get any better?

CHAPTER SEVEN

Justin breathed a sigh of relief and looked down at Vincent. "She said yes. I believe we have found the perfect assistant."

"Meow!"

"Yes indeed. Meow. She will be purrfect." He grinned at the cat, drawing out the word perfect with a slight growl.

Justin stood where Vincent lazed on the settee, absently fluffing the cat's fur. Yes indeed, Drusilla Montgomery was the perfect match for an assistant. No family to speak of. A job that, despite how she tried to make it sound like all was, well . . . clearly a drudge for her. That she lived alone was another plus. Aside from that, she was cute in a bookish kind of way. Take her out of the dowdy clothes and let her hair down, she'd be downright pretty if not gorgeous. It was good Drusilla knew Gabrielle's books, but that wasn't necessary for the position. No not necessary at all.

With a final scrunch of Vincent's fur, Justin strode over to the heavy oak desk and spent a moment studying the computer monitor before sitting down and picking up the phone. While the phone rang, he tapped an absentminded tattoo with his fingers and glanced at the computer clock. Madeline should still be at work in New York. With deference to the Gabrielle George school of writing and the fact that the publisher was on the East Coast while the famed writer was on the West, Madeline started work later in the day and often worked into the night, at least when they were on deadline.

When Madeline picked up, Justin cut to the chase. "She said yes!"

"Drusilla Montgomery?"

"Yes. I just offered her the job and she accepted."

"Great. Wonderful. So will you tell her?"

Justin thought for a moment. "No. At least not right away. Please make sure the people in the know back there don't say anything either. I want to be sure . . . I mean, she is perfect for what I'm looking for but I don't want any problems when I explain things to her."

"You don't think she'll figure it out beforehand?"

Justin considered that. "No. No. She's smart. That much is clear, but from the way she spoke about her job . . . well, more like how she sounded when she talked about it, I don't think so. She may figure out something is . . . different, but I have a feeling she'll be so pleased to have the position she won't go down that road."

"I hope you're right. It could turn out sticky if you aren't."

"Have you ever known me to be wrong?"

"Not in this century."

Justin smiled as he hung up. Madeline was well paid to make sure things ran smoothly. When it came to Drusilla Montgomery though, he was pretty sure he knew his girl. She would be a pleasure to work with.

Absentmindedly, he looked at the fireplace across the room and debated throwing on a few logs to take off the chill of the room. It wasn't bad. Just enough to remind him this was a 19th century Victorian and it was cold and rainy outside. Drusilla would fit in perfectly with his plans. She belonged here. In this house with its wood paneled walls, heavy but well cushioned chairs and candlelit rooms.

He sat down and opened a new file on the computer and began to write . . .

She belonged there. In that room, in that house, in his life. For far too long he had been alone. Alone with his secrets, his desires held close within his heart. Finally. Now. Without a qualm or doubt, he'd found the woman of his dreams.

But would he turn out to be the man of her dreams . . . or nightmares?

"I do write a good back cover blurb, don't I?" he asked Vincent. The cat turned and looked at his person with almost human intelligence clearly in his eyes.

"Oh don't give me that look. Even if you had opposable thumbs, I doubt you could write such eerie prose."

Vincent yawned, turned and curled up on the couch. Justin studied the cat for a moment. How wonderful to sleep at night . . . and day. To just be able to curl up and sleep without sometimes having overwhelming thoughts crowd his mind.

No, that wasn't true. Those thoughts and his ability to place them on the page were his life's blood. The motivation to create overrode the need or desire to sleep. Although when dreams did come, they were the stuff of Gabrielle's emotionally passionate novels. That yearning for the one person who made another whole . . . that was what those sleepless nights gave him.

Turning back to the computer Justin continued . . .

There she stood at the entry. All prim and proper in her travelling cloak. A charming yet discrete hat perched on top her . . .

"Hmm, what do you think, Vincent? Shall I make her a sandy blonde or give her the same deep brown shades of Drusilla's hair?"

Vincent cocked one eye open.

"Good point. Something in between . . .

. . . glossy auburn locks laced with hints of gold.

"How does that sound, Vincent?"

The cat slowly closed his eyes half way and opened them again before turning to settle in for a nap. Justin shrugged and continued.

She was the manifestation of the woman who haunted his dreams night after night. There she'd stand, just at the threshold of the room, he glimpsed her on the periphery as she stood a heartbeat away. His breath would stutter as he'd try to calmly take in his next breath.

The last thing he wanted to do, ever, was let her know how much he longed for her.

A step, just a step . . . no not even a step, but the mere thought of taking one toward her and she would vanish like a specter. Perhaps she was just that, a specter, a wraithlike spirit come to haunt him.

He'd lived for centuries, known hundreds of women, had them, enjoyed them, tasted their sweet nectar and then, brokenhearted, moved on. Was she perhaps an echo of one of those women? One who he'd taken too much for granted, enjoyed too much and left her to pass to the other realms. Was that why she haunted his dreams? Because she lived, almost as he did, between the worlds?

But now, here she was, the woman of his nightly imaginings, standing before him.

"I've come to inquire after the position." Her voice calm and yet oh so proper.

"Have you now?" He assessed her cloak — clean, neat but threadbare. Without her even parting its folds, he knew beneath it she wore a pale green muslin grown, modestly cut so only the hint of her breasts peeked over the top and only if she took in too deep a breath. The gown caressed her hips and fell in tantalizing folds down to her booted feet. She wore boots. Well-made boots as they would last longer than shoes, given the path she'd need to walk day after day, searching for a way to support herself. He'd support her. In a heartbeat, that self-same heartbeat that pulsed in his veins when he saw her in his dreams, he'd support her. She could choose. All she needed to do was agree to be his. His . . . now and forever.

"Y-yes." She stammered.

"Well then, please, have a seat." Gallantly he gestured to a chair beside his massive oak desk.

She glided into the room. Sturdy boots did not bind her to the floor. No, she fairly floated to the desk. Perhaps she was indeed an ethereal being, the spirit of a woman he'd loved and lost so long ago. How else could she so soundlessly seem to float over to the desk?

She sat, back erect, her reticule on her lap, knees together — not a hint of impropriety.

Gavin sat behind the desk. Better to hide the erection that the reality of her being here brought. He smiled.

She offered him a tentative one in return and then was once again all business. "I have references."

He didn't reach for the eggshell colored foolscap she presented to him. Instead he asked, "The agency told you what would be expected of you?"

She pulled the page back and held it over her reticule, not yet ready to concede that perhaps the position would not be offered to her. "Y-yes. I will maintain your papers in orderly fashion, take correspondence, arrange soirées and the like."

"Do you read?"

She blinked. "Why yes, of course."

"Have you read my books?"

A light blush crept up her cheeks. "Bits. They are . . ." she delicately cleared her throat.

"A tad lascivious?"

"Yes. Yes I would say that they are a tad . . . risqué."

"Will it bother you to read them? To know those words are going to be part of your everyday working life with me?" And that you will no doubt inspire perhaps more tantalizing expressions of those very words?

"No. At least I do not think so. The words . . . well if one is reading your books for . . . pleasure, that is one thing. As a lady I wouldn't venture down those roads . . . not that I know much about them, that is. But as part of my posi—job, well then they are just words, are they not?"

Gavin smiled to himself at her flustered jumble over the word position. If he had anything to say about it, she would definitely be part of those positions. "Exactly, Miss?"

He'd done it on purpose. It was part of his interview process. Until he made up his mind he didn't bother with names. They were too personal. Names connected him to the person and he may well leave those persons behind all too soon.

"Montgomery. Drusilla Montgomery."

Justin stared at the page. "Drusilla. Well that won't work now, will it?" He erased the name and pulled up a file labeled "women's names 1800s." He tasted each one. "Rose, Rosa, Nora, Emma, Lula . . . Emma. Emma it is. Now, Emma what? Ackerman? Emma Ackerman? Grady. Emma Grady." Yes, the perfect name for his heroine, absolutely perfect.

Chapter Eight

"Leaving?" Ottila Millan peered over her horn-rimmed glasses at Dru.

She noted wryly that Millan didn't wear the horned-rims because they were a fashion statement. The woman had worn them since she was in high school forty years ago. Fashions came and went, but Ottila didn't change a thing.

"Yes. I've accepted another position and well, here is my notice. Two weeks."

Ottila cleared her throat. "Your mother wouldn't approve."

"Ottila, my mother has been dead for three months and where she is I'm not sure she cares whether I work at the bank or not."

"That is terribly disrespective of you, Drusilla. Your mother would be appalled

"I'm sure she would, however, Ottila, this is my life and it's time for me to live it my way. By the way, I think you meant disrespectful. I'm not sure disrespective is a word. "

Ottila looked down at her desk, at the dark brown blotter that sat on top of it and picked up a pen. She gazed at the designer pen, replaced it on the blotter and watched it for a moment before gingerly touching it with her finger. "Your mother wouldn't agree. Drusilla, I knew your mother for many years." She clearly wasn't going to address her misuse of common words.

"Yes, I know. She came to work here the same day you did when the bank opened. She worked for you, here, for forty years. I know you were great, well not friends per se but close co-workers."

"Exactly."

"Well I'm not my mother and I do not want to wake up one day forty years from now and find out I've become her." Dru fought the urge to fold her arms over her chest and appear defensive or weak.

"There are worse things you could be." Ottila pointed her finger at Dru. "Martha Montgomery left you a legacy, a secure legacy. When you failed in school, when you could not make it in college, she went out on a limb and obtained this job for you. This is how you thank her?"

Dru sighed. "Ottila, I worked here summers in high school and I think it's time to set the record straight on my college days. My mother didn't want me to pursue the coursework I wanted in college. When she found out I wasn't sewing costumes, but doing something I enjoyed, she not only made a scene on the campus and told me she'd kick me out of the house if I didn't drop my plans to go into lighting design, she went further. When that didn't work, she contacted the student loan people and told them I falsified my application. She was convincing enough that they not only withdrew my loan but demanded it be paid back immediately. They never listened to what I said or tried to explain. I did *not*, as she was fond of saying, flunk out of college. *She* got me thrown out and made sure that my only choice was to live in her house and take the job here at the bank."

Ottila sniffed. "She always did say you never took responsibility for your failures. I cannot believe you would besmirch her memory by lying about what happened now."

Dru blew out a frustrated sigh. "Ottila, we're never going to agree on this. My mother lied to get her way. Most of the time she'd lie by omission, but when it came to me and when it came to college, it was definitely by commission."

"You are being disres . . ."

Dru put her hand up. "Ottila, I am leaving. I've given you the courtesy of two weeks' notice. I will be happy to train my replacement should you hire one and honor that two weeks of notice if you drop this talk about how my mother would be upset or offended, or how my leaving dishonors her memory. I am taking this new job and if it doesn't work out, fine. That's on me. I'm not going to spend the next two weeks hearing you talk down to me and glorify my mother. Take it or leave it."

Inside she cringed. She'd never in her entire life spoken up for herself like that. Damn though, it did feel good. And if she said go ahead and go—even better. She'd tell Mr. Hunt, Justin, she could start early and if he didn't need her, she'd take a little vacation, the first vacation of her life. Maybe to Mexico or Hawaii or New York—a vacation just for herself. If Justin said to start immediately, she'd be there and make plans for a really super vacation next year. Maybe even Europe.

She flashed back on the day her mother had shown up on campus, humiliating her beyond words. And that was before her mother called the student loan people and lied to them.

"All I ever wanted was a little girl!" Martha Montgomery lamented for the millionth time.

Dru looked down from the sixty-foot cherry picker where she was hanging lights in the college little theatre.

"Get down from there this instant," her mother yelled. Around her the other theatre students stood gaping at the woman shrieking like a banshee.

"I'll be down when I finish with this lamp," a rather stunned Dru called down to her mother.

"Drusilla Marie Montgomery. I am serious. I wanted a little girl. This is unacceptable."

Below her a few of the kids snickered. Dru was hard pressed not to join in. After all, whose mother showed up at school — a college — in the middle of the day to . . . what? Check up on her daughter? Pay a quick visit before going home for the evening? That might be it except it was two in the afternoon and Dru, like her classmates, came to the theatre between classes to do some rigging.

A moment later, Dru's professor ambled out of his office, spoke quietly to her mother and took Martha by the arm to lead her out of the theatre. Dru scurried down the ladder and with a quick apology to the lighting designer, hastened after her mother and professor.

" . . . but she said she was a costuming major." Dru heard her mother's bewildered statement. Martha sounded like she'd lost her best friend.

"Dru does need to take a costume design class, but she is my top lighting design student, Mrs. Montgomery," Professor Anderson told the older woman.

"Well you will have to change her schedule and classes. I wanted a little girl and my daughter is not going to be spending her days climbing ladders and carrying around dirty pieces of whatever."

"Lamps, lights. We call them lamps. And they aren't dirty. Listen, Mrs. Montgomery, Dru is over eighteen, isn't she?"

"Yes." Her mother sniffed now.

"Then it's her choice, isn't it? Her career, it's her choice, right?"

Before Martha could answer, Dru entered her professor's office. "Dr. Anderson is right, Mom. It's my choice and I love lighting design."

"But I want a daughter and what you were doing in there is hardly ladylike. I knew when you father dragged you under that car when you were just a child you were doomed. Doomed. Where did I fail?"

Dru knelt next to where her mother sat in the hard wooden desk chair. "You didn't fail, Mom. I am a daughter, a girl. I'm just a daughter who likes to do different things."

"Climbing a ladder is not different. It is masculine. It's what a boy does. You will stop that ludicrous ladder climbing or you will lose your happy home."

"Fine."

"What does that mean?" Martha started to rise from the chair Professor Anderson had given her. Dru knew that look and the accompanying body language. She'd seen it the first time when her *mother picked up a favorite doll, shook it and then pulled off its head, shouting she wished it were Dru. It was the kind of thing the crazy ladies in Gabrielle George's gothics did. The things that tormented her heroines and sent them into the hero's arms. Maybe her mother was crazy . . . but if that was so, the whole gothic thing didn't work out too well. No, not at all because no hero rode to Dru's rescue. They lived in an unassuming Eichler house in northern Marin. With its neatly tended lawn, carefully trimmed bushes and sturdy siding, it just didn't fit with the whole gothic image of a house on a dark cliff. Still . . .*

"I'll live on campus and make my own way." Dru tried for non-chalance and shrugged. Before she could say another word, Martha rose and stormed out of the office. For a moment, Dru felt a pang of sadness, which was quickly replaced with elation — if she had her own place she could buy as many romance novels as she wanted and her mother would be none the wiser. Hiding them in her room got tedious at times. That's what one of Gabrielle George's heroines would do. She'd go out, find herself a fabulous place to live, and meet the man of her dreams.

Actually, it wouldn't quite happen like that, would it? No. She'd find herself out on the streets, struggling, and a man would come along and try to take advantage of her. The hero would be a friend or acquaintance and . . ."Well anyway, her heroine would come out all right and so will I."

Much to Martha's extreme pleasure, Dru's theatre career came to a grinding halt.

Not exactly what would have happened to one of Gabrielle George's heroines. Nor would they have ended up working at a bank, standing side-by-side with their mother.

Otilla Millan finally spoke, making it sound like she was doing Dru a favor. "Fine. You can stay for the next two weeks. Understand this though, Drusilla Montgomery, once you walk out that door two weeks from now you will not be able to walk back in here and work for us again. Your mother's fine memory aside, once you *disrespect* her by taking this other job, no matter how high we esteem Martha, you will not work here again."

"I understand. That's fine."

Like she'd want to come back here again.

Just to be on the safe side she called Justin when she got home that night and confirmed her start date and time.

"Yes, Drusilla, I'm looking forward to having you start. Oh, did I mention our working hours?"

"Uh, no. Just the job duties, but I can do 8-5 or 9-5 or whatever."

"Wonderful, we work from 7:00 p.m. until 4:00 a.m."

CHAPTER NINE

Had she heard that right? Seven at night till four in the morning? When they ended the call, the last thing she said to Justin was, "Great, I'll see you on the 20th at 7:00 p.m. Give me a call if anything changes."

And he answered, "I'll see you that night."

If she misunderstood or was wrong he would have said so, right?

Dru replaced the receiver. Well that was that. She'd be working nights. Not that the hours would be a problem. She'd always been a night owl. It was one of the reasons theatre work held her interest—most of the time they did their rigging at night and, it was when her mother proclaimed lights out when Dru would turn in, that she escaped into whatever world her heroes and heroines lived in be it to the distant past, to the wild west with hot cowboys and sexy Indians, to contemporary mountain cabins and far into the future. For years she fell asleep imagining herself as each of those heroines, believing someday she too would meet the man of her dreams. Now, here she was, twenty-eight years old and hadn't ever been out on a real date. Oh Martha found guys for her to go out with. Like the "Martha stamp of approval" equated with once in a lifetime romance. So not true.

Each of those set ups she went on—every one she could remember—she'd come home and tell her mother what an awful time she had. And each time, as she walked in the door, wanting a bath to wash away the residue of another awful evening, she'd tell her mother, "That was one of the worst times of my life. He was just gross."

And her mother would immediately respond with, "You didn't go to bed with him, did you?" Like bad sex was the reason the date was awful. Like Gross Gordon.

That date was a fiasco from the git go. Despite the chilly fall night, he was sweating up a storm when he arrived. In the car going to the movies he kept smacking his lips . . . thick lips that couldn't seem to hold back his tongue. And he smelled. He smelled like he hadn't bathed in days.

During the movie he kept trying to put his arm around her and Dru had to keep squirming away from him. He suggested dinner after and given the toss-up between the rest of the evening talking to her mother or getting a bite to eat, she went for the meal.

And quickly regretted it.

He chewed with his mouth open, had no qualms about complaining, loudly, of what he felt was wrong with his meal and really, it was a small town diner. They weren't sitting in a five star restaurant. He also made it clear he'd be more than amenable to getting intimate with her.

So was not going to happen.

She finished her meal as best she could. Gordon took her home and tried to wrangle an invitation into the house.

Dru pleaded a migraine . . . one that had her on the brink of getting sick.

Gordon hustled away.

Dru slipped into the house, called goodnight to her mother and headed to bed where under cover of darkness, she escaped into her most recent romance.

The next morning, true to form, her mother's first question was "you didn't have sex with him, did you?"

Over and over she'd tell Haley about her mother's fixation on her having sex with guys she couldn't wait to get away from. Martha definitely had a disconnect on what Dru was saying.

Conversely, Martha would also tell her that if she wanted something from a man, *that* was the time to sleep with him. Once she was married that was. Her mother firmly believed in waiting until you were married to have sex.

Which was odd because there was every indication that her mother had been quite free with her favors . . . at least to Grayson. Ah yes, Grayson, the great love of Martha's life. Clearly she hadn't held the same place in his.

"Well it's not part of my life now, is it? Nope. Now it's *my* life to do what *I* want with and if working for Gabrielle George means I go vampire and sleep days, so be it."

Work at the bank became more and more tedious each day. Two short weeks turned into the sludge of two centuries. At least it felt that way.

Each day since she gave notice, at least three times a day, Ottila repeated her mantra that Dru would be miserable at her new job and if she left the bank she would not be welcome back. And each time she'd also remind her that her mother, more likely than not, was rolling over in her grave, which would have been a neat trick since she'd been cremated.

Those mentions gave her pangs of sadness. Getting away from the bank and the memories of her mother's death would be so freeing.

And they brought back the memories of what happened the day her mother died. That day Martha moved a little slow in the morning. She barely finished her coffee, hardly touched her cereal and let Dru drive to work. Martha never let anyone else drive. Not even her father. Dru chalked it up to her mother's control freak nature.

Whatever it was, that day Dru drove.

They'd walked into the bank, pulled their cash drawers

and were ready for the first customers to come in when all of a sudden Martha grabbed her chest. The next thing Dru knew, she was kneeling by her mother's side, trying to give her CPR while one of her co-workers dialed 911. The paramedics made it there in no time and assessed her mother while wheeling her to the waiting ambulance. Ottila gave Dru a ride to the hospital and for the first time, didn't make any nasty comments or shoot her any knowing looks. They arrived moments after the ambulance, and Ottila waited in the waiting room with her. They didn't have to wait long before the doctor came out. Martha was dead. Dru was on her own.

In the days after Martha's funeral, Dru seesawed between guilty elation at finally being free from Martha's domineering ways and an unsettling confusion as to what to do next. Here she was, for the first time, able to plan her own life. To do what *she* wanted and she had no idea what that was. She found herself laughing at herself when she didn't immediately run out to the bookstore and buy every romance in sight or that she didn't tear the house apart and toss out all of Martha's belongings, especially all her religious tracts. Instead she went through the motions as if Martha were still there commanding her every move. Haley told her sometimes you just had to go with what you knew. It didn't even occur to Dru to ask, "What would one of Gabrielle George's heroines do?"

With no other family, it fell to Dru to settle her mother's bills, transfer the utilities into her own name and make what other notifications were necessary. She went back to work the day after Martha's funeral for no other reason than to find some sort of normalcy. Haley came by pretty much every night with tears in her eyes. It seemed Haley missed Martha more than Dru.

"It's funny," Dru told her friend one night about a week after the funeral. "She's gone physically but I still have this feeling she's still here, still running my life."

"I suppose that will go on for a while. It makes sense you'd be numb. In my psychology class, we talked about needing to be normal in the face of grief."

Dru sighed. "I guess."

Long last, her final day as a teller came and a few of the girls took her to lunch. No one told Ottila and in deference to their own self-preservation once Dru was gone, they left in pairs minutes apart from each other. The retaliation if she knew they celebrated with her would go on for weeks if not months.

Janice Tom, the assistant manager, privately told her, "Once Ottila is gone, if you decide you want to come back to the bank, I'll hire you in a heartbeat."

"Thanks, Janice. I hope when she does finally retire they do give you the manager's job. You definitely deserve it."

"You do," Melissa Howard told Janice. "Thing is, even if Ottila dies on the job, I don't think anyone will notice. She'll haunt the place for years to come."

Chuckles erupted at the table and the women launched into their favorite uptight Ottila story. To herself, Dru reflected that pretty much everything they said about Ottila she could also have said about her mother. Pretty sad commentary that.

Haley picked her up after work that night and together they headed out to dinner. They picked a favorite restaurant in town and feasted on crab salads topped off with a decadent dessert and cappuccinos.

"This means a lot to me, Hale."

"You deserve something special, Dru. You know I'm concerned about whether this job is the right thing, but if it's what you want, I want it for you."

"Thanks, Hale."

"So what are you wearing Monday? You know, for your first day?"

"Actually I bought a new skirt, a dark purple pencil skirt and lavender silk blouse."

"Sounds pretty."

"It is. Justin said dress is casual but to start . . . well . . . anyway, the blouse is sort of Victorian, a high collar, puffy sleeves on top and some delicate lace at the wrists and collar. Very feminine. At least on the first day I want to kind of live up to the characters she's known for. You don't think that's too much, do you?"

"No. Not at all. You definitely deserve to be feminine or do what helps you to feel that way. So, how does it feel? You know, to be done with the bank, to be leaving that part of your life behind?"

"Good. Hales, it feels so good. I feel like I'm about to start a whole new life. That the best is about to come my way."

"I hope so, Dru. I really hope so."

Justin rose a little earlier than usual Sunday night. Dru would be starting the next evening and he wanted things situated just right. His secrets had to be carefully kept, at least for the time being. No hint of the reality of Gabrielle George's life could be seen until he knew Dru was on board with things.

Not that he expected her to go beyond the ground floor and the office space.

Still . . .

Vincent followed him up to the third floor and into the turret room where Gabrielle created some of her darkest dramas, the white knuckled gothics. With long, full, and billowy sheer panels of lace peeking out through velvet curtains so dark a red they appeared almost black, the room had a mysterious aura. The slightest breeze caused the sheer curtains to flow and flutter yet look majestic when sitting still.

The king sized, four-poster bed complete with canopy and

matching, hanging red satin drapes sat in the middle of the room. Plush carpets in muted reds, golds and black covered the hard wood floors and heavy maple furniture made it the epitome of a gothic bedroom.

Justin walked to each of the nightstands and checked the white tapers sitting in the heavy silver candleholders. It was the kind of room one of Gabrielle's heroines would find herself in after arriving at a wealthy landowner's estate on a cold, dark and rainy night. Too bad there was no rain forecast for the next few days. That would definitely add to the drama of Drusilla's arrival and starting to work.

He closed the turret room door and walked down the hallway to check first the small library set up on the third floor. With its floor to ceiling bookcases and deep, heavily cushioned chairs, he'd spent many hours in here reading, researching and considering Gabrielle's plot lines. This room too he closed off and with a click of the key, locked against someone wandering by.

The third floor bathroom held a claw-footed tub although it was modernized with a built in shower and a pedestal sink. Monogrammed linen towels sat beside a water pitcher and bowl on a dark wood vanity table. It would be safe for Dru to come in here . . . but really, for now, there was no reason for her to go beyond the first floor.

From there Justin took a quick look in his own room. There was no concern that Dru would make her way here, not any reason for him to explain why he lived in Gabrielle George's house. Not if he was reading his new employee correctly. The shy and retiring Drusilla Montgomery wouldn't venture far without permission to do so.

With Vincent on his heels, he headed down to the second floor and the bedrooms there. Early on in her career Gabrielle outfitted each bedroom in the motif of each genre she wrote in from medieval to western to Victorian and dark gothic. She said having a space that reflected the time as accurately as possible made writing that period easier. The gothic was definitely different from the others with the accoutrements she'd chosen.

The bathrooms as well reflected each era Gabrielle wrote about. While each had hot and cold running water and the latest in plumbing conveniences, they were accurate to period in terms of form and design. It took her time and at times careful saving, but bit-by-bit she designed each room. Likewise, the bookshelves in the rooms contained not just Gabrielle's, but the books of her friends for each era. Justin had fresh flowers delivered weekly to sit on the vanities in each room. No detail was spared. Ever.

If Dru ever found her way to the second floor, all she would find were the epitome of style, grace and each time period Gabrielle loved best. No worries here.

Downstairs was another story. With its ultra-modern kitchen where the latest appliances covered various counter tops, it was a chef's dream. Not that Justin cooked. Frothy foam for a latte was about all he managed.

Satisfied that all was ready and that Dru would see nothing untoward or suspicious, he proceeded to the office to do some work. Smiling to himself, he sat at the desk and booted up the computer. This book would most likely be the easiest he'd ever written. How often did a story write itself? He should have hired an assistant years ago.

Gavin checked each of the mansion's rooms to ensure everything was in its place. Mrs. Storer, the housekeeper, had suggested a mirror in the new girl's room. The thought of one near enough to see him in it terrified Gavin. If he wasn't careful, so very careful, she'd see and know. How did one explain the lack of a reflection? The rest he could control. His nocturnal hours were easily justified as was the fact he did not dine with his staff . . . and Emma was his staff, at least for the near future.

Ahhh, the future. The future with Emma . . . It would be

delightful. He knew it. Once she came to know him, to care for him and he told her the truth, he had no doubt she would look forward to a long, long future with him.

Mrs. Storer had arranged for fresh flowers to be placed in the rooms Emma would spend her time in. As well, she laid in a supply of foods he hoped she would enjoy. By this time tomorrow the woman who he would spend the rest of his life with would be in residence. She would leave behind a dull and dreary way of being and enter into his world where they would be limited only by their imaginations.

Justin reread the last sentence. "Imaginations" wasn't quite the word he wanted. After all, not even the most powerful paranormal could make everything imaginable happen. "Hmmm, what would they be limited by? What do I put so that whatever was feasible was possible? Feasible . . . feasible. Hmmm, that's going to take some thought."

Deciding to let that idea percolate, Justin turned to the email correspondence that had come in the past few days. Even if it was only a simple thank you note, she always answered each piece of fan mail.

Early on she'd done some guest appearances, but as time passed, rather than appear as an older woman, she adopted the persona of a recluse. It served her well on several levels — it built up her mystique while at the same time kept her from the public eye. Not making guest appearances also enabled her to have more time to write. But answer her mail she did. So now Justin turned to the emails . . . he'd have Dru answer the snail mail. She had a softly flowing and feminine style that would serve well in the handwritten notes.

Yes, Dru would handle that task, as well as the others, quite well. He knew, without a doubt he'd chosen well with his new assistant.

CHAPTER TEN

Dru took a few minutes to stretch and roll about in her bed the next morning. Glancing at the clock, she corrected herself—it was early afternoon. Over the weekend she stayed up later than usual, slept in and took a few naps to acclimate herself to working nights. She'd also had her car tuned-up, tires checked and filled the gas tank so nothing would interfere with the start of her new job.

Even though she'd be working for Gabrielle George and would probably have access to all of her books—after all, didn't an assistant get to read those wonderful stories?—Dru bought her latest book and read it—twice. Okay, the hero was the stuff of dreams and she had to admit, she'd imagined herself in the role of Minette and Justin as Mason the brooding aristocrat turned pirate, if only in her own private thoughts.

Unsure what Justin would do about food—did he eat breakfast when the work night started, or have a meal break a few hours in? He hadn't said anything about a meal break, so she figured she should be prepared. Dru made herself a sandwich and grabbed a juice pack and apple to bring with her.

Ready an hour before she needed to leave, Dru gave herself one last look in the mirror. The dark purple pencil skirt fit perfectly. The skirt showed her curvy hips, but not in a blatantly sexual way. The pale lavender blouse with this fluffy ruffle was feminine yet looked professional. A quick check of her makeup and Dru took off. The sun was setting as she pulled on to the freeway. With the sky pinking to one side and a full moon rising to the other, Dru felt as if something magical was about to happen.

"You goober. Something magical *did* happen! You got the job! You got the best job in the world working for the hottest guy you have ever laid eyes on. Now if you can only keep yourself from looking and acting too frumpy you will be on your way."

Closer to the bridge, Dru saw the fog rolling in over the bay. The moon hit its zenith against the dark sky. With its full white light, the fog appeared to glow from within. There were no words to describe the bay's beauty at that moment.

Driving through the avenues toward the park, the fog dissipated to softly curling tendrils close to the ground. Dru smiled to herself at the thought that the fog would be waving at her, cheering her on.

"Oh yeah, I've become Ms. Fanciful here. Hmmm, I wonder if everyone feels this way about their dream job?"

Minutes later she pulled in front of Gabrielle's stately Victorian. Once again a parking place sat vacant right out front. Once again not another car traversed the street. Nor was there another person out and about in the neighborhood. *Maybe it's just this neighborhood. I'll check with Justin about it . . . maybe. Although, with the way my life is going this could just be my own good fortune.*

The black wrought iron gate creaked as she pushed it open, the sound inordinately loud in the otherwise still night.

As on her previous visit, Dru looked up to the garret window drawn to it by the shard of white moonlight glowing above. Tonight no light glowed within the third story room. No sign of a woman watching out the window or sitting in the room. Maybe tonight Gabrielle would be in the office working beside them. After all, wouldn't she want to meet her new assistant? Even if the assistant was actually Justin's? Justin had said it didn't matter but still . . . she was a stranger coming into the author's home.

She stood outside the front door for a moment wondering if she should knock or just walk in. With a shrug, she reached for the heavy brass knocker. If Justin wanted her to just walk in, he'd tell her when the time came. She waited to a count of twenty before raising the knocker again. This time she heard footsteps coming down the hall. The porch light flipped on and the door opened to reveal Justin smiling before her.

"You came." He sounded almost surprised.

"Well, err, yes, you expected me to start tonight, didn't you? I mean, if I'm here early" . . . *I hope I'm not a few days late . . .* "like on the wrong day I can come back . . . on a better day . . . or night."

"No. No, you are scheduled to start tonight. I just lost track of time for a while there. You know how it is, you get on a roll with something and where are my manners? Come in Drusilla, please come in."

He held the door open a bit wider and gestured for her to enter. "By the way, I had a chat with Vincent and told him he needed to be on his best behavior for you."

Dru smiled, "And what did he say?"

"Meow." Justin's smile did what Dru never imagined was possible. It made him even more handsome. The man did things to her libido she didn't know could be done.

"And is that cat-anese for 'you got it?' " She smiled up at the dark haired man who had become the main attraction in her dreams and fantasies the past few nights.

Justin laughed, a solid, healthy and full-throated laugh. "I'll have to use that in a book."

"Oh, are you a writer too?"

"Writer . . . well what I mean . . . well yes, I dabble a bit. Sometimes the lines between Gabrielle and I blur. When you work with someone as closely as we do for some time, you can easily take on their manners, words, etc. Know what I mean?"

"Yes. I do. I hope to share that closeness soon too." Boy did she ever.

"Great. Well, I've set you up at the main desk. I'll work over here to the side. Just put your bag down and I'll give you a quick tour of where things are."

As instructed, Dru put her purse by the side of the heavy oak desk Justin had used the night she interviewed and turned to follow her new boss. She swallowed to keep from making a fool of herself while she eyeballed his compact, perfectly formed butt. His stonewashed jeans hid nothing but definitely fed the imagination.

"The downstairs powderroom is here." He opened a door mid-way down the hallway to reveal a half bath complete with a dry sink along with the requisite water bowl and pitcher as well as an array of decorative soaps. Antique perfume and lotion bottles sat clustered to one side, a shallow dish filled with potpourri sat to the other. Small hurricane lamps sat on either side, but at least in this room Dru noticed there was a light switch. It was going to be interesting to work by the candlelight in the office although, given the computers, printer and other office equipment, the house clearly had electricity. With a mental shrug, she figured the candles were more to set the mood than anything else.

The kitchen, however, stopped her in her tracks. Talk about a trip to the twenty-first century! The espresso maker alone was equal to one weeks' salary at her old job. The side-by-side refrigerator filled a good couple of feet against one wall. An eight-burner stove stood across from it and in the middle sat a large butcher block table with four stools situated around it. A bowl brimming with fresh fruit sat in the center.

Justin strode over to the refrigerator and pulled open one side. "I didn't know what you ate or liked so I had a fairly decent selection of foods ordered. There's eggs, cheese, milk, a few kinds of fish in the freezer, chicken and some pre-made pastas. Just let me know what you like and I'll have it delivered."

"Wow, that's great. I mean this is really nice of you. I, uh, brought a sandwich for tonight . . . you don't need to, you know, feed me. Um, Ms. George won't mind?"

"It's no worry. I should have told you earlier, meals come with the position, so just let me know what your favorites are and I'll be sure we're stocked up."

"Actually." She eyed the bar pump espresso machine. "I'd love a latte if that's possible."

"Of course! Non-fat, whole or half and half?"

"Non-fat. Here, let me try so I know how to do it."

Justin stood to the side while he measured out the beans to ground. "By the way, I have a key for you so you don't need to knock. Just let yourself in at night when you arrive. If I'm not already up . . . well downstairs, I'll have left instructions for what to do on the desk for you."

"That sounds great. That should work out well. Um, do you live here?"

Justin stared at her for a moment. He seemed startled but recovered quickly. He hadn't meant to tell her about his living situation just yet but . . ."Actually yes. I do. I uh, I moved in a few years ago. Gabrielle thought it might be better because uh, of, you know, her writing, the hours she prefers to keep." Justin drew in a breath and seemed to collect himself rather than ramble on. "You'll see that because we're on the West Coast and our agent and publisher are on the East we work slightly different hours. And, as you know, Gabrielle is reclusive. So because of timing of calls back East and how she works and since the house is so big, she suggested I move in. Made sense to me."

Dru nodded. "It would to me too."

"Good."

Feeling almost at home, Dru reached for the milk. "So,

foam for two?"

A startled Justin turned to look at her. "Foam?" Then realized what she asked. "Oh, no, none for me. At least not at the moment. Maybe later."

Dru finished preparing her latte and together they walked back to the office.

"I thought first we'd get you started on thank you notes. I know that probably sounds dull, but Gabrielle has always put her fans first and since many of the long time readers still don't use email, we try to answer the snail mail fan mail first."

"What a great way to see what I remember from which book—not that I'd be talking about . . ."

"Actually that would be a great approach. Many of them write about not just the latest book, but what happened in a prior one, especially with the different series. If you feel comfortable talking about the earlier books—and are sure you are talking about the right one, that would work well."

Justin directed Dru to the desk and showed her where the note paper and envelopes were. She was pleasantly surprised to see the antique-looking foolscap and fountain pen. "I didn't think anyone used these anymore."

Justin stared at the pen a moment and cleared his throat. "We considered using a quill for effect but the fountain pen works just as well . . . I . . . Gabrielle prefers the turquoise ink. She feels it looks more feminine than black or blue."

Dru opened the pen and wrote her name on a piece of scratch paper. "It is pretty. I'll get to work then. Did you want to look at the first few to be sure I'm on the right track?"

Her question seemed to surprise Justin, but he only explained, "Um, sorry, I've worked alone for so long it takes me a minute to think about what would work best. You're right. That would be helpful, at least at first."

He nodded to her then walked over to the smaller workspace, sat down and seemingly oblivious to her, began typing away on the keyboard. For the next several hours, Dru answered letter after letter, making note to refer to not only the book the writer mentioned in his or her letter, but referred to an earlier one in the series or simply said the writer's words reminded her of a character in another of Gabrielle's older books.

Justin sat at the keyboard, typing non-stop for several hours. When Dru glanced up now and again, it seemed the only part of him that moved were his fingers. His gaze locked on the monitor, he was definitely in his own world.

Finally, curious as to what he was working on — after all, if he were editing one of Gabrielle's books, wouldn't he stop now and again? It seemed he was writing long passages. She stood, picked up several of the responses she'd written, and ambled over to Justin. He looked up, startled, and quickly exited the document so quickly, all Dru saw were the words, *Head bent over the foolscap she wrote page after page, acknowledging the adoration* . . .

CHAPTER ELEVEN

"**W**onderful," Justin told her as he looked over the completed thank you notes. "These are exactly what Gabrielle would have written. You certainly have a grasp on her personality."

"Thanks," Dru told him. "I guess part of the difference between an okay writer and one who evokes intense emotion in her readers is allowing part of your personality into the characters. I've always felt like I knew every one of Gabrielle's characters—that they were people actually in my life. Does that sound crazy?"

"No. Not at all. That's high praise that she's creating realistic characters. She'll be very happy to hear about that. Are you ready for a break? A bite to eat?"

From the hallway the grandfather clock chimed twelve times. It struck Dru as odd she hadn't heard the clock chime the past few hours passing. She had a sense that time in the old house seemed to run at a different pace than the outside world. The night she interviewed the two hours raced by and seemed like minutes. Again tonight, it felt like she'd just started to work and here it was, midnight. "Dang, it's midnight I had no idea it was so late . . . or early. I was so wrapped up in the letters."

Justin looked over at Dru's desk and nodded. "It looks like you're going to be done with that batch in no time. At the rate you're going I'd say by the end of the week you'll be through them."

"Oh."

"Don't sound so sad. More always come in and you haven't seen the emails she gets yet, and Gabrielle answers every one. Even the quick ones that just say 'loved the book.' And when she gets reviews or readers post comments on them, she responds to them as well. You'll be in "thank you land" for quite some time. At least till we're caught up. But don't worry, there will always be more notes to answer and then, maybe we can set you to writing up some blog posts . . . at least a few interviews."

"I didn't realize there was so much to it."

Justin leaned back in his chair, stretching. There was something primal in his move, catlike with the hint of a predator preparing to stalk its prey. That simple movement left her mouth dry and her thoughts going where they had no business going, especially on her first day . . . night . . . with her boss.

"Writing is a lot more than just putting pen to page or fingers to keyboard. Success depends on a connection to readers, good marketing without overwhelming readers. It's gotten harder and harder the last several years with so many new authors and ways for people to become published."

"I don't think Ms. George has anything to worry about. She's always been the grand dame of romance. At least I think so."

Justin smiled. "We like to think so too."

Before Dru knew it, the clock chimed three. Somehow the last three hours sped by as quickly as the earlier part of the evening. She'd nibbled on some fruit and ate her sandwich while she continued to work. Not that the passage of time mattered but tomorrow night . . . or tonight . . . she'd pay more attention to the hours and whether or not the clock chimed.

An hour or so later, Justin yawned and reached to straighten his papers. "The sun should be up soon. I don't know about you, but I'm ready to turn in. Are you all right to drive?"

Dru likewise began to shut down her computer. "You bet. I feel totally energized. Actually, if you wanted, I could go for a few more hours."

Justin shook his head and finished tidying his workspace. "I need to turn in and not that I don't trust you to work on through, but tiredness does hit you when you least expect it. I predict you will sleep sound and deep today. And, we want you well rested for tonight."

"I'm looking forward to it. Tonight. I had a great time tonight."

"Easy to entertain, are you?"

Dru chuckled. "Not that easy. Overall the bank was kind of dull but you had to think and be sure of what you were doing. We balanced to the penny every night. But this, writing letters, it was fun."

"I understand. I know when I write the thank you notes at times I feel like I become someone else — not just Gabrielle, but someone else entirely. It becomes its own fictional world."

"Glad to hear that's normal. I have to admit a few times I thought about what it would be like to be Gabrielle. At least who she is when she's writing."

"Let's hope you feel that way six months from now."

"Have you had other assistants who lost their momentum?"

"No. You're the first I've . . . we've hired. You have no idea how much it will help to have you here."

"That's good news for me. Even when I first went to work at the bank, I didn't feel half as good as I did last night working here."

"Then we'll do it again tonight."

Justin walked beside her down the hall, past the stately grandfather clock, to the door. Dru took a moment to glance back at the clock. The pendulum silently swung back and forth marking time with tireless dedication.

With a flourish of sorts, Justin pulled the door open, seemingly oblivious to Dru's fascination with the clock.

"Well, goodnight. Or good morning." Dru chuckled.

Justin stepped outside the door and started down the walk beside her.

"Justin, is everything all right?"

"Yes. Why?"

"My car is right there . . . I . . ."

"I like the chance to do the gentlemanly thing now and again. I may not be up every time you leave but when I am, I'll escort you to your car."

He stood at the back end while Dru climbed in. Adjusting her seatbelt, she glanced in the rear view mirror but saw no sign of Justin. "He was standing right there. Right behind me." She shifted in the seat and looked out the back window and there he stood, arms crossed over his broad chest, a slight smile on his face. Once again she glanced in the mirror . . . not Justin . . . yet there he stood. With a shrug, she started her engine and headed down the street. Whatever was going on with the mirror was a thought for another day.

The streetlights winked off as she approached and passed in rhythm to the blooming dawn. As she looked in the rear view mirror, it seemed that each one blinked out when she was past. Like silent sentinels they seemed to light and guard her way. There had to be a simple explanation for what she thought she saw. "More like than not it's just tree branches blowing and covering the light. Of course. That's what it is."

The fog greeted her, thick and low to the ground, just outside the park presidio tunnel. Along the curved road to the entrance to the bridge, she watched, fascinated, at how the fog seemed to play in her headlights. Like a living thing it played, twisting and turning in the dim glow of the lamps. There may not be real magic in the world but this job was definitely open-ing the doors to her imagination.

CHAPTER TWELVE

Justin took his time heading back up the walk to the house.
The slight nip in the early morning air invigorated rather
than chilled him. He was probably being fanciful, but Dru left
him feeling warm. Even with her on her way home, her presence lingered.

He locked the front door behind him and started toward
the stairs. At the bottom step he stopped, momentarily lost in
thought. He'd gotten quite a bit written tonight. It seemed being around Dru energized him. A quick look down at Vincent,
accompanied by a smile, and he headed back into the office,
rebooted his computer and began to type.

*He stood at the portal, the dark fence posts with their ornamental
yet deadly finials reaching skyward on either side, watching, watching, watching until her carriage rolled out of sight. So absorbed in
watching the carriage grow smaller and smaller, he didn't notice the
snow begin to fall in the chilling air.*

"Sir?" His butler, Vincent, called to him. "Sir?"

When he didn't . . .

"Hmm, do I use didn't or did not? What would Gavin use?
Smug little pecker he is . . ."

*When he did not respond, did not move even a blink of his eye,
Vincent scuffed at the pebbles in the walkway. Gavin turned ever so
slightly toward him and reached for the cloak he knew his trusty old
butler would have in hand.*

"What do you think, Vincent? Shall I make you my butler?"

The cat stared up at him, an incredulous look in his eyes.
At least that's how it looked. For all he knew the cat

understood every word he'd said.

"Well, butlers are intelligent, you know? They are the ones who truly rule the world. Don't worry. I'll give him a big part in the story. Perhaps a lady love he wins in the end as well?"

"She will return, my lord."

"You sound sure of yourself, old friend."

"Have you ever known me to be wrong?"

There was no response to be made. Vincent knew him too well along with the uncanny ability to know the future. That he wanted Emma was beyond question. The issue was whether or not she wanted him – or would want him once she knew his secret for there was no way for them to be together if she did not know. She would need to be one with him in all ways.

A short time later, pleased with the scene, Justin stretched. He hadn't felt this inspired in ages.

He logged off as the clock chimed five. A quick glance out the window showed the sun was about ready to break through the bit of dawn that still lingered. He'd stayed up longer than he planned, but the scene he'd written flowed so easily he couldn't help but continue to write. With a quick glance about the room making sure all was secure, Justin strode up the stairs and to his room. Pulling the heavy black velvet drapes tight across the window, he again considered his evening's work. Gabrielle would be pleased.

Dru yawned as she pulled into the driveway shortly after five. Only twenty-five miles from the city and the stately Victorian, the weather was startling different. Not much warmer, but the sky was clearer. A few early morning stars dotted the sky. She let herself into the house, dropped her bag at the door and after checking the locks, headed to her room. This morning, for the first time in a long time, she didn't avoid her mother's room. Not like she had since Martha died.

The moment she walked into the room she felt like a weight

had been lifted. Actually just applying for the job with Gabrielle George was freeing, this made it more so. This morning the simple act of walking into her mother's room freed her even more. She decided with her first paycheck she was going over to the bookstore and loading up on every brand new romance on the shelves.

After her mother's death she had ordered some floor to ceiling bookcases and cleared out the spare bedroom in preparation of creating a library. Her mother had a few interesting books on the shelves in the living room. For the most part, however, they were ones she bought at her various churches and then searched for the platitudes that would support her latest theory or bid for attention. When Martha died, Dru donated most of those to the library. She supposed they could have gone back to the church, but the idea of walking in there just creeped her out.

"No more sneaking books in the house and reading under the covers with a flashlight. Never again."

Standing in the doorway, Dru reflected on the days after Martha first died. At a loss for what to do, Haley offered to help clean out her mother's belongings. The library idea though was something Dru wanted to do on her own. Her library was going to be a work of art with books in alphabetical order by author in the year they were written, and chock full of the romances she liked best of all. The online bookstore became her best friend. With the house long paid for her bills were minimal, so money to do what she wanted, within reason, wasn't an issue. "Okay, so I can't recreate the Library at Alexandria in one fell swoop. At least I'm making a start."

She walked further into the room and sat at the edge of her mother's bed thinking about Ottila and how she'd been more than ready to step into her mother's role. If Dru thought Martha micromanaged her, Ottila Millan mini-micromanaged her. At the bank Martha would stand there counting coins with her. Otilla had her do it twice. When she moved a pencil out of the way one day, the woman demanded Dru tell her why. For some reason it being in Dru's way wasn't a good enough reason for Otilla. She had been slowly fading away, day-by-day at the bank.

After a particularly uncomfortable question-answer period with Ottila asking why she did this or did that, almost like the woman was trying to creep into her brain and know her deepest thoughts, Dru took a breath and looked around the bank. Nothing ever changed. Not the off-white walls, not the black and gray floor tiles, not the wood that lined the windows, not the gray banker lamps at the officers' desks. Each workstation was a mirror of the one next to it. Not one personal item could be seen at any workstation.

But it was the women who worked there that she noticed most of all. Each one's pallor was a decided shade of gray. Whether it was because of the low wattage lamps Ottila favored or simply because they had worked there so long, each one looked washed out and drained. They smiled at customers, but the smiles didn't reach their eyes. Only on the rarest occasions did any of them go to lunch or on break together. Only two were married and their husbands looked as dour as they did.

She stifled a giggle at the thought of customers coming in one day to find Ottila dusting the staff off because they'd become statues and froze in place at their workstations.

And she knew, knew without a doubt, she had done the right thing getting out of there. Not just by going home for the night, for the weekend, but by getting another job. And Justin, had she ever tingled down to her toes just thinking about a guy? Dru shook her head when she thought back on the night and how many times she had to remind herself to stay focused on the thank you notes than on gazing across the room at Justin. Working with him was going to be a combination of heaven and hell, pleasure and frustration because what red-blooded woman wouldn't want to climb up in his lap and have her happy way with him? She so needed to keep lusting over her boss out of the work place.

Shaking off her musings, she looked around the room and softly said, "I love it, mom. I love this new job and I'm going to succeed. Too bad you aren't here to see it. Too bad you would have never supported it."

She knew if Martha were still alive and there in the room with her, she would have done all in her power to stop Dru from pursuing her dream yet again.

With a tired sigh, Dru left her mother's room and headed toward her own where she quickly undressed, washed her face, pulled on her pj's and climbed into bed, musing on how answering Gabrielle's letters tonight wasn't all that different from her drama classes. The first few letters were a tad difficult to get into but once she pretended to be Gabrielle, the words just flowed. Having read all of the author's books, usually two or three times, helped to respond to most of the questions and comments the readers made. Of course sitting across from a guy who could easily have been the hero in any one of those romances made coming up with toe curling responses to some of the letters very easy. She fell asleep imagining a close and very personal relationship with Justin, working side by side with him in the years to come.

She woke before the alarm in the early afternoon, showered, made some toast and coffee, sat down with her meal and then called Haley. "Can you talk?"

"Sure! I'm due for a break. How'd it go?"

"Great. Hale, this is going to be the best job ever. I just know it."

"So did you meet the great Gabrielle George? What's she like? Did you get a sneak peek at her newest book? Was Jason there?"

"Jason?"

"Isn't that his name, the assistant?"

"Ah, no it's Justin. And no, I didn't get to meet Ms. George. Maybe tonight. I think she turns in early. The upstairs window curtains were closed up tight when I got there last night and even though there was some creaking downstairs I didn't hear anything upstairs."

"Did you get a look at what she is working on now?"

"I don't know about her latest book. Most of last night I spent getting used to the office, finding things and answering snail mail fan letters."

"*That's* what you'll be doing? Answering a bunch of letters?"

"In part. Justin figured that would be a good way to start out getting to know her style. I figure it's also a good way to see just how much I know about Ms. George's books. The letters aren't just thank you notes, I get to add a little personal bit here and there like talking about the book they mention—if they mention one. Then I bring up another one—a nice kind of marketing tool. It's subtle. Tonight I'll be finishing up the paper letters and starting the emails. Justin also said I might be writing some responses to blog posts, you know, when I get to know what she'd say and all."

"So you're sort of pretending to be Gabrielle George?"

"Kind of. Know what the best part is?"

"What?"

"I sit like six feet away from Justin and Haley, he is hot. We're talking major hot. Last night he had on these stone-washed jeans that had to have been washed a zillion times because parts looked really soft, almost threadbare. Not threadbare in a poor way but like way sexy. And they didn't hide a thing. He's got the best buns you've ever seen. When he bent over, girlfriend . . ."

"Seriously?"

"Uh huh. And his shirt . . . well when I got there he had it buttoned up to the very top but as he worked he unbuttoned a few of the buttons. I don't think he knew he was doing it . . . for the most part he just sat there staring at his monitor and typing away and then occasionally he'd reach up and unbutton a button. By time I left this morning I had a decent gander at his chest."

"And?"

"It's fine, mighty fine."

The women giggled in shared delight. It felt so good to be away from the strictures of her mother and Ottila Millan at the bank.

"I'm glad you like it so far, Dru. It's only been a day though so keep your options open."

"Hale . . . don't."

"I'm just saying every job starts off great and then people get to where they can't keep up the happy side. You start to see where the seams are a bit frayed. Just be ready to find out he's not all that and more or that the job isn't what it's cracked up to be."

"Now you sound like my mother." Dru got ready to hang up the phone.

"No I don't. If I sounded like your mother, I would tell you that you only imagined last night was great and that you probably didn't do that great of a job and he only said that because he felt sorry for you. Then instead of telling you to keep your eyes open I'd tell you to quit so no, I don't sound like your mother at all."

"Well don't burst my bubble. Let me enjoy this." And because Haley had already started to sound a tad negative about the job, she wasn't going to tell her how Justin walked her to her car last night.

Or what she saw on his computer screen before he closed out his program at the end of the night.

Or that he seemed to fade in the mist as she pulled away from the house.

Chapter Thirteen

Since Justin told her dress was casual, on her second night of work Dru wore slacks with a nice blouse. It wasn't as formal as her outfit the night before but she wasn't quite ready to wear jeans and a sweater. Maybe next week she'd relax her dress style.

The sky above the bridge was clear as she drove across the Golden Gate and she was more surprised when a car drove down Gabrielle's street just as she turned the corner than when none had appeared the night before. Odd that this was her third time on the street and she'd already accepted that the traffic patterns were a tad different.

By time she pulled into the parking spot Justin encouraged her to use in back of the house, darkness was setting in. Not yet comfortable enough to use the back door, she followed the path to the front of the house, taking a moment to glance up at the third floor turret room and once again in what appeared to be flickering candlelight, saw the shape of a woman at the window. Okay, if she was being honest it was because she wanted to see if she could get a glimpse of Gabrielle George. She was delighted to see a woman's shape in the window and waved but received no response. Maybe Gabrielle didn't wave at strangers and since they hadn't met, Dru was still a stranger to the author.

She hesitated at the door, considering whether or not to use the key Justin had given her. Deciding she'd go for it and use it, Dru had just lifted her hand to insert it in the door when Justin pulled it open.

"Hello!" He sounded genuinely glad to see her. Standing there in his form-fitting jeans and white fisherman's sweater he looked positively gorgeous. For a fleeting moment, Dru contemplated wrapping her arms around him and planting a long, hot, wet one on those seductively sensual lips of his. That's what the heroine in the current book she was reading would have done. Gabrielle's heroines were always feisty women who knew what they wanted and exactly how to go after it.

Tonight though, here in the real world, common sense won and she returned his greeting, "Hi, yourself."

Together they started down the hall and after Dru dropped off her purse, they by tacit, unspoken agreement, headed to the kitchen. Once again she made herself a latte and Justin refused any food. He casually told her he had prepared a chicken breast stuffed with walnuts, feta and spinach for her dinner and when she was ready, it was warming in the oven. Apparently he'd already eaten but still, he'd taken time to make an extra serving for her. Inconsequential as it was they chatted about her drive home that morning and how little traffic there was. She figured telling him how she fell asleep imagining him in bed beside her doing all kinds of delicious things, wouldn't be her best idea. The evening commute into the City was a different story and Dru was glad she left a little early for work to make it in on time.

Back in the office, Dru asked, "So how was your day today?"

Justin cleared his throat. "Day? Oh, well, quiet. I got a few phone calls answered before you arrived."

"I saw . . . at least I think I saw Gabrielle upstairs when I arrived. Will I be meeting her tonight?"

"Gabrielle? Upstairs?" His brow furrowed in concentration. "Ah. No. She ah, well, it will be a while. She left on a vacation last week . . . didn't I tell you?"

"No. At least I don't remember it. Well as long as you're both happy with what I'm doing it doesn't really matter when we meet."

He seemed relieved. "Exactly. I have no doubt she'll love you. This may sound a bit premature but you are definitely her kind of person."

"That's good to know. But then who . . ."

He quirked a brow at her and she decided to let it drop. She stammered, her shyness coming to the fore, to explain why she'd been looking for Gabrielle probably wasn't such a good idea. Besides, it could have been her imagination. "So . . . well . . . then . . . I guess I'd better get to work."

Justin smiled and nodded then turned to his own computer and once again, his gaze fixed in the monitor, began typing himself.

Dru pulled the basket of letters to be answered to her and applied herself to answering the fan mail. When she'd stop to take a sip of her latte, she'd glance over at Justin. His gaze never seemed to waver from the task at hand. No wonder Gabrielle valued him as an employee and trusted his judgment hiring an assistant for himself. He was diligent about whatever his portion of the work was.

A few hours later, Justin rose and stretched. "Are you getting hungry?"

Momentarily startled, Dru looked up from the letter she'd been writing. "Actually yeah, a little. Are you?"

"Me? Ah, no. Not right now. Anytime you're ready just go ahead and grab your dinner. There's drinks and such in the refrigerator. Just make yourself at home."

"Thanks." Dru stood and twisted side to side working out the tiny kinks that had started while she'd been sitting for the past few hours. Justin had stopped typing, his fingertips resting on the edge of the keyboard and was looking into space, lost in thought. She didn't want to disturb him so she headed to the kitchen by herself. Along the way she stopped to look at a few of the portraits in the long hallway to the back of the house. She told herself she was being fanciful, thinking each one looked like Justin dressed in bygone eras. Each of the men bore a strong resemblance to the dark-haired man working away at his computer. And how could that be?

When she returned to the office, Justin rose and came over to her with a stack of papers in his hands. "I meant to give you this earlier. It's a galley for Gabrielle's upcoming release. If you get a chance to read it the next few days, I'd . . . we'd be curious what you think of it."

"Seriously? I've never read a galley before. This is way cool. Can I take it home?"

"As long as you don't show it to anyone. We like to keep these things under wraps till they're released."

"No problem. I'll start it tomorrow. You sure you wouldn't like some of this chicken? It's fabulous." She chuckled to herself. "I guess you know that being you made it, huh?"

Justin smiled back. "Yes. I've had it before. It is good. I didn't mean to interrupt your meal, take your time and as the mood hits the next week or so, if the mood hits, read it."

Electing to take a real meal break, Dru settled down to eat in the kitchen and instead of waiting, started reading Gabrielle's galley. She knew immediately it was going to be a good read because it was a historical western romance—one of the genres her favorite author did best. As she read she could clearly see Justin in the role of the half-breed Indian hero who was adored by the town he lived in by all but the woman he loved.

Full from her dinner she went and made another latte before settling back in for the next few hours of work.

Once again at the end of the night, Justin walked her to her car. This morning he'd logged off before she had so there was no tantalizing glimpse of whatever work in progress he'd been so absorbed in. What he'd given her to read had no resemblance to what she'd seen on his screen the night before. They seemed like two entirely different books. If he was editing or proofreading the most recent book, what was the one he'd given her?

On the drive home she'd put the two different books out of her mind. Arriving home a short time later, Dru treated herself to a few more chapters of Gabrielle's galley, telling herself over and over one more chapter and then she'd sleep. Before she knew it, it was mid-morning and she hadn't slept a wink. She double checked the alarm and dozed off with thoughts of the torrid love scene she'd read a short time ago, imagining she and Justin in the roles of the hero and heroine.

Her dreams started out with her riding the plains, sitting before a half-naked Justin on his horse. The scene morphed into the present day with them sitting in the office. When Justin looked over and smiled at her, she rose and started to walk over to him. When his smile turned into something a tad more sinister and fangs popped out of his mouth, she woke herself up with a short scream.

Heart beating a tad faster, Dru sat up in bed and looked around. There was no sign of Justin — not that there would be. He was a nice normal guy who lived in San Francisco and had no clue where her house was. The western galley sat on her nightstand where she left it. Clearly those love scenes melded with Haley's negative comments and the stately yet gloomy Victorian, to turn into a gothic paranormal with Justin in the role of a vampire.

"Now wouldn't that be a good read? A Heathcliff type vampire would be delicious. Maybe I'll suggest it to Gabrielle when I meet her." Although Dru remembered one interview she read where Gabrielle said while she occasionally enjoyed reading a good paranormal with a brooding vampire or a virile werewolf, it wasn't a genre she was interested in writing.

Her favorites were factually accurate romances without anything speculative to them.

"Maybe I can write it!" Dru giggled to herself. "Of course I can."

Something about the gothic vampire niggled at the back of her mind but she couldn't quite put her finger on it. Mentally putting the dream and thoughts about a brooding creature of the night aside, Dru settled back down under the covers and drifted off to sleep again. When the alarm rang, she was surprisingly wide-awake and eager to get to work.

While showering, her mind drifted once again to the galley she'd been reading and how it was nothing at all like what she'd seen in the few glimpses on Justin's computer. She puzzled on it a few minutes and then hustled to get to work on time. In the car, crossing the bridge her mind returned to the galley. In a moment of clarity, she smacked her palm against her forehead. "Of course! Justin said Gabrielle puts out four or five books a year. The galley is almost ready to go to press—he's doing edits on her next book. No rest for the romantically wicked in writing!"

Justin listened as the downstairs clock chimed four in the afternoon. He was up a bit earlier than usual, but he was rested and ready for work. The words on Gabrielle's latest story were flowing beautifully. Of course it helped that the book was pretty much writing itself, given his really cute assistant. All he had to do was glance over at Drusilla sitting there at her desk, her attention on the computer screen, the glow of the monitor shining on her face and hair, and ideas just came to him. He was pretty certain Gabrielle would be pleased with his new assistant.

Speaking of Gabrielle, remembering Dru's question about the author, Justin headed up to the third floor and unlocked the turret room. There was a slight chill brought on by the evening's fog. He walked over to the bay window and knelt on the cushions of the window seat. He studied the street and front walk, imagining what Dru saw when she approached the house.

In the dim light, he turned and looked deeper into the room. A painting of Gabrielle hung on one wall, the glass covering it polished to a clear glow. The headlights of a passing car might hit the glass . . . but it certainly wouldn't produce the image of a woman standing in the window. He continued to stand at the window and took in the items in the room, his gaze finally locking on the wig stand. Over the years Gabrielle had acquired a number of stylish wigs and hairpieces. The latest one was a bob, the style a woman in her 70s or 80s might wear.

Vincent peered around the corner of the room and looked up at him expectantly.

"I'm not sure what she saw, fella, but let's pull the curtains closed just to be on the safe side. We don't need our assistant asking certain kinds of questions just yet, do we?"

Vincent meowed in response.

With that, Justin pulled the drapery cord, sealing the room in complete darkness. With Dru due to arrive in a few minutes, he looked over the room one last time, pulled the door shut, locked it and started downstairs.

Dru walked up as he returned to the first floor. He smiled to himself as he saw her fumble with the key through the stained glass front door. Despite her being in her late-20s there was the innocence of another time in the woman. Something he liked very much.

"Oh, Justin, hi!"

"Hi yourself. Have a good day?"

"I did. You?" She smiled.

"I did. Slept like a baby." Together they headed toward the office. "Are you sleeping okay?"

"I am. I've always been something of a night owl—staying up reading way past when I should have been asleep has been a way of life for me. At one point I thought I'd like being a dispatcher because they work nights but, well, I never really pursued it. The hours here are actually pretty perfect because they fit so well with my body clock."

"Good. Good. It was a concern Madeline had—adjusting to working nights can take a little time but you seemed to do so quickly."

"I did. Did you have problems when you first started?"

"No. I'm like you—a night owl. You know, if you're ever too tired in the morning, just let me know and we can put you up here for the night. In fact, now that I think of it, you may want to bring a few things over just in case."

He noticed her surprised look and hastened to tell her, "It's just a thought. Since the house is so big, there's always room. No pressure."

"It's a good thought. I appreciate it. Thanks."

Over the next few weeks Dru learned more and more about Gabrielle's life as an author as well as the publishing business. It was so different and such a welcome change from life at the bank. Working for Gabrielle she felt valued. Ottila never complimented an employee. Do something wrong and she'd jump on you as soon as she could to berate you. But do something right, get a compliment or a thank you from a customer? Not a word. In fact the woman would spend hours looking at a spreadsheet or a group of transactions just to see if she could find something wrong to write up an employee for.

One time Dru had told Ottila that it was demoralizing when all you ever heard was what you did wrong. Ottila merely said it was her management style and if Dru ever got to be a manager she could adopt whatever style she liked.

Justin, on the other hand, always took the time to let her know when she'd done something well. What a welcome change.

As Justin had said, she moved from the snail mail fan mail to the emails and began to write some comments on review blogs. Justin still handled answering interview questions.

He seemed to anticipate her when one evening he told her, "Gabrielle has given so many interviews it's pretty easy for me to pull out the information she wants to include. I draft up the answers and then she reviews them."

"Ah, I see. So is she home?"

"Home?"

"From Europe?"

"Oh, ah no. Actually she's decided to stay in Europe a little longer. I send her the information before I turn in in the morning and she sends it back to me a day or so later. She's aware of all we're doing."

"I guess she's happy with my work?"

"Oh yeah. Totally. I guess I should have said something but I get so absorbed sometimes I lose track of time. I did let her know things are working out really well."

"Glad to hear it."

He stood and came over, leaned a hip on her desk and toyed with a pen. "You're okay with things here? You enjoying what we do?"

Dru nodded. Despite the sometimes-odd happenings inside the house, it really was a great job. And more than that, Justin was much better to look at than the staid wooden teller windows at the bank and Ottila sitting across the way just looking for anyone to make the slightest mistake. It felt good, just so good to let some creativity into her life. "Honestly it's the best job I've ever had. It's like not working at all."

"That's how it should be. At least with writing you need to work your passion."

Dru nodded again and rather than make a fool of herself by either reaching out and showing him how she'd really like to work her passion and grabbing in a torrid lip lock, she turned back to the review comment she'd been working on. Working her passion was an understatement. Although she wondered what Justin would think if he knew he had become the main focus of her dreams the past few weeks and those dreams were getting hotter and hotter. Like a well-written Regency, in her dreams, they danced around their attraction with ever growing sexual tension. There were times, like tonight, when her body reacted to just being in Justin's presence. Just the thought of the man turned her on and being around him . . . well she had no doubt if he touched her she'd go up in flames. Working her passion was definitely one thing she wanted to do with this man.

And it's time to drag my mind out of that gutter because if I don't I'll be sighing and otherwise embarrassing myself big time. And I'm not sure which team he plays on now, am I?

"And I keep meaning to tell you, I love the book . . . the galley . . . you gave me to read. I'm not sure how you do it, when you proofread her books and I probably should have asked — I, well I read it through once and now I'm going back through it much more slowly looking for typos and things like that."

"That sounds about right. So you got into the story?"

"Justin, it's probably the best book she's ever written."

He gave her a broad smile. "I'm glad to hear it. Knowing how much you read, especially Gabrielle's work, that's high praise."

"It is, Justin. She's the best in historical romance. When I read her books, I feel not only like I'm there but sometimes I feel like I'm the heroine."

"You do?" He looked completely surprised by her statement.

"That probably sounds crazy."

"No."

"Yeah, it's okay to say it does. It's the way she writes . . . you get so pulled into the story, so deep into the heroine's thoughts that you feel not only that you *know* her but that you could *be* her."

"I don't think it's crazy at all, Drusilla. An author wants a reader to be completely immersed into a story. If . . . we're doing that, then we've accomplished our goal."

Dru nodded. "And I can see how she's changed, grown I guess, from her earlier books."

Justin raised his eyebrows in surprise and scrubbed his hand across his jaw. "Is that so? Does it . . . do you get the sense it's still Gabrielle writing or . . . well, does it seem like it's someone else?"

Dru thought about his question for a few moments. "No, it's definitely her. The change has been gradual, like she's been honing her style. I can't wait to see what she does next."

With that, Justin returned to his desk and the pair worked, each in their own world, into the early hours of the morning.

Ever the gentleman, despite her parking out back, each morning Justin still walked her to her car. Sometimes he followed her down the driveway and stood at the edge of the street until she pulled completely out and drove from sight. There didn't seem to be a rhyme or reason when he'd do this but each time he'd stand there, he'd seem lost in thought. This morning was no different.

Over the first few weeks Dru and Justin developed a solid working relationship and style. Despite her desire for more adventure in her life, Dru did like routine and her job gave her both. Each night she arrived for work, parked behind the house and, with Justin's approval, walked in the back door. Sometimes he'd be in the midst of making her a latte while other times she'd set about making her own before joining him in the office. Half way through the night, she'd stop for dinner. It seemed like Justin ate before she arrived each night because he never joined her for a meal.

And they'd joke. Justin had a great sense of humor and timing, and would have her in stitches over some oddball comment. He spoke little of himself or of Gabrielle for that matter, except to occasionally relate an incident that came up while working on an earlier book. Rather than talk about himself, he often asked Dru about events from her own life. She had no doubt they were developing a solid friendship and that worked just fine . . . as long as she didn't let on how he filled out her very rich and full fantasy life, that was just fine.

Surprisingly Dru's own innate wit, kept buried for so long, emerged, and she'd have him laughing as well. A few times he'd stop her in the middle of a story about her childhood and tell her what she was saying was too good and he wanted to make notes—that maybe someday Gabrielle would want to use something similar in a story . . . with her permission that was. It thrilled her to think an otherwise minor event from her life was worthy of mention in one of Gabrielle's stories.

Life was good. The job was everything she ever wanted. There were a few times she wished she could tell her mother how happy she was. But then her mother wouldn't share her joy, not at all. Never at all.

Still, she got to talk about how happy she was when Dru and Haley caught up with each other on weekends. A few times she met the women from the bank for coffee and each one of them told her how happy they were that at least one of them escaped Ottila.

Her dreams took her to far away times and places—with Justin in the role of hero in each one. Occasionally a not so great one would creep in with him parting his lips to reveal fangs. But then another dream person, who also looked like Justin, would appear and rescue her. The man definitely gave her a rich and full fantasy life.

Yes, life was good. Dru was truly happy for the first time in her life.

And then one morning life came crashing down around her.

Chapter Fourteen

Dru rolled over and snuggled up against the warmth. So warm, so enticing. Suddenly the man behind that warmth moved, shifted ever so slightly so that he could hold her closer. Dru opened her eyes and met the rich brown ones of Justin Hunt. He smiled, ever so slightly. The five o'clock shadow of his beard made his teeth look even whiter. The slight crinkling at the corners of his eyes caused her stomach to flutter in anticipation. He'd done this before, come to her bed in the middle of the night and woke her with gentle kisses. Kisses so gentle, so feather light she felt she almost imagined them except the imprint of his lips lingered.

With a hand on her hip, he pulled her to him and whispered as if in prayer, "Drusilla. Drusilla, I need you."

"Oh, Justin, I need you too. I've needed you for my whole life."

"I'm here now, love. I'm here now."

She felt his manhood rise against her belly. Hot and thick with his need. Dru reached between them leaving only the slightest of spaces between their bodies. The rush of chilled air caused from that ever so slight separation from him made her nipples peak and harden. Not that Justin's ministrations didn't help that growing need to abate. His every move set her on fire, burning ever more strongly for him.

She feathered a touch at the tip of his penis. A just-barely-there caress that caused his breath to catch.

Justin closed his eyes and drew in a shaky breath.

She stroked downward, to the core of his cock while he

matched her soft, yet oh so firm stroke on her breast.

He placed a quick kiss on her lips before dipping his head to take a nipple into his mouth. Justin moaned with need as she slowly, so erotically, stroked his length up and down. His cock heated in her hand . . . a tiny pearl of his nectar beaded at the top. Without looking she unerringly brought her finger to the tip and spread his cream along his length before sliding her hand lower and cupping his balls. Dru moaned with pleasure at the treasure she held.

He wouldn't give an inch. He would match her move for move and without lifting his lips from her breast, he rolled her over and brought his other hand up to caress her other breast. Dru writhed beneath him.

"Justin . . . Justin, I can't . . . when you touch me like that . . . I can't . . . I want . . ." She grasped his balls, made ever so slightly tighter by her ministrations, and fondled him.

"You can't what, love?" he asked against her lips.

"I can't focus on you when you . . . ahhh, Justin."

"Then don't. Just let me . . ." He slid into her. Hilt deep, he rested on top of her a moment before kissing her deeply. With his tongue he showed her what he would do with his hips, his cock, how his body pleasured her beyond words.

"Justin . . . mmm, Justin . . ."

The alarm jarred Dru awake. Sleepily she fumbled to turn it off. Only it wasn't the alarm . . .it was her phone!

Ticked at the interruption, she let voicemail pick it up then turned her head on the pillow looking for Justin. She slid her hand on the side of the bed, momentarily to find it cold to the touch. Had he come and gone? "Justin?" She raised her head and called out. "Justin?"

Disappointed, she dropped her head back down on the pillow. Of course he wasn't there. It was a dream. Yet another dream about Justin Hunt. The man she worked for. Her boss. The man who was becoming one of her best friends and who she secretly lusted after.

At least she hoped it was still secret. That wasn't something she wanted him to know. Not at the risk of losing her job.

Dru shook her head at herself. This had to stop. Every night since she met him, he'd appeared in her dreams and each one became hotter and hotter. Most of the time they were akin to scenes from one of Gabrielle's books, the ones where the lovers would come close, so close to physically consummating their union just before the door would close and the chapter end.

The dreams the past few nights had intensified, becoming more and more erotic. This one was the closest she'd come to a climax. This one . . . it was the first time he entered her in the dream state and it felt good. So good.

But it wasn't going to be a reality. She was his employee and for as nice as he was, Dru knew she wasn't quite Justin's type.

Not that she knew his type. But when a guy was that gorgeous, that sexy, that masculine, he didn't go for a plain Jane like Drusilla.

Down the hall she heard a male voice droning on the answering machine. She couldn't place the voice but was pretty certain it wasn't Justin. For him she would have gotten up and run to the phone. With a glance out the window, she saw it was still rather early in the day. Justin would certainly be asleep.

In the future she'd silence the machine before going to bed. Haley was usually the only one to call her and she knew Dru was working nights and wouldn't call so early. "Probably a telemarketer getting an early start on the day."

She closed her eyes with the hope she'd fall back asleep without much effort and that the dream would resume.

"If wishes were horses . . ." Dru rolled over and pounded the pillow. The ordinarily quiet neighborhood seemed to have a massive construction project starting if the sounds she heard were any indication. Between the banging and the sound of her phone ringing yet again, it seemed she wasn't going to make it back to sleep any time soon. "Maybe I can catch a nap before I leave this afternoon.

Once again a man's voice could be heard on the answering machine and the banging got louder. Giving up on sleep, Dru realized the banging was on her front door. She grabbed a robe and headed to the front of the house, ready to give the intruder a major piece of her mind.

She dropped her jaw when she saw who stood on the other side of the door.

CHAPTER FIFTEEN

"M-M-Mr. Armstrong?"

His lip curling, the dark haired man looked her up and down and sneered. "Miss Montgomery."

Dru pulled her robe closer and retied the sash. With a moxie Dru wasn't aware she possessed, she questioned her mother's sleazy attorney a bit more nicely than she felt he deserved. "What are you doing here?"

He ignored her question and simply stated, "You are making a spectacle of yourself. Your mother would be appalled to see you standing there in your undergarments."

Dru looked down. "Uh, this is my robe, not quite my under . . . excuse me, I don't see how that's your business."

He pushed at the door, edging past her. "Might I come in before you embarrass yourself?"

Her moment of bravado passed and she answered, "Uh. Sure. Fine." She held the door open to let the attorney in and pointed him to the living room. "If you give me a minute, I'll throw on some clothes."

"Of course."

Striding into the living room as if he owned the house, Armstrong didn't seem to be giving her a second thought.

Dru hurried down the hall and locked the bedroom door behind her. Not that Armstrong would pull anything . . . at least he wouldn't have while her mother was alive. Something felt wrong about him just showing up on her doorstep unannounced at ten in the morning. She'd always felt he was up to something, but her mother adored him. They had, of course, met at one of her myriad churches. Most of the parishioners didn't stick at that particular church for the long term but Armstrong did. He'd never done anything overt, but something about the man just creeped her out.

She quickly threw on a sweatshirt and some jeans, washed her face, brushed her hair and teeth and then headed out to find out why her mother's attorney just showed up out of the blue. The estate was settled months ago, and he should have been long gone.

Armstrong turned from the bookcase where Dru had placed some of her latest acquisitions—pretty much every new erotica on the market—when she walked into the room. From the look on his face, he clearly wasn't pleased with her selection of books. Before she could say a word, he asked, "Is there a reason you do not answer your phone?"

"Excuse me?"

"I tried to reach you three times this morning. Is there a reason you are letting your voicemail pick up? Your mother certainly would never have done that."

Dru sat. Well that explained all the ringing noise while she was trying to sleep.

She wasn't about to offer him any coffee. Not with an opening salvo like that. Enough was enough. Gathering back some of her bravado and sense of self, she answered, "Not that it's any of your business, but there are a lot of things my mother wouldn't do that I have no problem doing."

"She would be appalled."

"Mr. Armstrong, my mother is dead. She has been for several months. It's time for me to be making my own way. If I've changed some things, it's because it was a long time coming. What I do is none of your business."

The man shook his head and seemed to be on the verge of shedding a few tears. "This is a sad situation."

The teary part had Dru feeling contrite. "I'm sorry. This got off to a bad start. I was only asleep for a few hours and you kind of startled me awake."

"That's partly why I'm here this morning. Drusilla, I'm concerned about you."

Odd how when Justin called her Drusilla it sounded like a caress and it curled her toes, but when Armstrong called her that it came across like a reprimand.

"I'm fine. Actually I've never been better. Life has been pretty good."

"Without your mother?"

Dru thought about the question for a moment. "I miss her, of course. But life goes on and I'm doing what I think is best with mine, so there's no reason for concern."

"Actually, Drusilla, there is." His arrogance back in place the man rose and hands in his pockets, ambled over to the front window and back again to stand in front of her.

"Mr. Armstrong, I'm twenty-eight years old. I've got a great job, my bills are all current. I'm healthy and life is good. I can't see any reason for concern. It was kind of you to come by . . ."

"Drusilla." His tone stopped her in her tracks. "There *is* a concern."

She leaned back in the chair and crossed her arms. "I'm listening." And hoping he'd get to the point quickly so she could get on back to sleep and those dreams of Justin.

He turned and headed back to the chair he'd been sitting in. "I've been hearing things."

"Uh huh."

"I heard you left your job at the bank. A good stable job your mother obtained for you. One that would have secured your future. I understand from a credible source that you leave the house just before dark and are out gallivanting most of the night and that you spend your days sleeping. At least from what I've seen this morning it does, indeed, appear you are sleeping away your days not at all unlike a cheap whore. That doesn't sound like someone whose life is under control."

Now she was getting royally pissed at the attorney, "Not that it is your, or your not-so-credible source's business, but yes, I did quit my job at the bank because I took another one. I work, nights, as an *administrative assistant*. I'm making more money than I made at the bank and love it."

"You. Work. Nights? As an administrative assistant?" He couldn't have sounded more incredulous than if she'd told him she'd been spending her days entertaining hot men with two penises from Mars.

"Yes."

"Well it must stop. Now, I've spoken with Ms. Millan at the bank and she is willing to give you your job back. There will, of course, be a slight cut in pay and you'd need to start your tenure over again with only five vacation days a year instead of the ten you had been earning when you left . . ."

"No."

His mouth popped open and for the first time since she'd met him he seemed to be without words. Finally finding his voice, he asked, "Excuse me?" He was truly shocked.

"No. I'm not going back to the bank."

Armstrong huffed out a breath. "Let me explain."

"There is nothing to explain. I'm happy with my life right now. I have everything I want and life is good."

"But you will not have it for long unless you do as I'm going to tell you."

Was he bullheaded or what? Dru shook her head. "Mr. Armstrong, you aren't making sense."

"Please, just listen."

At her nod, he continued, "Your mother owned this house outright. The title was in her name and her name only."

"Right. And on her death title reverted to me." This discussion was pointless . . . why wouldn't he just leave? Better yet, why had he come in the first place?

"In a manner of speaking. The way her will reads is that you may remain in the house *only* if you continue to work at the bank until it is time for you to retire. Your remaining in the house is contingent on continuing to live the life your mother lovingly carved out for you. If you intend to keep living here, you will need to resign your position—whatever it is you are doing—and immediately return to the bank. As I said, you are fortunate Ms. Millan is willing to accept you back."

Dru was too stunned to speak. Her head ached like a shard of ice had sliced into her mind. The house, her home, was tied to her remaining at the bank? How could that be? She swallowed and rethought everything Armstrong had said to her.

"Drusilla?"

Her mind spun and she groped for words. "Mr. Armstrong, are you certain? That my continuing to live in my house, my home, is contingent on my working at the bank? How can that be?"

"It is how your mother laid things out in her will. My job is to ensure it is carried out to the letter. So, shall I tell Ms. Millan you will be returning in two weeks?"

Chapter Sixteen

Dru studied the document Armstrong left with her. No matter how she looked at it the words still said the same thing . . . she had to work at the bank or lose her home. Leave it to her mother to find a way to continue to make her life less than what she wanted, even from the grave.

"I should be sleeping. I should be sound asleep and dreaming about Justin Hunt and some fabulous future for myself, not worrying about losing my home." She raked her fingers through her hair.

Oblivious to the cold coffee that had sat in front of her the past few hours, Dru rose from the kitchen table and paced back and forth in the room. It might not be much, but it was her kitchen . . . or had been. "I can't go back there. I just can't. I'll wither away and die at that bank."

Her stomach cramped with the grief coursing through her. Grief for the loss of her life, the life she wanted for herself. She could either have a roof over her head or a job she was quickly coming to love. It wasn't like she could buy the house because her mother owned and encumbered it. Knowing Martha, she had some sort of condition that if Dru lost the house because she wasn't working at the bank that she couldn't buy it outright. And really, where would she find the money for even the down payment? Gabrielle paid her pretty well. Excellent in fact, but her savings were minimal. Certainly not enough to even start to buy the house outright.

Despondent, she looked at the clock. Haley should be getting off work soon and she had some time before leaving for her own job. Fighting her growing despair, she dialed her friend.

"Dru! What's up? Read any juicy chapters yet?" Haley asked when she heard Dru on the line.

"What? Oh, chapters. No. Haley, I need to talk to you. I've got a problem. A major big problem and I don't know what to do."

"Problem? What's up? What can I do?"

"Oh I don't know. Got an extra $30,000 or so laying around?"

"You aren't making sense. $30,000? For what?"

"My house."

"Your house? Did something happen?"

"Martha happened. My own mother happened."

"How?"

"Her will. Haley, her will stipulates that I can keep the house and all her belongings *if* I remained working at the bank. Otherwise it goes off to one of her church charities."

"Huh? Are you sure? That's kinda weird, isn't it?"

"I don't know. I don't know anything about this kind of stuff."

Haley huffed out a sigh. "Well that's your mom for you."

"That isn't helping me."

"I'm trying."

Dru took a shaky breath. She'd been so numb with the news, tears hadn't even formed until she heard Haley's voice. "My mother . . . she always had to be in control and this was her way of controlling me from the grave. If I didn't do as she demanded, I lost my home. If I obeyed her from the grave dictate, while I'd have a home, I'd be miserable. Just the way she liked my life to be. Miserable."

"Oh Dru, that's not true. She loved you, I know she did."

"No? Think about it. She always found a way to manipulate a situation so I felt like I was in the wrong and she always had to be perfect, always the put upon victim. She always held back some crucial piece of information, something I needed to know to make a decent decision, so of course I'd make the wrong one or one she could look all superior about when something went south. And now this."

"Dru, listen, I'm on my way over. Order up some Chinese and I'll be there in a few."

Needing to talk to Haley and get some of her angst out, Dru called Justin and left a message that she'd be a little late. Hopefully he would understand. She'd never been late before and hadn't missed any days in the two months she'd worked for him.

True to her word, Haley arrived just as Dru finished dressing for work. Justin hadn't called her back, but she wanted to be ready to take off as soon as she and Haley were done talking. She had two weeks to figure something out and in that time she could continue to work for Gabrielle George. And then . . .

Dinner arrived at the same time Haley pulled up. Together they opened up the cartons of fried rice, mushu pork and garlic shrimp.

"Tell me what happened. Start from the beginning." Haley pointed with her chopsticks.

"My mother's attorney, Mr. Armstrong, came over this morning. Woke me up like 10:00 a.m., half way through what's now my night. He wasted no time telling me what the terms of the will were and he said I needed to quit my job with Gabrielle George immediately and return to the bank. He looked like Snidely Whiplash with this sickly smile and assured me that as a favor to my mother, because of her long-standing relationship with them, the bank would be happy to have me back. Apparently he had a conversation with Ottila before he came over here and I think was going back after we spoke to tell her what happened."

"What did you say? Are you going back?" Haley wriggled about on the couch where she'd been sitting to eat. It was something Martha would have never allowed—eating anywhere but at the kitchen table or, if it was a fancy event, the dining room. Eating from cartons in the living room was one of Dru's little bits of rebellion, not that Martha would ever know about it.

"I told him I'd think about it and sent him on his way. Instead of spending my day getting some much needed sleep, before returning to work tonight, I've been sitting here trying to figure out what to do. I suppose I should have started to look for a new place to live. I have two weeks to, as he put it, come to my senses or leave."

"Seriously?"

"Yes. Totally seriously. And you know what surprised me most?"

Haley shook her head.

"That she gave me two weeks to decide. She must have been feeling sick that day because that so isn't like my mother. The Martha I knew would have made it happen immediately."

"Dru, that's not so. I told you before, your mom loved you. I know she did." But Haley didn't sound all that sure of her words.

"No, Haley, she loved herself and only herself. It was all about her. You can't believe someone wouldn't love their child and want the best for them, but when it comes to my mother it was all about her and only her. She probably put in that two week grace period so she'd look good in front of Armstrong or his staff because she'd never give an inch to me."

"What are you going to do?"

Dru sadly shook her head side to side. "I don't know. I honestly don't know. Right now I'm too numb to make a decision and I don't really have enough information."

Haley picked up the will and looked it over. "Looks pretty straight forward to me. Plain and simple—it says you continue to work at the bank until you are, hmmm, 62, and then you get to keep the house. If you leave the . . . oh *that* church. The one where they wore those white dresses on Wednesday nights is the one that gets it."

"You remember that?"

Haley finished chewing a piece of shrimp and swallowed. "Yeah. Remember how she'd get all duded up in those long white gowns, like a prom dress or some virginal sacrifice? And the time she brought us for some sort of induction or celebration or something and she was mincing up the aisle like it was a wedding or something?"

"Wow, that's the first time I think I've heard you talk about her church stuff like it was ludicrous. You used to always be saying it wasn't all that bad."

"Yeah, well times change. I've seen how happy you are working in the city and for Gabrielle George. You've been different since you've been there, Dru. A lot happier. You used to have moments but since you've been there it's like you're a whole new person."

"Do you like this . . . new me?"

"I didn't dislike the old one but yeah. You're a lot happier, you kinda glow and all, especially when you talk about Justin. Say, do you think he could or would help?"

"Hale, I don't want him to know. I don't want him to even have an inkling that my life is less than stable in any way. The job is still too new and either he or Gabrielle is eccentric enough that I don't want to take any chances of losing it. And then there's those idiosyncrasies of his."

"You mean the not eating and drinking thing?"

Dru shook her head.

"I wouldn't worry so much about that. I mean, everything

else with him is good, right?"

"Yes."

"But this business with Armstrong, you will lose the job if you go back to the bank," Haley pragmatically told her.

Dru sagged back in her chair. "Haley, I'll die if I have to do back to the bank. I just know it."

"You mean like you'll be standing there and just keel over?"

"Haley, come on. No. I mean it will keep sucking the life force out of me. Justin may be a hot bite-me-in the neck vampire, but Ottila is a psychic vampire—sucking me dry bit by bit until there is nothing left. I was miserable there. From the very first day I was miserable and it never got any better. Between Ottila and my mother constantly looking over my shoulder and micromanaging every little move, I was suffocating there. You know how paranoid she was always asking, 'What are you doing?' 'Why are you doing that?' 'How did you decide you were going to do that?' I couldn't move a pencil across the counter to get it out of my way without her asking about it. And Ottila! She was a hundred times worse. She probably taught my mother how to be a consummate micromanager. Martha was always looking up to Ottila like she was something so wonderful."

"Hmm, do you think they . . . you know?" Haley twirled her hand in a circle implying Ottila and her mother may have been an item.

"My mother and Ottila? Ohhh no. Grayson, Grayson Harrington was the great love of her life and even though he's been long gone and probably dead for years, she'd never even consider cheating on him and trust me, even having a coffee with Grayson was high romance for her."

"Never know."

Dru laughed. "Hale, that is totally the ick factor. Please, no more. My boss writes romance, not horror and my mother and Ottila would be horror."

"Glad you are laughing a bit. Are you feeling better?"

"Yeah, a little." Dru looked at the clock, "I gotta go! I told Justin that I'd be a little late but I don't want to be too late."

"Go. I'll clean and lock up for you."

Dru grabbed her purse and ran out to her car. On the way to the city the events of the day replayed over and over in her mind. Armstrong waking her up, giving her the news about her mother's will, insisting she return to the bank and give up the life she was carving out for herself. The fog blanketed the bay, seeming to call out to her.

Dru slowed as she approached the Golden Gate Bridge. Not just because of the lower speed limit but because she wanted to enjoy the moment, the way time seemed to suspend itself when the fog settled in. The span symbolized her old life from her new. Each night when she crossed it was a reaffirmation that she was not in control over her life.

By time she arrived on Gabrielle's street, Dru knew that somehow she had to find a way to stay at this job. The house was just a structure, a place where she lived but it wasn't a home. Not really her home. It was her parents' home . . . Martha's really. For Dru, it was just the place she went to at the end of each day.

She could move! She could live anywhere. Not just Marin — she could move to the city, rent a house or an apartment, get a roommate if need be. There were possibilities upon possibilities.

Time and distance from the house helped to see beyond the moment and that there were options for her. That was something that never happened when Martha was alive. If anything, her mother would have belittled the options. She would have diminished them and tried to make Dru feel like she was incapable for any kind of independent thought.

Amazing how a simple drive across the bridge could

change her whole perspective! Well, that and the fog. Some people expressed annoyance at the fog or found it made them uneasy. Dru found it comforting in its way. In a manner it cocooned and carried her away to another place.

By now she took the stillness of Gabrielle's street as normal. It no longer seemed eerie to her. The grandfather clock chimed seven when she walked in the door. Not that Justin was a stickler for her comings and goings, and she had called that ahead, but she still hated to be late. He was more than generous about that. More than once he'd told her he knew she worked hard and the man was more interested in her diligent writing and taking care of administrative details than the more mundane aspects of a job like clocking in and out precisely on time.

He looked up from his desk and smiled when she walked in. Despite working here for two months and seeing that smile five nights a week, he could still melt her with a look. Not that Dru would ever let on. That could well cost her the job or at a minimum make things decidedly uncomfortable for both of them. Better that she sat at her desk keeping her lascivious thoughts about her boss to herself. Sometimes though . . . when she'd read a particularly scintillating scene where the hero brought the heroine to bed for the first . . . or second time . . . she couldn't quite see anyone's face but Justin's or imagine anyone else wrapping their legs around his but hers.

"How are you doing?" Justin asked her, a concerned look on his face.

"Good. You?"

"Excellent. Are you sure you're all right?"

"I am. And I'm sorry I was late. Something came up that I kind of had to take care of. I promise it won't happen again." *I hope.*

"No worries. The rest of the world is conducting business while we're sleeping so I completely understand how there will be times when you need to deal with a day time business."

"Thanks, Justin. I still feel bad . . . hopefully if something comes up again, I'll have a little more notice so I'm not ditching you at the last minute."

"Seriously, not a problem. Now if that's settled, if you are okay with it, I have a few chapters for you to look over tonight. It's the first love scene between Christina and Derek in her current work in progress. I need . . . Gabrielle . . . needs to know if it works. She tried . . . well, she's trying something a little different with it."

"I'm looking forward to it." Dru put down her purse and started for the door. Christina and Derek weren't the names she'd seen on Justin's computer nor in the galley she'd been going over, but as she considered before, it stood to reason Gabrielle would have several books in different stages at different times. Authors probably were no different than readers who needed an occasional break from historical romance to read a good cozy mystery before wandering back into romance.

"Is it okay if I grab a coffee before we get down to it?" More like she needed a few quad shots tonight.

"Sure. Take your time. Oh, and we got a delivery from Hastings Market today. I saw one of their quiches in there and it looked pretty good."

"Mmm. I might take a look at it now. Did you want a slice too?"

"Um, no, I'll ah, I'll pass for now."

"Okay, well, let me know."

Justin had already turned back to his monitor, and Dru stopped to study him for a moment. With his head bent ever so slightly over the keyboard, the glints from the ever-burning candles coupled with the monitor's diffuse light, soft gold highlights shone in his hair. At times, like this, despite the deep brown of his hair, he reminded her of the Scots warriors Gabrielle often wrote about. Justin never showed any interest in her beyond work and a bit of friendship—which was fine because it was, after all, her job. But he never got calls from women and none ever came by while they worked. He was discrete, if nothing. Which begged the question—did he like women or did he relate to them?

Well, it didn't matter, did it? As long as the books sold and sold well and she had her job, it didn't matter at all.

Vincent followed her into the kitchen, and Dru took a few treats out of his jar for him before starting to work on her latte and warming her quiche. Vincent looked up as if studying her between bites of his treats.

"Yeah. I not only have a job and a job I really, really like, but I'm not sure about my home. I tell you, Vincent, some days I think when I come back in my next life, I want it to be as a cat."

Vincent stared up at her and gave a soft meow.

"Gotcha. Cats don't all have it all that easy, do they? A lot of you have to worry about a home and food and everything. Maybe that's why we get along, huh? I understand your plight."

The timer buzzed on the oven, signaling the quiche was warmed, and Dru finished frothing her latte milk. Vincent followed her back to the office.

"I left the pages on your desk," Justin told her. "No rush, just sometime this week if you can give them a look-see."

Dru slid into her chair and took a sip of her latte. "I'm caught up on both the snail and electronic fan mail and have a few interviews done, so I'm more than ready to be transported to another time and place."

Justin smiled. "Transport away."

"I will. By the way, I'm almost done with the galley you asked me to read."

"And? What do you think?"

Dru scooted to the edge of her chair and leaned her elbows on her knees. "Justin, I told you before, I think it's the best book I've ever read. Gabrielle has outdone Gabrielle. It's fantastic. The tension between Rachel and Corey is palatable. You can feel their desire through the pages. My toes curled and haven't uncurled since."

Justin chuckled. "That's a great line—haven't uncurled. I've said it before but it bears repeating, you have a great sense of wording."

"Why thank you! But if I can say good things about the book, it's because the book is good. Trust me, if it wasn't a great read I'd tell you."

"And the time period? Does it work for you?"

"Oh yes! I love post-civil war stories that take place in the West. At least the romance ones. Gabrielle brings the trials and tribulations to life and the romance . . . Justin, if you lived back then, would you have wanted a mail order bride?"

Justin chuckled. "I might. It would depend on the woman. She'd need to be a reader, particularly a reader of romance."

"You goof."

"But a goof you like working with."

"That is true. Very true." With a smile, she picked up the pages Justin had given her and fanned them, "Well I'm thinking I've got some more good reading ahead of me."

"Enjoy." Justin turned back to whatever he was working on at his desk.

Dru dug into the chapters, turning page after page, only occasionally making a notation in the margins. Oblivious to everything else around her, the coffee and quiche grew cold. If she noticed the slight clicking of Justin's keyboard, it became part of the story. It wasn't until the stocky candles sitting on the desk beside her flickered out, she realized how dark the room had become. She looked up and the room was almost entirely in darkness. Across from her Justin sat in the pale glow of the monitor, his expression unreadable, watching her.

She took in a quick breath and again glanced around the room and then back to the man who sat there so silent, so still. If ever a romance hero came to life it was Justin Hunt.

Granted, she had no idea about the man outside this room, outside this house. But his looks, his manners, his way of speaking was the epitome of what every romance writer she'd ever read poured into the men who filled their pages. He was handsome with a devastating smile, a body that any woman would want in her bed, polite, courteous and just enough mystery about him to make him intriguing. And in his own way he was a hero — after all he gave her this job. The job that may well cost her her home.

Unsure what to say or do, Dru quickly glanced at the clock on the computer. It was almost 4:00 a.m. She'd been reading for hours completely oblivious to everything around her but the couple finding each other on the pages of Gabrielle's latest book. She hadn't even heard the grandfather clock in the hall clock chime once through the night.

"Well," Justin broke into her thoughts, "either the book is so bad you can't believe you are reading such dribble or it's so good you can't tear yourself away from it."

Dru rose and headed over to him. "Justin. It's fantastic. Gabrielle has another best seller. I'm sure of it."

He looked up at her and studied her face as if seeing her for the first time. "Is it?"

"Oh yes. Justin this has to be one of the best Gabrielle's ever written. In fact I think it is the best romance I've ever read, well, aside from the galley I've been reading. In this one, the hero just breaks my heart. The way he yearns for the heroine even though there is no way they can ever be together. The way he talks about how his heart will break again and again if only for a moment with her. How he feels he will never deserve her no matter what he does and how he risks his life time and again in the hopes that maybe, just maybe, she might open up to him ever so slightly."

Justin gave her a small smile before she continued.

"And she's so wonderfully written. I've read shy heroines before but the pain of being that shy, that unsure . . . I've never seen it so sensitively written. It's still Gabrielle George. That much comes through in the story but it's different. Totally different in voice than anything else I've ever read."

"I'm glad you like it."

She looked into his eyes and was surprised to see the need in his gaze. "I love . . ." She bit her tongue to keep from saying "you." "Justin, I love this story. I can't wait to read all of it."

He smiled. Not his usual killer sexy smile but a softer, sweeter one. A smile that reflected the need she was seeing in his eyes. "Soon. I have to decide how they will consummate their relationship. He . . . I've decided, that is, Gabrielle has decided, the hero has a secret. One he is sure will destroy the fragile love between them."

Dru sank onto the desk chair beside Justin. "What kind of secret?"

"A deep, dark one. One that has destroyed relationships for him before. One that even he cannot bear. One that if a woman told him was something in herself, he doesn't know if he could get past it."

"Something he could die from? Or other people could be hurt by?" she whispered as if they shared a secret between them.

"Yes. Exactly. It is a secret that would destroy so many if they knew."

The hall clock chimed five in the morning. Justin looked up and toward the window, startled. "It's morning. Time to turn in. I need . . . you need to go. It will be light soon."

"Oh. Uh, right. I lost track of time. I'll let myself out and uh, see you tonight?"

Justin began to shut down his computer. With quick strokes, he saved the document he'd been working on and began to log out of his programs.

The moment broken, Dru walked over to her desk and did the same process of logging off and out.

As usual Justin walked her to the door but instead of stepping out as he usually did, he stood just inside the threshold. "Drive safe. I'll see you tonight."

For some reason the man had hurried her out of the house. The sun began to peak through the nighttime clouds as Dru crossed the bridge. He'd always been conscious of when it was time to end for the night but this morning he seemed more hurried. Perhaps it was because the days were getting longer. Still, it was odd how he seemed to hide from daylight.

After her day the day before and the long night lost in another time and place, the lack of sleep began to catch up with her. Looking for something to focus on to keep her away until she arrived home, Dru thought about Justin. She'd found fantasizing about her boss tended to keep her awake . . . and inspired. This morning her thoughts went to his hands. Strong hands with fine, long fingers. She imagined those fingers on the keyboard and then the words she'd seen on his screen came to her . . .

It was coming time to tell her. Gavin had no doubt once Emma knew of his true state, she would flee. Their time together would be done. He'd kept his secret for generations. Oh he'd known women, been with women and left them before they could take his heart — and he did have a heart. They said one of his ilk had no heart. That when he'd been changed, become a creature of the night that his heart was forfeit. Little did they know . . . he still had a heart and it still hurt when he had to part from one he loved.

Loved . . . it had been too long and despite his best intentions, he'd fallen in love with his quiet little assistant. She was so sweet, so kind, so good but not so compassionate as to love him despite the dark side of his nature.

Yes. It was time . . . time to tell her and then, before she ran from him . . . change her.

CHAPTER SEVENTEEN

"Hmm, is Gabrielle starting to write paranormal?" Dru asked herself. The few times she'd seen what was on Justin's screen, the hero appeared to look very much like the relationship between him and the heroine was a lot like his with her.

Right. Now she was being fanciful because there was no way Justin Hunt would be attracted to Drusilla Montgomery. No how. No way.

"But dang if I don't wish there was a way." Dru took in a deep breath and slowly let it out. The hero in that book, as compelling as he was, had a dark side and if there was one thing about Justin Hunt she knew, he didn't. At least she didn't think so. In fact the way he looked at her tonight, he looked ever so lost. And she almost told him she loved him.

And that wasn't possible.

Sure, it happened in books. In romance novels. But in real life . . . so didn't happen. So clearly what she felt for Justin was lust. Pure lust.

Right?

She was exhausted when she pulled into her driveway and it wasn't the time to be thinking about whether or not she was in love with Justin. She could fantasize all she liked, but it ended there. It had to. She just needed to keep a lid on the all too frequently lascivious thoughts about him.

Right now though, all Dru wanted to do was climb into bed and sleep for the next three days. That wasn't going to happen, however, because she had to find a place to live. Pronto.

As of yesterday she had thirteen days to find a new home and move in or she'd find herself on the streets. Knowing Armstrong and her mother, there was no doubt about that.

After taking off her makeup and getting ready for bed, Dru went online for a few minutes and ordered some moving boxes. At least she'd be prepared to store some of her things before losing her home. She couldn't go back to the bank, she just couldn't.

And then she turned to the online housing list and began to note the places she could rent. Several hours later, unable to keep her eyes open another moment, Dru went to bed. Instead of daydreaming about Justin or the latest hero she was reading, she thought about finding a new home. The task was daunting—first and last month's rent, security deposit. Where was she going to get the money to pay for it?

She woke early enough to make a few phone calls or send emails about the apartments she'd seen for rent. Since most everyone else was at work she'd need to wait for them to return her queries. Hopefully Justin wouldn't mind her making and taking a few personal calls the next few nights. Just because he said he was good with her taking care of some business that could only happen in daylight, she wasn't about to push it. Hopefully over the weekend she'd be able to hunt down a new place to live. In a world where things happened the right way, she'd find a place Saturday and move on Sunday. Packing up the house . . . well that was another thing. She figured she'd need to hire a company to do that. For a fleeting moment Dru debated telling Justin about her problem, but if he thought she had troubles, she might lose her job as well. He wouldn't want a loser working for him . . . or Gabrielle.

Of course that would solve the housing issue because then she would have to return to the bank at least for the time being. "What a quagmire." She smiled to herself. "Wouldn't

Gabrielle like that? Quagmire."

It wasn't until she pulled on to Gabrielle's street later that day, Dru remembered the words on Justin's computer the night before. With the changes in favorite genres so many writers seemed to have, it made sense Gabrielle would have to change as well. Clearly she was looking at a darker story.

When she arrived, Justin immediately noticed she wasn't firing on all cylinders and came over to sit beside her. He reached out a hand and laid it on her arm, sending tingles of delight through her. "Drusilla, are you all right?"

"Oh, I'm fine. Just a little tired, that's all."

"You sure you aren't feeling a little under the weather?" He looked into her eyes as if answers to her health lay in their depths.

"No, really, I'm fine." He nodded and went back to his desk. With a look in her direction, he bent down to his own keyboard. With that, Dru settled down to work and after picking the same letter up and putting it to the side for the fourth time, Justin stood and walked back over to her desk.

Once again, he sat and reached for her hand. "Drusilla, something is wrong. Are you sure you're all right?"

"I'm fine. Really."

"You can tell me anything. I think it's safe to say if I haven't done it, I've seen it."

She smiled up at him. "I know. Well I don't know that you've done everything, but I know you care. I just don't like to mix work and personal life things."

He glanced over at his desk as if considering sharing a secret of his own. Was it a dark one like Gavin in Gabrielle's latest book? Finally, he seemed to make a decision. "Sometimes our personal lives can impact our work and vice versa. Tell me."

Dru took a deep breath and traced a pattern with her finger on the desk. "It's nothing really."

"Then it shouldn't be that hard to tell me, should it?" His voice was soft, like a lover's caress rather than her boss probing into her personal life.

"Okay. So here's the deal. I'm going to lose my home."

Justin leaned back in his chair, looking stunned at her statement. "Lose your home? Do you need a salary advance for rent or a mortgage payment?"

"No. Nothing like that. The house is all paid for. No. This has to do with my mother's will."

"I see."

"You do?"

"Well, no, not really. Dru, you were clearly tired last night and tonight I can see rings under your eyes. Why not start from the beginning?"

That made her chuckle. "You're sure about that?"

"I am. Dru, we're more than co-workers. At least I hope we are. I consider you a friend and friends stand by each other, right?"

"Yeah. Well here's the story. My mother makes the queen in Snow White look like an angel. I know you shouldn't say rotten things about your parents, especially if they're dead, but my mother was . . . difficult. She was very controlling. My whole life, every time I wanted to do something that didn't fit with her paradigm of what a daughter did, I'd hear about how all she ever wanted was a little girl and how badly I'd let her down. I had to drop out of college because of a tantrum she had. To be honest, the whole reason I ended up working at the bank was because she'd badgered me so much I finally gave in and took the job there. The bank was her be-all-and end-all and because in reality I think she thought I was just an extension of her, she pushed me to work there was well. It was stable, but stifling. That's why, when I saw the ad for the job here with you, I jumped on it. I finally had a chance to do what I want with my life."

"And now your mother is somehow threatening to throw you out because of it?"

"Not exactly."

Justin's brow rose in question.

"Like I said, my mother is dead. Her will apparently has a clause in it that the only way I can remain in our house is if I continue to work at the bank. To be honest I had a copy of it when she died, but never read it. Why should I since it was just she and I? The whole thing seemed pretty straightforward to me. It was just she and I and when she died I thought I inherited everything. Oh she left a few little bequests to the church she was going to at the time, but the rest was mine. The attorney never said there was anything else to consider. Now though, the issue with the house, well, her attorney assures me it's an ironclad clause. So I either have to quit my job here or find a new place to live. I love this job. I really do. Justin, this is a dream job for me and I don't want to lose it so I spent today, at least part of it, looking for a new place to live. That's why I was late last night. I found out yesterday morning and needed to get my head on straight about it before I came to work. My friend Haley came over and helped me figure out things, at least about where I was at, yesterday. The house hunt won't interfere with my job. I promise you."

"Drusilla, I wouldn't fire someone because they have a problem at home, especially one like that. Things happen. Are you absolutely sure the will can't be broken? I know it sounds awful but can you prove she was competent when she made it?"

"Wouldn't trying to break it or proving she was nuts take time?"

Justin nodded. "I believe so."

"As of this morning I've got twelve days. She had a two-week grace period in the will for me to make a decision and I've already used two of those days. I did look for a few places online today and am hoping something comes through in the next day or so and maybe I can move over the weekend. So I don't think there's enough time to prove anything."

Justin rose and paced across the room, rubbing his jaw. Even in his jeans and pale blue sweater, his every step reminded her of a man from another time and place. Justin was the epitome of the Regency gentlemen Gabrielle wrote about.

He returned to where she sat and said what only the lord of the manner in a Regency would say, "You'll move in here."

"What?"

"You'll move in. Here. With me."

CHAPTER EIGHTEEN

Spoken like a true Regency period Lord. It occurred to Dru that after so long of reading and writing a time period, authors probably started to sound like their characters. Thing was, Justin wasn't the author, Gabrielle was. But then again, he edited and read all her work so . . .

And then her mind wandered to all sort of illicit and delicious scenes sharing his bed. Justin on the bottom . . . his hands tied to the brass posts above while she had her merry way with him . . . in what she suspected was at least one clawfooted bath tub . . . Dru on the bottom with her hands caressing that scrumptious butt of his. The pair of them laying side by side, legs wrapped around each other, sweat-slick chests sliding along each other, lips locked in a heated kiss . . .

As if reading her mind, he smiled her way.

Sanity reigned and put a damper on her thoughts and a lock on her lips for the time being. "I'm not sure that's a good idea, Justin. What about Ms. George? What if she doesn't approve?"

"Ms. George . . . oh, uh, yeah. Well, she won't mind. In fact, she'll think it's a great idea." He ran his fingers through his hair, taking a moment to think. "Look, you have almost an hour's drive each way. Gasoline is expensive, there's wear and tear on your car. You have to move anyway, why not move in here?"

Not once did he blink as he said those words. He merely looked into her eyes, mesmerizing her, as if seeing into Dru's very soul.

She swallowed and fought the urge to lean into him, grab hold of his hips and demand he have his naughty way with her and focus on the actual, very practical words, he was saying. "I'll think about it."

It wasn't like he was coming on to her. Not really. If anything, he'd been a consummate gentleman from the moment they'd met.

"Is it a problem living with me? Well, not exactly with me. I live here in the house. I'm talking about the cottage."

"Cottage?"

"Yes, we have a cottage out back. You must see it when you park in back? No?"

"Cottage . . . in the back . . . the yard. No, I hadn't noticed but then when I get here I'm more focused on work or getting to work."

"Ah. Well we have a pretty nice cottage back there. Electricity, heat, indoor plumbing. It's actually modern and up-to-date." He chuckled.

He'd offered her a room, period end. Not his body, which in all likelihood she wouldn't have refused. Just a room. Actually, a cottage. She had some thinking to do. Maybe she could have it all.

The next morning, she arrived home about five. She hurried into the house and dozed until she was sure Haley was awake and called her. They met for breakfast and Dru told her about Justin's proposal.

"Dru, living with a man you aren't married to? What would your mother say? And what about that whole creature of the night thing?" A frown on her lips, Haley shook her head while stirring her tea.

"Haley, I'm thirty years old. What Martha said or thought, should have been a non-event ten to twelve years ago. Martha's greatest fear was being left alone. The woman couldn't handle being in the house by herself for more than ten minutes. By pushing me to work at that stupid bank with her, she pretty much had company all the time."

"People thought you two were close."

"Come on Haley, you know better. And we've had this conversation before . . . many times. You know what she was like and don't look at me like that. It's a cottage, not in the house."

"Have you seen it? And like I said . . . that vampire thing?"

"No, I haven't seen it, not yet. Justin said we could check it out when I get into work tonight."

"He couldn't show you last night?"

"Well . . . no. It was dark when we talked about it and he . . . well he . . . you know, he's not much for being up when the sun is out."

"Right, yeah. The sun. You notice I notice you aren't addressing that aspect?"

Dru waved her hand. "He's not a vampire. It's all because of Gabrielle being reclusive and her traveling and when it's the best time to contact her."

"Sure. Okay. Then what happens if the job doesn't work out though? Have you thought about that?"

"You mean like if Justin or Gabrielle suddenly doesn't like how I do my job?"

"Exactly. How stable are these people?"

Dru breathed out a sigh. "Her former assistant was with her for years. At least she . . . or he . . . had to be stable since whoever it was retired. Although if Justin is, you know well that thing I'm sure he's not . . . well then he's been with her for years. In any event, if Justin didn't think I was doing a good job, I don't think he would have asked me to move in."

"Either that or he wants to get into your pants and see if you're any good in the sex department."

She briefly pondered just how Justin would enter her

pants.

It wasn't exactly her pants she wanted him in. They were more or less the gateway to where she wanted him.

"To be honest, Haley, I wouldn't mind getting in his pants — but that's not in the cards. He's totally and completely professional. And, if for some reason the job doesn't work out, well, I can always stay in a hotel while I look for an apartment and a new job."

She sighed. "Well, good luck. I wish you the best, I really do, Dru."

Not very encouraging for a best friend.

CHAPTER NINETEEN

Later that day, the fog cresting over the hills to blanket her in its embrace, Dru arrived at work, suitcase in hand. If Justin was serious about letting her stay in the cottage, she might as well start moving things in right away. Not that she'd have that much to move. Most of the furniture and household items could be put in storage. But she'd do that over the weekend.

When she let herself into the main house, she was greeted with the mouth-watering scent of what turned out to be the most divine breakfast for supper consisting of a feta cheese, bacon and avocado omelet. The bacon was done just right and the cheese ever so slightly melted in contrast to the still cool avocado. It would not have surprised her to hear that Justin had stood watching from the window for her to pull up before promptly setting about making her meal. To the side was perfectly toasted sourdough bread and real creamery butter. A non-fat latte with a luscious foam top sat beside the covered dish.

Vincent sat on the side chair near the desk. There was no sign of Justin, however, but Dru dug in anyway. With Vincent's help, they polished off the meal. Dru hadn't realized how hungry she'd been after a few days of picking at her food. The stress of her mother's will and what she would do had been weighing more heavily than she anticipated. That was one of the great things about Vincent, now that she'd gotten to know the fluffy black cat — he was always there to help out with a good meal.

When Justin came downstairs a few hours later, he stared at her suitcase, making her think perhaps he'd forgotten he invited her to move in. Or perhaps Gabrielle objected to the idea. At times lately, she wondered if what she thought was Gabrielle sitting in the window when she first began to work here was a life-sized cutout. Surely, in their emails back and forth, Justin had mentioned to Gabrielle the possibility she might move in. A moment later, Justin softly called her name and offered to show her the cottage.

She followed him back outside the house to a charming cottage. Rose bushes that would bloom in the spring were arranged in front. There was a porch, wide enough to accommodate a porch swing and a pair of white wicker chairs. A few potted plants were interspersed between the chairs and a couple of matching tables.

Justin unlocked the door and flicked on the light switch to reveal a cozy living room with hard wood floors, a Victorian fainting couch, chairs and a plush couch that looked like a body could lie down, snuggle in and read for hours. A few bookcases covered the walls on two sides of the room. Dru smiled at Justin and nodded to his unspoken question. The cottage was perfect.

From the living room he led her to the kitchen where there was what appeared to be a brand new four burner stove, double-sided refrigerator and walk-in pantry. "The washer and dryer are through that door," he told her, pointing off to the side. There's no food stocked up now but we can order whatever you like."

"Oh, Justin, you don't have to . . . I'm happy to go to the market and buy whatever I need."

He looked confused for a moment as if the idea of food shopping was a foreign concept and then nodded. "Well then, there are two bedrooms. Just pick whichever you want. We've got extra linens for the beds in the main house."

The bedrooms were mirror images of each other, both with canopied king-sized beds covered with a number of fluffy pillows, down comforters and lace curtains. The cottage was completely feminine in appearance and Dru felt like someone had visited her dreams and created it just for her.

Dru chose the room with ruby velvet drapes covered with what appeared to be floor to ceiling windows on two walls. As with the main house, thick, stout candles adorned the tabletops; not an electric light to be seen, although Justin assured her the house was fully wired. An antique looking eggshell-white timepiece sat beside the bed.

Vincent jumped up on the bed and stared at her. Clearly he liked the space and was hoping he'd be able to spend some time in there as well.

"Gabrielle chose thick drapes for the bedrooms so the rooms are dark enough to sleep during the day should it be necessary or desired," Justin explained while scruffing Vincent's ears. "The bath is through here."

He led her into a room that rivaled a Roman spa with a sunken bathtub large enough for six. Dru made a mental note to try out the individual jets evenly spaced around the tub. Naturally, her imagination flew to an image of Justin, naked, in that tub beside her. Together they'd engage in all manner of sensually pleasing activities using those very jets.

An array of soaps and oils filled a built-in shelf in one of the tub's walls. A glance at one told her it was one of those with the delightful option of being used as a massage oil or to help matters glide along during a particularly pleasing sexual encounter.

Two sinks in a marble-topped vanity covered the wall opposite the tub. The mirrors were set just high enough that the tub had no reflection in either, not that she'd want to watch herself bathe. However, if Justin ever did join her in the tub, watching him do some exquisite things with her body . . . well that would be a whole other story. Not that he had any leanings in that direction with her. This was, after all, San Francisco.

At the time, she noticed only in passing, Justin did not enter the room himself. And that brought to mind the lack of mirrors anywhere in the house, at least that she'd seen, except in the downstairs half bath.

"Did you want to take some time to unpack now? If you are staying the night tonight that is," Justin asked.

"Sure. I'd like to officially move in tonight. It won't take more than a few."

"It doesn't look like you brought too much tonight but take as long as you need to settle in. We can outfit the cottage with whatever you want or need in the next few days, just let me know."

"Justin, thank you. You have no idea how much this means to me. I appreciate it more than you could ever know."

In the dim light she saw him blush but he also gave her a small smile. "It's my pleasure. You work so hard, do a great job, it's the least I can do. If you don't mind, we'll pick up some linens before you leave in the morning."

As they walked back to the main house, Dru reflected on how at times when she arrived Justin was nowhere to be seen. She was never quite brave enough to wander about the house on her own. There were times she was sure she was still the shy and timid Drusilla and dutiful enough to just march in, sit at her desk and get to work. Now that she would be living here, she supposed it was all right to take a peek now and again . . . maybe.

Before they left, she took a few minutes on their way out to look at the paintings in the cottage. "Justin cleared his throat and told her, "Just family photos. Feel free to bring whatever you like and hang them on the walls."

Family photos? Of who? Justin or Gabrielle's family? He'd

explained early on how Gabrielle had offered him a place to live while he was working for her and he'd moved in. Justin definitely was completely at home in the main house. She supposed it stood to reason that adding another staff person to the residence made sense.

She peered at a few of the pictures and briefly noted not a one had glass covering it. Not that you'd want to be looking at your reflection in portrait glass, it just struck her as yet another oddity about Gabrielle's house. And not that she knew much about art, but shouldn't something at least protect them? They all appeared to be family portraits dating back to at least the Gold Rush, if the clothing they wore was any indication. The resemblance from portrait to portrait was uncanny — the men looked almost like twins marching through time; the women all looked like Gabrielle on the back cover of all of her books. She'd looked the same for the past four decades. Justin had never said so but there was a definite resemblance between he and Gabrielle. That likeness was even more noticeable in the photographs here in the cottage. It would certainly explain why he was able to run her business with as much freedom as he did. Not that a close assistant wouldn't also work that closely with their employer. Well in any event, it didn't matter.

There'd be time to look more closely at the photographs after she moved in. With a shrug and a smile, she told Justin they should be getting to work.

When they entered the house, the clock chimed seven, long past time for them to start work.

They stopped in the kitchen so Dru could make herself a coffee. She offered a cup to Justin and, as usual, he declined. It seemed he would never eat or drink in her presence.

Her latte in hand, they walked into the office and Dru sat down at the desk to resume the edits she'd been working on the night before. It was kinda cool being a BETA reader for a famous author. Surely, now that she was living under Gabrielle's roof, she and the famed author would meet sooner rather than later. Or at least whenever the author returned from Europe.

It seemed that Justin spent most of their work time either typing for hours on end or combing through books and Internet sites doing research. She supposed that given what a stickler Gabrielle was purported to be, she'd have a research assistant of some sort. It made sense Justin would do that research.

Before Dru could begin working that night though, he came and stood beside her and leaned his hip against the desk. For a moment, Dru imagined reaching out to cup his groin and see where it would lead. Then just as quickly resisted the urge, because that could so get her fired and now her home would be at risk.

Still, he stood so tantalizing close, close enough that his scent enfolded her. It wasn't cologne. It was pure Justin. He smelled good. In fact, so very good she'd joked to herself he must wear eau de pheromone cologne. The man was walking sex and acted as if he didn't know it.

He toyed with a pen on the desk. "I spoke with Gabrielle today."

Oddly, that surprised her. Not that he'd seen or at least spoken to her, but that it was during the day. He'd been insistent that he never woke before the sun set and she'd never seen him in the daylight hours.

"How is she?"

"Good. She's doing really good." He paused and looked around the room as if seeing it for the first time. "I told her you'd be moving in."

"What does she think about it? Was she angry or upset that you didn't ask before you offered me the cottage?" Not that they had anything special or illicit going on. Weird maybe, but certainly not illicit.

"She's still out of town, traveling and she has no problem with you staying here."

She noticed he hesitated, still toying with the pen before continuing, "Gabrielle trusts my judgment."

"But she's okay with me staying here?"

"Staying . . . yes. She thinks it's a good idea." He began to seem distracted.

"And?" Was he going to fire her? Of course not. He just said Gabrielle thought it was a good idea. Martha had certainly done a number on her so much so that even now Dru second-guessed herself on just about every decision she made. No, if he were going to fire her he would have called and told her not to bring her things.

"I told her you were the best assistant ever. When I told her you'd read all her books and while we were working, you'll tell me something happened in such and such a book so it couldn't really be used again. She said she hopes to meet you soon."

"She did? That's great because, well aside from the fact I'd like to meet her, I do like working for her."

"Yes. Glad you'd like to."

"Oh, Justin! Like to? That would be a dream come true! Yes, I'd love to meet her! When?"

"Um, well, as I said, she's still traveling. Soon. I promise you, soon. Before I forget, let me grab some linens for you."

He returned a short time later with sheets and towels, and placed them on the sideboard by the office's entryway. "Feel free to use the kitchen here until we stock up yours."

"Thank you, Justin. I appreciate it."

With that, he abruptly turned and walked away leaving Dru to her proofreading. He took his seat across the room with his laptop where he sat working steadily till the clock chimed five. He rose abruptly when the final chime echoed through the house. "Do you need anything?"

Startled from the passage she'd been reading, Dru shook her head. "No, I'm good."

"I'll see you tonight, Dru." With that, Justin hurried out the door.

"See you tonight." But he'd already left the room.

On her way out of the room, Dru walked by Justin's desk and caught sight of some handwritten notes sitting there. Ordinarily she wouldn't be caught dead snooping except she saw her name on one of the pages. Taking a closer look, the document seemed to also describe her to a T.

Sitting down in the chair she began to read . . .

It was getting harder and harder for Gavin to keep his hands . . . and teeth from her. In those moments of rest between the sun times, she was in every thought. She cared for him. There was no doubt Emily cared for him. She was attendant to his needs, courteous, always making certain he was fed. Well, at least offering to feed him — but it was human food. Dishes he had long ago forgotten and that she would soon cease to need.

Tonight he came close. So close. Standing by her side, her scent caressing him, calling to him. His heart pounded, pounded so hard he was sure she could hear it. The temptation to take a sip . . . just a sip . . . almost overwhelmed him.

She was his! There was no doubt about it. If she wasn't, why did everything fall so neatly into place? She'd been the first to answer his query for the position and when she arrived that first night, his lady was all he expected and more. The signs were all there . . . even the cat, his big black familiar . . . knew what and who she was to him.

Then when she had no choice but to move into his home! He could not have orchestrated the situation more neatly. She was his! His and only his!

So why did he hesitate? Why did he hold back from taking her and making her his lady for all time?

All was silent. Except for the ticking of the clock, there wasn't a sound to be heard. The sun peaked through a tiny opening in the windows.

Dru walked over to the window seat and settled down on the plush velvet cushions and pulled the drapes aside.

Pale morning sun filtered into the room. Not yet high enough to warm her face, her hands. Just enough to cast its glow in the room making it a little less eerie than a shard of moonlight.

No, it wasn't the sun that made the room seem other-worldly. That was purely of Dru's making—Dru's imagination and what she'd just read.

Was Justin writing a story using figments of Dru's life?

Or was he writing about his reality and a future . . .

Those questions he asked that seemed to come from no-where.

The times he said her quips would make for some good threads in a book.

No. No, it couldn't be.

It had to be a book that just sounded a lot like Dru's life. Except her life wasn't that interesting. Not many heroines had these fabulous lives they left for a less fabulous one? None. That's what romance was—a woman living a dull humdrum existence who suddenly finds herself with the man of her dreams. Just like Dru, except her excitement came from imagining a hot and heavy romance with Justin.

So if it was just a book . . . a story . . . what about the other things? Once again she wondered why she saw no mirrors in the house. And why didn't he ever eat a meal with her?

She sat, considering that, when a tap at the window startled her. With a gasp, her heart in her throat, she turned and looked out the window. As quietly as possible, she turned to look more closely out the window.

The tap came again and with a start she realized a branch had blown against the window. No cars traversed the street, but plenty of dried leaves, some still attached to branches, flitted around. A sliver of sunlight lit the walkway just enough to illuminate a tendril of fog as it wound its way across the walk. Mesmerized, she watched the gray haze wrap itself around a bush, cover the sidewalk and wend its way toward the main house. Like a living thing the fog fascinated and comforted her. There were times Dru felt like that cool gray mist was a part of her. Watching the vapor-like tendrils as it covered the front of Gabrielle George's lawn, it seemed to encase it and cocoon them in a magical place away from the everyday, mundane world.

She thought back on the mornings she'd returned home to Marin. There might have been a hint of fog when she left on those mornings, but it was more like a light damp mist. It might cover the bay like a big downy comforter, but secure in her little car the way was always clear.

Her imagination caught as she stood there by the window, watching the fog roll in. Beyond the border of the ornate black fence, the street looked clear. It was as if the fog's intent was to surround the house, encase it, hide it and its residents from view. She half expected to hear a wolf howl, but this was San Francisco and they didn't exactly have the kind of neighborhoods a wolf would wander about in.

At least not a real wolf.

She shook her head. What on earth was she thinking? She didn't even read those kinds of books—the kind with the hyper sexy alpha male who hid his werewolf nature in the guise of a hunky guy. Her preferred genre was historical romance— hence Dru's life-long love of Gabrielle George's books.

Shaking the fanciful thoughts from her head, Dru headed to the cottage, her new home, to sleep. As if aware of her thoughts, stately grandfather clock chimed six times. Had she really been standing, gazing out the window for almost an hour?

To the east, a purple-blue light appeared heralding

morning and the sun. Her neck began to itch and suddenly she was tired, so tired.

At the cottage door she fought back a scream before she realized the black blur that flew by her was Vincent, racing by on the path to the cottage. He paused on the porch and stood waiting for her to let him in.

Now she was really starting to think about those crazy thoughts about Justin. It had to be crazy, overtired thinking, because if that wasn't why she suddenly felt detached from her body, almost watching herself from a distant point, it meant something else, something sinister, was going on in this house. It would be nice to have the fluffy black cat sleeping nearby.

Why do I only see Justin at night? Why doesn't he eat or drink? Why aren't there any mirrors in this house? Where is Gabrielle George? And why do all the people in the portraits look so much alike?

The thoughts raced through her mind. Clearly, she was tired. It had been a rough week, an emotional week and plainly she was tired.

She told herself, over and over again, it was only her imagination, her way overactive imagination and that she was tired, bone tired after the stressful week she'd had. Between hearing she would lose her home to looking for a new one to moving in with Justin and still keeping up with her job, it was a difficult week. Still . . . creatures like . . . dare she say it? Vampires? Didn't exist except in books. Right? It was all her imagination and there were perfectly logical reasons why Justin did the things he did. He just wasn't ready to tell her.

And the book he seemed to be writing? It had to be fiction. Plain and simple, just his own active imagination writing a story . . . that strangely mirrored her life.

But that vampire thing . . . *Okay, so in modern literature they're depicted as dark, dangerous and positively gorgeous men. Okay, okay, so maybe literature is stretching it — and I will admit to delving into a few of them. I mean, have you looked at those men on the covers? Who wouldn't want to get bit by one big time?*

She looked down at Vincent. "Seriously, if Justin wanted to take a bite out of me, I'd lay down so he could easily suckle both sides and then some."

The cat merely gazed up at her a moment before turning to lick a paw. He clearly wasn't concerned.

She quickly stripped off the comforter and made up the bed, taking a moment to tell the cat, "I'm doing some crazy thinking, aren't I? Justin's just a night owl and does his best work at night because that's when Gabrielle does hers or it's easier for her to communicate to him from where she's traveling, right? So it's daytime wherever she is and it's most convenient for us to work nights, right? Right. He's a normal, healthy guy who just happens to be the most sinfully good-looking man I've ever seen. And besides, he's her assistant. Just because he resembles a few of those guys in the paintings doesn't mean he's related or anything like that. If I were a rich and famous romance writer, I'd hire the most gorgeous guy I could find as my assistant. Right?"

Vincent strolled to the foot of the bed and looked up at her.

"Are you waiting for an invitation?"

The cat continued to stare as if considering her question.

Dru laughed at herself, or tried to. "Well see now, that's a vampire thing. They can't come in unless you invite them. *You* are a cat, not a vampire so if you're waiting for an invitation because you're polite, that's one thing. If you are doing it to make me think you're a kitty-vamp, that's not going to work."

With that, Vincent jumped up on the bed and laid down. Dru in turn walked into the ensuite bathroom, brushed her teeth, pulled on her flannel jammies and climbed into bed. "Yes, Vincent, flannel jammies . . . the sexy ones are for when I get to know Justin a little better and I'm certain Gabrielle wouldn't be venturing in to check on my suitability to live in her home with her yummy assistant just down across the yard."

Across the yard?

She looked as Vincent sidled up to the pillows. His eyes widened with the kind of intelligence only a cat can have. "So, Vincent, just where does Justin sleep?"

Vincent turned and lay down. Clearly, he wasn't going to share.

An hour or so later, as she lay in the comfy, big bed, unable to sleep, Dru replayed her earlier conversation with Justin along with her thoughts on the book he seemed to be writing. "A girl has to think of something if she doesn't want to imagine being locked away in a haunted house with a vampire now, doesn't she?"

The walls had no answer for her and neither did Vincent sleeping soundly on the pillow beside her.

"And she should probably stop talking to herself, shouldn't she?"

The silence still had no answer for her.

Then again, until Justin had raised the prospect of meeting Gabrielle, she hadn't slowed down her mind to look at the other things that went on in the house. Not really. She'd completely dismissed the fact that it was odd an employer hadn't met her employee. No, she'd focused on just putting one foot in front of the other and hadn't thought about Gabrielle or her life. She just hadn't let herself think too much about the oddities of the old Victorian. Aside from how rude she suddenly felt not asking after Gabrielle the night she met Justin, there were things that, had anyone else told her were going on, she would have told them to run like hell. Oh she'd asked about Gabrielle, but nothing in particular — like her health.

The eerie clock chimes from the stately grandfather clock in the hall noting time she wasn't aware passed, had taken a back seat to any other considerations. The neighborhood's stillness was a tad odd too. This was San Francisco for Pete's sake! At least you'd hear a car honk its horn somewhere on the street now and again.

Time seemed to move at a different pace here in Gabrielle George's painted lady. There she'd be most nights, working away, maybe glance at the computer clock but the time never registered. Not until the antique clock, the one that was clearly from another time, would chime five in the morning. Justin would immediately rise and say goodnight, or good morning, or whatever it was he said at the end of the work night. Only then would Dru realize how much time had passed. She'd never worked a job where she didn't know what time it was or that she was so lost in the moment. Granted, it was easy to get lost in Gabrielle's stories. She'd buy each new release, bring it home, crawl into bed and read from start to finish in one sitting. Dru devoured Gabrielle's books, unable to put them down until she had read every last word. Then she would read it again just to make up for anything she missed and to savor the words.

Now she saw the stories unfold, chapter by chapter . . . waiting for the end. When she asked Justin how the latest book they were working on ended, he smiled, that killer smile of his, and in a moment of total meanness said, "They live happily ever after."

That was mean of him. Very mean.

Of course they lived happily ever after! It's a romance! She was pretty sure he saw her surprise and chagrin because he then told her Gabrielle didn't know how the stories ended until she got there. He said they'd have to wait, anticipate and see. Which brought to mind the story Justin had been working on, the one that seemed so much like a page out of Dru's life — would that heroine have a happy ending?

Sleep eluding her, she rolled over. Thoughts about the strange activities in the house kept running through her mind.

The no mirror thing? Come on. A guy that looks like Justin not ever looking in a mirror? And what was with the soft shoe he did, not walking into her bathroom when he showed it to her?

"No! No how, no way!"

She sat up in bed and felt her neck.

Smooth as ever. Vincent grumped something at her from his place on the bed.

"Okay, now I am letting my imagination run wild." Or had it itched when she stood at the window downstairs?

Still . . . she rose and went into the bathroom and looked in the mirror.

Her neck looked fine. Just fine.

So what . . .

The door to the bathroom creaked open. A dark shape formed in the shaft of moonlight that filtered in. A second later Vincent meowed.

Dru swallowed a scream. Realizing who it was, she slowed her breathing, bent down to pick him up and cooed, "Hey, baby. I thought you were in bed. Do you want to look in the mirror too? Want to check your neck too?

Vincent meowed again. A plaintive sound that seemed to echo through the cottage.

Vincent snuggled against her for a moment and then wiggled out of her arms and back on the floor. Dru followed him out of the bathroom and down the hall where he scratched at the door to be let out. With the sun shining brightly in morning sky, Dru stepped out the door and followed the cat to the main house, figuring he was probably hungry. She made a note to bring some of his food into the cottage just in case he wanted to take up residence with her and stay there on occasion. He'd followed her here last night so why not take up at least part-time residence with her?

Together they walked into the house, but instead of sitting

down in the kitchen for a snack, Vincent dodged up the back stairs to the second floor. Dru turned to head back to the cottage but a crash upstairs caught her attention. She headed up the stairs after the cat where he stood staring at a little statue that, just like the night she interviewed, had apparently fallen off one of the little tables in the hallway on to the floor.

"You have to be careful of these things, Vincent. No rocking the tables, right?"

The cat looked up at her, blinked his eyes, which seemed to take on an almost eerie glow in the early morning light, and resumed walking down the hall. Mid-way he stopped in front of a door cracked ever so slightly open. Before entering the room before him he looked back at her and softly meowed.

Unable to resist, she followed the cat inside. Absently she felt for, and found, a wall switch. She looked around the room. Like all the others she had seen in the house — not that she'd seen that many — it was charmingly appointed. Fine chintz love seats were paired with what had to be original Chippendale chairs. Crystal ornaments sat on end tables beside each of the seating groups. Photographs seemed to cover each flat surface.

Unable to resist, she walked over to look at them. She recognized a younger Gabrielle from her book covers. She'd been a lovely young woman. There was a strong family resemblance to each person in the pictures, especially in the group ones. Dru took in each one, studying each for a few moments before alighting on one of Justin.

She peered closer.

"Oh my god."

CHAPTER TWENTY

Dru replaced the photograph. Clearly, she was losing her mind. Sneaking around Gabrielle George's house in the middle of the morning, when she should be asleep, was pure lunacy. What she needed to do was get her butt to bed so she could do a decent night's work that night, especially after the rough start she'd had on her week. Saturday night she'd get together with Haley and regale her with stories of her latest nonsense. They'd have a good laugh at her vivid imagination. But for now, bed . . . her own bed in the cottage . . . was the order of the day.

The photograph of Justin had to be a recent one. Certainly he'd been dressed for a costume ball and the photographer had just made it look like an old tintype. There was no way that was an original 18-something photograph. Right?

Because if it was an original then Justin . . .

"It's probably his great grandfather or something, right? Right. Okay, Vincent, let's grab some food for you, get back to the cottage and get some sleep, huh?"

Vincent followed her back down the hall and back out to the cottage. This time when she climbed into bed, sleep surprisingly came quickly.

Remarkably she slept till the alarm and for the first time in a long time, hit the snooze twice. Clearly, sleeping in the stately Victorian cottage was peaceful enough to give her a good night's sleep. That and how exhausted she was from all the drama the week before. Dru tried to beat Justin into the kitchen for breakfast . . . or whatever the evening meal would be.

He was, however, already sitting at his desk in the office busily typing away when she entered with her toast and latte. He seemed almost surprised to see her when she walked in. Collecting himself, Justin asked, "Sleep well?"

Dru walked to her desk and while she put her plate and cup down, told him, "I sure did. I think it's the best night's . . . or day's sleep I've had in months."

"That's good to know."

"I'll say. I don't know if it's this house, the cottage . . . you know, how peaceful it is here or that super comfy bed or just that . . . well . . . the past few months have been different."

Justin stood and walked over to her desk. "You mean because of your mother's death?"

Dru looked down at her lap, considering his question. The man was very perceptive, perhaps more so than she was herself about what had been going on with her. "You know, for as awful as she could be, yes, sometimes I do miss her."

"Your mother? You said before she was quite awful."

"I suppose we all think our parents are awful at one time or another, you know?"

Justin shrugged. "It's probably different for guys."

"Maybe. Anyway, I'm here now and it looks like a slew of emails came in about the upcoming book so I'd best get to work."

Justin continued to study her a moment. "The emails will be there later. They'll be there next week and there will always be more."

Dru did something she never did before going to work for Gabrielle. She joked. "Job security?"

Justin chuckled. "Exactly."

"Good to know."

"Seriously, your life growing up was . . . hard?"

"No. No. Not hard. My mother was difficult. She had her

way about doing things and wasn't really open to doing things any way but her way. Sometimes the highway looked pretty darn good."

"Ah, the old my way or the highway philosophy?"

"You got it."

"What about your dad?"

"Hmm, you know, I think he loved my mother but . . . it's not nice to speak ill of the dead." She thought about the old-fashioned photograph upstairs. "Although if you were talking to a vampire, what would he think being undead and all?"

"You mean someone speaking ill of him?"

"Or her?"

"I don't know. Hmm, that's something for the books to reason out, isn't it?"

"And what would he do? If someone said something nasty about him, would he bite them and run the risk of inheriting some mean-faced blood? He wouldn't want to turn them, would he? Because then the mean-faced jerk would be a vampire."

"Mean-faced?"

"Well sure. Everyone knows vampires are hunks and a half so someone who said nasty things about them would have to be ugly . . . wouldn't they?"

Justin chuckled. "I think it would depend on the story. Nosferatu was portrayed as pretty damn ugly."

"That's true. I'm thinking more of the romantic type vampires."

Justin studied her a moment. "Do you think vampires are romantic?"

Dru considered his question for a moment. Her mind traveled back to the night before when she checked her neck. "I uh, well, I think it's the man, not the hmm, being? I think anyone can be romantic if they set their mind to it. Think about Cyrano. He was one of the most romantic characters of all time and yet portrayed as ugly on the outside."

He leaned toward her. "But do you think a vampire can be romantic?"

"Sure. The author just has to write him that way, right?"

Justin rose only to settle more comfortably into the desk chair beside Dru's desk. Instead of answering her question, he said, "We've been working together for almost three months and it occurs to me I don't really know that much about you."

"Or me about you." And given how attracted she was to him that was something she definitely wanted to know. She wanted to know all about Justin Hunt—starting with was he married or otherwise attached. And then there was that whole vampire thing.

Just as quickly as the thought entered her mind, Dru shoved it aside. He was her boss and unless she wanted to lose the best job ever, she needed to put those thoughts about him aside. The ones about marriage and especially the ones thinking he was a vampire.

"Since we're going to be living together, in a fashion, why don't you tell me a little bit about you personally?" Justin asked with a smile.

"It's pretty dull."

"And you think my life is all exciting?"

"Yes."

"Really?"

Eyes lowered, feeling shyer than usual, she answered, "You work for my favorite author."

"As do you."

"But you've done it for much longer."

"Hmm, yes. Tell you what. You tell me about you and then we'll talk about me. We'll see who has the more boring child-hood memories."

His words were dry, but his eyes danced with mischief.

"Okay, you got it."

CHAPTER TWENTY-ONE

"I suppose in a way my parents had kind of a romantic start. Martha, my mother, was in love with this man, Grayson. Personally I think he was married and cheating on his wife, but she disagreed. Vehemently, I might add."

"What made you think that? Something your mother said?"

"Yeah. She would get this dreamy look on her face and tell me how he used to come by her desk at work — she was a secretary at a bank, a different one from where we... I worked ... at the time, working for the vice president or some such. All I know is that he was in management somehow. Anyway, she'd wait for him to come by on Friday nights to go out. Never any other day during the week. I asked her about that one time, and she admitted that once or twice she tried to bring it up to him and he'd tell her it was that old school-night thing. You know, like you don't go out or do anything exciting on a school night. So she'd sit and wait till the end of the day on Friday and then he'd come by and ask her out. Or not. Then he'd take her someplace nearby, no place with reservations or anything like that."

"He ever say anything to her about marriage?"

"No. Not that she told me and believe me, my mother would have told me. You know what she was like?" Dru leaned forward as if ready to confide something secret.

Justin shook his head.

Dru chuckled. "No, I suppose not. She was like the mean housekeeper in a gothic. You know the ones I mean? Dark hair pulled back in a severe bun, dark dress with a collar that is so high and tight their chins would drop if the collar didn't hold them up. Kind of like Charmella in Ms. George's book, Bronze Door."

"She dressed like that? Charmella was gruesome to put it mildly." She could see Justin working to keep a smile from forming.

Dru giggled, "No. Not quite. Although I have to say she would have loved to dress me in that kind of drab dress. She was all about making me look and dress as plain as possible."

Justin toyed with a pen on her desk, pushing it back and forth with his finger.

For a moment Dru wondered what it would feel like if he did the same over her nipple.

"Do you know why?"

"Not really. I asked her more than once what the deal was and if she answered at all, it was something to the effect of me needing to know someone wanted me for myself and not because I was easy. She'd say things like girls who wore panty hose were just asking for it or short skirts or whatever wasn't what she thought the best way to dress. Trust me, if she saw the jeans I wear to work here, she'd bust a gut."

"There's nothing wrong with how you dress. Don't take this wrong, but you've got a great figure, cute smile and any guy would be lucky to take you out."

"Thanks, Justin. Coming from you that means a lot." And damn if she didn't feel a sensual swirling in her tummy at his words.

He blushed and for a moment turned his attention back to the pen he twirled in his hand. "So, your mom? The bank? Were you a love child between her and this guy Grayson?"

"Oh that's a snort moment. Not even close. At least that I can think of. She still, after like thirty years of marriage, had Grayson's picture on her dresser. We, Grayson and I, share nothing resembling each other. No, he was a Friday-night-go-someplace-dark and dull kind of guy. She told me that some nights he'd just give her cab fare home. Kinda sad given the time period."

"You make it sound like the horse and buggy days."

Dru chuckled. "I guess I do. And you give me great images of it."

With a smile he said, "Just doing my job, just doing my job. So where does your father come in? Did you know him?"

"Oh yeah! My folks had me a little later in life and he died right after I graduated high school but he . . . my dad was . . . he was special, Justin. He was really special. He loved me more than life itself. Sometimes I think having me, or just having a daughter, was the dearest thing in his life. I don't mean in a creepy way, but in the way of a parent who truly cherishes his child."

"Where did your folks meet?"

"Believe it or not, at a Valentine's day dance."

"Sounds romantic."

"I suppose it could have been. I know it was for my godparents."

His brow furrowed in the unspoken question.

"Since Valentine's wasn't on a Friday that year, Grayson, of course, didn't ask my mother out. It was on a Saturday night or there was a dance on that Saturday — I don't remember which but my Aunt Margie, my mom's best friend, told my mother she *had* to go to this dance. Aunt Margie, that's my godmother, used to say it made the battle of Bull Run look like a board game with how hard she had to push to get my mother to go. When they got there they met these two guys, my dad and my Uncle Al. Uncle Al took one look at Aunt Margie and knew she was the only girl for him. They were married like 3 months later and even after forty years or so of marriage they still dote on each other."

"They're still alive?"

"Yeah. They're in their 80s, live in Florida, but still going strong and still as in love as they were when I was a kid. They kinda make me believe that there is a happily ever after if you find someone you really love."

Justin studied her a moment before murmuring, "That's what romance is all about, isn't it?"

Dru nodded. "Well I believe it. I honestly believe some day I'm going to meet the most amazing man and he's going to love me for myself and I'm going to be the only one he could ever want or need."

Clearly seeing her momentary discomfort, Justin prompted, "So Al and Margie got together . . ."

"And my dad asked my mom to dance. He used to get all dreamy eyed himself and tell me how he danced every dance with her and my mom didn't disagree. At the end of the night he asked to see her again, and she said she was involved with someone. He asked if it was serious and before my mother could say yes, my Aunt Margie said that there was only a guy who just called on my mom now and again. My dad said and I quote, he "wanted to throw his hat in the ring" and he started to take her out after that. According to both of them, he called her pretty much every day and took her out every Saturday and for drives on Sundays. He'd take her out on a Friday night if Grayson didn't pick her up and then my dad asked her to marry him."

"And so they married."

Dru nodded. "It's sad though, my mother told me, many times, actually, that the only reason she agreed to marry my dad was she thought it would get Grayson to commit. She held on to that hope till almost their wedding day to see if Grayson would come around but he never did."

"Did Grayson try to stop them?"

"Nope and six months to the day after they met my parents

married. They tried to get pregnant for a few years and finally I was born. It's kind of sad but I think my mother was jealous of me and not in a natural way. She'd get nasty — I'd do something less than perfect or my dad would compliment me on a grade in school or project or something and she'd get this mean look on her face and tell me that he always loved me best. She acted like it was some kind of contest to see who he loved more rather than just seeing it was the way a parent *should* love a child. He never did anything creepy. Nothing like that. Just when I needed a book bag or new backpack, he'd take me to get one or if there was a dance at school and my mother didn't want me to go — she never did — he'd not only make sure I had money for a ticket to get in but would give me money for a new dress and a ride to the dance. She'd get angry after that but that was between them."

"It's sad he didn't live to see you be happy."

"It is." She swallowed as if it would make the memory go away. "One of the last really great times we had was during my senior year of high school. He went with me to check out this college I was interested in and he went with me to talk to the dean. They were looking for someone to sew costumes and because I've always been such a big historical romance reader, I talked about period dresses and all. The dean had admissions guarantee me a slot while we were still there. Like I said, my dad died right after I graduated high school . . . really just a few weeks before college started."

Justin raised a brow. "Natural causes?"

"Oh yeah. This is my life we're talking about, not a gothic romance with a nefarious step-mother looming in dark hallways."

Justin put down the pen he'd been rolling back and forth between his fingers while they talked. "You know what though? It *would* make for a great story."

Dru took a sip of her now cold latte and considered his

words. "Maybe. But not starring me, that's for sure!"

"Oh, you'd be surprised." He seemed lost in thought for a moment before continuing, "Anyway, it does have some great elements that would make for a good plot."

"I guess. I'd need to see it first."

"And what did your mother do when your dad died? Did she look up Grayson again?"

"Ah, now that's an interesting bit of history. At least in terms of a romance gone awry. My mother never stopped carrying her torch for Grayson and when he died not long after my dad, she lost it. I don't think they ever spoke again once she got engaged to my dad. I mean they would have talked at work, but not outside business dealings. When my mom married, she changed branches to the one closer to home and away from Grayson. That's where she met Ottila. Once she heard Grayson died though, she really carried on something awful. While my dad was still alive he simply shrugged at some of her antics. When my dad died, she carried on like he never existed. I suppose in some ways that's what I've done since she died."

"Does that bother you?"

"No, not really. This is going to sound really bad on my part, but it was a relief when she died. I . . ."

Justin reached out and slid his hand along the side of her head, absentmindedly slightly entwining his fingers in her hair. "What?"

Dru released a long, slow breath. It was a tad hard to focus on her story and talking when what she really wanted to do was lean into Justin and give him a soul-searching kiss. It seemed he had no idea of his effect on her.

Dru blinked. "Her death . . . I think it freed her from whatever she'd spent her life running from and it freed me to be who I really am. To do what I really want."

Justin considered her words a few moments before asking,

"What was she running from?"

"I, I'm not sure. I just had this feeling that somehow she was running from something or someone. She'd never be alone. There was nothing worse for her than to be alone. If for some reason she needed to be home alone, she'd start calling everyone she knew and talk to them for as long as they'd stay on the phone. When they had to hang up, she'd call the next person in her phone book. It was like something bad was going to happen to her if she wasn't in contact with another person for very long. I think that's why she interfered with my college education and wanted me to work at the bank with her. It wasn't so much that she wanted and had a daughter or a child but that she wanted a warm body that was an extension of her. Just to have someone who would always be by her side."

"Please don't take this wrong, but you're right, she does sound like the stoic housekeeper in a gothic novel."

Dru smiled and nodded at Justin. "That sounds exactly what she was like! Always looking down her nose at anyone who didn't live up to her standards or her way of doing things. It was always her rules, her way and if you didn't do what she wanted, when she wanted, she'd get you for it. Somehow, some way she'd get you back for it. That sounds pretty awful to say about my mother, doesn't it?"

"No. Not really. People who hurt other people to make themselves feel better . . ." Justin shrugged. "Well they do become the fodder for a villain in a book now and again. I'm glad you found your way here."

"Trust me, I wouldn't have if she was still alive."

"And that's what you mean when you say it freed you?"

"Exactly. If she was still alive, I'd still be living in her house, working at the bank and having to sneak the kind of books I like to read into the house and hope she didn't find them."

Justin shifted on the desk. "What kind of books did she want you to read?"

"Generally religious, metaphysical books. She was big on spewing platitudes about what good people did. She could out "Phil" Dr. Phil. Just don't tell her she's not one of them. But yeah, if she was still alive, I'd be working at the bank and would never have found the ad for the job here and trust me, this is a dream job. I hope we . . . you need an assistant for a long time and that I'm the best one for the job."

"At the moment I think I can safely say you are the only one we'd want in this position. You are pretty near perfect, Drusilla. Pretty near perfect."

CHAPTER TWENTY-TWO

Justin returned to his desk and sat down. Out of the corner of his eye he watched Dru. The way she tilted her head as she proofread the manuscript in front of her. The way she held her head, the slight tilt and curve of her neck had him feeling things Gabrielle's heroes felt, initially tried to run from but what ultimately captured their hearts. That, however, was not him. Definitely not him. Not until he met Dru. Those few creamy white inches of neck begged to be kissed before he worked his way down to her breasts and lower. Surprised at his arousal, Justin shifted in his chair. Not that he didn't usually find himself growing hard looking at a lovely woman, especially Dru since she'd been working here. No, this was pure and simple reaction to Drusilla.

What caught him off guard was his growing attraction to his assistant. When he read her resume, he knew she was pretty much an open book and someone who could be taught and molded to be a fantastic proofreader and editor. Then when he met her there was something so desirable about her. Not one for snap decisions, he knew the moment she stood in the doorway that he was going to hire Drusilla Montgomery. The only reason he waited to offer her the job was so he didn't want to look overly eager. For now, things had to be kept strictly professional. The question was, for how much longer could he keep up the façade of being Gabrielle's assistant and having no interest in his new housemate?

Ah, now that was a delicious way of looking at it . . . his housemate. His mate.

Justin turned to the computer and began to write . . .

She looked so innocent, so fragile sitting there while the police inspector posed his questions. Gavin knew she hadn't killed her mother. No, Emma was too delicate, too delicate take the life of another. That fell to him. When he'd heard about how the elder Juliet treated her daughter, shutting her away and playing her deadly psychological games on the young woman, it enraged him. His thirst for blood took on new meaning and on that cold and foggy night, he waited for the older woman. She never knew what hit . . . or bit her. Her blood wasn't the most flavorful he'd ever drank, but a sweetness caressed his palate anyway. The lingering sweetness of revenge and making right a wrong.

When the time came to make Emma his, he would savor each moment. Emma would taste sweeter than anything he'd ever drank. She'd rejuvenate then enliven him. She would be all to him.

When Emma told him she sought the position in his home as part of her freedom, it seared him. For a man who prided himself on keeping his lust under control, of never hardening without having decided to partake, the woman made him lose all sense and control. Whenever she walked into a room, no not even into the room itself, but the thought of her even walking by, he hardened. Their mating would be one that was completely mental, physical and spiritual.

For now he only needed to bide him time . . . and soon, very soon, she would seek him and his bed out. Of that he had no doubt.

The words of the story flowed and for the next few hours Justin's fingers barely left the keyboard. He tried to tell himself what he was doing was wrong, but how could anything this easy be wrong? Dru made the perfect heroine. Well Dru's personality, her characteristics were absolutely perfect for his heroine. Maybe asking her to live here at the Victorian with him wasn't the smartest thing to do. There was too much history here, too many secrets, secrets that could drive her away. But telling his story had become a compulsion. Night after night as he learned more about her, came to know her, the story grew.

For the first time in several hours, he looked over at Dru only to realize she'd fallen asleep sitting at her desk. Clearly, the week had been harder on her than she'd thought. With a smile, Justin rose and walked over to his assistant.

The small smile on her lips made her even prettier than he'd originally thought. There was an innocence to it . . . one he'd need to put into the book along with how that smile incited the hero to need to possess her even more.

His gaze moved to her neck, pale, slender, begging for him to lower his lips and suck at the shallow pulse point. Once again his groin tightened in anticipation of being skin to skin with her. Without really thinking of his actions, Justin tugged his sweater down past his hips. With how soundly Drusilla slept she wouldn't wake to see his bulging hard on but still . . . it was the gentlemanly thing to do.

Gently he bent and scooped her up. That Dru didn't wear perfume was one more thing that made her so appealing to him. Her own scent was tantalizing. He licked his lips. Damn but he wanted to kiss her! And that would be wrong. Gabrielle would have a fit if she knew what he was about.

Then again, she would, in reality, with a sly smile, encourage him.

He contemplated waking his assistant and telling her to make an early night of it, and head on out to the cottage and go to sleep. But while that would allow him to touch her, it wouldn't be the same as gathering her in his arms and holding her close. Justin glanced toward the door and stairs beyond. With a nod to himself, he decided he'd carry her upstairs. If she woke, he'd set her down and explain. If she slept on, he'd tuck her in in one of the second floor bedrooms.

His plan decided, Justin gently shifted her in his arms and headed upstairs to one of the rooms on the second floor. He decided he'd leave her a note explaining what he'd done, so in case she woke before evening and was confused, she wouldn't panic. Vincent rose from his place on the couch and trotted up the stairs behind him to the second floor, and room he thought Dru would most like. With care, he laid her on the bed. Moving carefully he removed her tennies and placed them on the floor beside the bed. For a moment he studied her, wondering if he should remove more than her shoes. The temptation to strip her naked and cuddle up beside her in the bed almost destroyed his common sense. Lying beside her wouldn't do more than tempt him to do more. She might not mind a few kisses, but kisses weren't going to be enough for him. That was one thing Justin was sure of.

Vincent hopped up on the bed, shot him a look as he walked up to where Dru's head rested on a pillow. Deep asleep, she rolled to her side and curled toward the cat. Vincent's purr could be heard at the end of the bed.

"Don't get cheeky," Justin whispered.

Vincent blinked at him.

"I mean it. Enjoy yourself now because one of these nights it's going to be me with his head on the other pillow."

The cat turned away from him and rested his head near Drusilla's shoulder.

Justin shook his head, and quickly wrote a note he placed near her pillow. At the door he turned down the single light in the room and pulled the door almost all the way closed. She'd probably be surprised to find herself in the bed when she woke. Hopefully, it wouldn't startle her too much.

He hoped she wouldn't mind that he carried her upstairs and not woken her to turn in herself.

Holding her those few minutes coming up the stairs was a mere taste of what he wanted from her.

Justin walked to the end of the hall to the dormer window that overlooked the front of the house. One of the long, low moans that were known to sound, shuddered through the house. He stood at the window looking out at the velvety dark night. A few stars that looked like brilliant diamonds showed against the black expanse. They were fortunate in this part of town that while the streetlights shined from sundown to sunup, the city's lights didn't obliterate the beauty of the night sky. The sun wouldn't rise for a few hours yet. There was time to get a bit more work done. Not that writing about her effect on him would diminish the arousal he felt just from holding her.

Maybe he should look ahead in the book and begin writing their first love scene. Yes, tonight would be a good time to describe how that first time he lay between Drusilla's legs would feel.

Drusilla's legs? This needs to stop. It is Gavin who will pleasure Emma, not me who will lay beside Drusilla. Not unless I want this arrangement to end badly.

CHAPTER TWENTY-THREE

Dru woke early while the sun was still high in the sky the next day. Slightly disoriented, she rolled to the side to find herself looking into a pair of demon yellow eyes surrounded by black fur. "Ack! Vincent . . ." She huffed out a breath. "You scared the crap out of me."

The cat blinked and stretched out a paw, resting it lightly on her shoulder.

"Well I'm glad you're okay with it."

Vincent closed his eyes and began to purr.

Coming more awake, Dru looked down at herself and realized she was still in her clothes from the day before . . . and not in the cottage. "What? Where am I?"

Vincent raised a paw and began to groom himself, clearly disinterested in her plight.

"Well clearly you don't find it odd that I'm in a strange bed with my clothes on." She shifted to sit up. "At least I took my shoes off. Or someone did. I don't suppose that was you?"

With the kind of poise only a cat could have, Vincent continued grooming himself as if the woman in the bed beside him didn't exist.

"Yeah, for as talented as you are, lifting someone more than ohhh, twenty times your size isn't in your bailiwick, is it?"

Vincent still ignored her.

"So then how did I get up here?" Dru scratched her temple, thinking over what could have happened. She didn't feel sick, her stomach was fine, no headache, so what happened? The last thing she remembered she was reading Gabrielle's manuscript, glancing over at Justin typing away a few times. So what happened?

She rose and padded over to the window and pulled the heavy black out curtain aside. She mused on why pretty much every room she'd been in had heavy drapes or, in the case of her bedroom, the blackout curtains. Why would someone want to keep out the daylight from virtually every room in the house?

Absentmindedly she felt her neck and made note that it still felt smooth. Shaking her head, she headed for the door and downstairs to the cottage. At the threshold she spotted the note Justin had left, went over and read it. With a smile, she stuck it in her pocket and headed out the door.

As she tiptoed down the hallway, the temptation to peer into the rooms on what she realized must be the second floor almost stopped her progress back to the cottage. Instead she pushed her curiosity aside and headed to her new home.

Inside her bedroom she padded into the bathroom, thinking that maybe a shower would bring back the memory of what happened the night before. If nothing else, it would wake her up a bit more. If something weird did happen, at least she could get a start on her work tonight and make up for the lost time.

In the en suite bathroom she climbed into the shower with the hope that the plumbing was a bit more modern than some of the Victorian throwbacks in the house. "Not that beggars can be choosers. After all, I could either be back at the bank or on the streets looking for a new house to live in." To her delight the showerhead was modern with a great massaging unit attached. With plenty of hot water in a steady stream, the shower worked wonders.

Toweling off, she glanced at her makeup case sitting on the counter. "So do I do makeup like usual or, since I'm living here do I bypass the whole dressing for work thing?" That was going to be a whole other issue. Justin was always casually dressed in jeans and a button down shirt or sweater. The few times she bumped into him it occurred to her that she wouldn't mind seeing him in a t-shirt or rather what the t-shirt might reveal. Even with his shirts and sweaters, it was clear Justin had a pretty fine chest. Even when she interviewed, he wasn't dressed for success but for comfort. It took her a few weeks to feel comfortable wearing casual slacks and sweater and then only because Justin suggested she might be more comfortable in jeans. He, however, was a guy and the boss.

So if she put on makeup was it being professional? Or would Justin think she was hitting on him? If she didn't, would he think she was slovenly? Or after whatever happened last night that she was sick?

She looked in the mirror at herself. "You know, sometimes being a woman isn't the easiest thing to be. What do I do?"

Vincent ambled into the bathroom and jumped up on the counter. Spotting a tube of lipstick, he began to bat it around until it landed on the floor. He shot her a quick look and proceeded to hustle out of the bathroom, pawing the tube ahead of him out of the room.

"Well that answers that now, doesn't it? Some moisturizer, a little mascara and a smidge of blush and I'm set for work."

Without knowing what time she'd fallen asleep the night before—or how she'd ended up in the bed in the house, Dru decided she really did need to get an early start on the night's work. While her latte perked, she scrambled up some eggs and with her breakfast for dinner, she headed into the office to work.

Despite her resolve to keep from sneaking looks where she had no real business doing so, after setting down her dish and cup, she wandered over to Justin's desk. After all, he may have left instructions for her over there as well as on her own desk, right?

Right.

"Just keep telling yourself that girlfriend, just keep telling yourself that."

The desk was, as usual, clear of everything but a pad of paper, pens in a penholder, the ornate turn of the faux 19th century telephone and computer. The pad of paper, however, caught her attention. A list, written in Justin's precise handwriting, sat on the top page:

1. The mother, only child or siblings?

2. If siblings, were they also control freaks?

3. Abuse — only emotional? (Probably best to leave it at that regardless due to genre and reader age).

4. Dietary habits?

5. Alcohol?

6. Physical appearance? Fat, thin, gray hair, frizzy hair.

7. Attempts to break free?

8. Cemetery scene — how does Gavin feel when he sees the heroine at the cemetery?

9. Will she, or does she go to the cemetery? If not, how to bring our visceral reactions of going?

10. Gavin wouldn't really mind now, would he?

Dru stared at the list, not sure what to think. Was Justin curious about *her* past? And if so, why? Did he feel sorry for her? There was no reason to since right now she was living the kind of life she'd wanted to have for a long time.

Okay, not exactly *the* life she wanted. If it was *the* life, she and Justin would be partners of the romantic type, not an assistant to an assistant. There'd be sensual caresses, hot kisses and passionate lovemaking until the early hours of the morning . . . or night as the case may be. They'd be skin to skin and there'd be no need to imagine what his chest and ass looked like in the buff. With how he buttoned up his shirts or the high-necked sweaters, she didn't even know if he had hair on his chest or not.

Not that it would make a difference. Not when the rest of the package was beyond gorgeous male.

Then again, if the list wasn't about her per se, and it sure sounded like her, why was he making it? Did it have anything to do with the book he'd been editing or writing or whatever? That wasn't all that comfortable. Did Gabrielle George know about this? Was there a reason for her to be aware if Justin was writing his own book? Or was it research for one of her own? But why would either care about a plain Jane, every day kind of girl from Marin County California?

Confused about what her employer might be up to, Dru walked back to her desk and sat down. While her computer booted up, she again considered the list she'd seen on Justin's desk. Needing to talk to someone, someone who would at least tell her she was nuts, she picked up the phone.

"Dru! What's up?" Haley asked, clearly knowing it was Dru from the caller ID.

"Me!"

"I can see that."

"Yeah, well that's figurative and literal. I don't think I've been up this late or early as the case may be since I started working here."

"And you haven't burned to a crisp yet? Does that mean you can still walk into a church and see yourself in the mirror?"

"So not funny. Yes, I can see myself in a mirror. In fact, I put some makeup on this morning."

"Why would that be, I don't know, something different?"

"Cause I work from home."

"Uh huh."

Dru toyed with the phone cord while thinking. "It's, I don't know. This is my new home, you know?"

"Right."

"But it's still my job and even though no one comes to the house I do have a boss . . ."

"Who happens to be a major hottie, right?"

"Right."

"And you don't want to ugly-up for a guy that makes you near-to-swoon, right?"

"Right. But I didn't call to talk about my nearly perfect boss."

"No?" Haley chuckled.

"No. You free Saturday? For lunch or dinner?"

"Sure. Are you inviting me to the city?"

"Uh, I hadn't thought about that. I'll have you over . . . soon. Definitely as soon as I have a grip on things. When I have a better feel for the ground rules."

"No problem, so what's up? Just want to talk?"

"Yes, but no time right now. Saturday though, I need to pick up a few more things from the house and since it's going to be sold, I need to take some sort of inventory and find a storage space and all that."

"They're selling your house?"

"That's what the will says. If I leave the bank, I lose my home and the house gets sold or whatever that church wants done with it."

"Wow, your mother gets worse and worse. I had no idea. She always seemed so great."

"That was her other people persona. Haley, I tried to tell you for years what she was like, but no one listened. You never listened. You only saw the image of the woman she wanted the world to see, not the person I lived with."

"I guess. So you need my help with packing and all?"

"If you're offering, definitely. And then dinner cause I do need to talk."

"Sounds good. Meet you at your . . . the house . . . at?"

"How's two work? It will give me a little time to sleep and

in case traffic over the bridge is nasty, time to get up there."

"Two it is and we'll find a fun place for dinner."

"Thanks, Hale. You're the best."

"I try."

Dru stared at the phone a moment after she hung up. She glanced at the door . . . because Justin was in the house and the last thing she wanted to do was tip him off that in her eyes things were, at best, strange.

Across the room, one of the figurines sitting on a Chippendale end table shivered as if cold and suddenly fell to the ground, startling Dru. Dru gasped and looked over at Vincent, who reclining half asleep on the couch, lifted a lid to gaze at her a second before returning to his nap.

"Did you see that?" she asked the cat.

Vincent didn't move, not even a twitch of his eyelids or a whisker.

"Well you had to have heard it." What is it with things in this house falling over?

The cat still did not move.

It wasn't the first time something had fallen for no reason. It was the first time it happened when she was alone and saw the object tremble before falling. Justin never seemed to notice, except if it happened in the office and then he'd stand up, replace the object and go back to work as if nothing happened. Maybe there was a ghost who wasn't happy to have Dru in the house.

The cat never twitched a muscle when a low howl would course through the house for a few seconds. There were times when she wondered if Gabrielle was sitting up in that tower room and not really in Europe researching her next novel. Not for the first time, Dru wondered about Gabrielle and the story behind her absence from the house. Was she really in Europe? Or was she a prisoner in her own home? Or had something more nefarious befallen her? Or was Gabrielle dead and her

ghost haunting the house and engaging in poltergeist-like activities to scare Dru away? Or . . . rather than scare her away,
get her to investigate? Now that was something to consider.

It seemed Dru was the only one who ever noticed the
sounds or objects shifting on tables. Maybe she was losing it.
After all, her mother wasn't the most stable person in the
world. Maybe her family was disposed to some sort of quirky
mental illness.

Slowly she rose and walked over to the side table. She
stopped a moment before picking up the figurine. It was just
a statue, right? That was all. Just a little china statue that fell
off the table, probably because a truck went by outside. Never
mind that large trucks weren't allowed on the street without
a permit and advance notice to the residents. "It's just a little
china statue." She tried to assure herself.

"Actually, it's porcelain."

CHAPTER TWENTY-FOUR

Dru screamed.

Justin crossed from the threshold to where she stood, still mid-scream, and pulled her into his arms. "It's okay, Drusilla. It's just me. I'm sorry. I'm so sorry."

"You scared the hell out of me!"

He had the audacity to laugh and then repeated himself. "I'm sorry."

Reluctantly, she pulled out of his arms and punched the one nearest her. "No you aren't. You scared me and you think it's funny. It's not. You almost gave me a heart attack."

At that, Justin stopped laughing and studied her face. "I'm sorry, Drusilla. You didn't hear me coming down the hall? Are you all right?"

She gave a half-hearted attempt to move away from him and then decided it felt pretty damn good to be so near the man who made passionate love to her in every imaginary scene she had the past few weeks. "No. I'm fine. Sorry for . . .

"Please, don't be. I just never saw anyone turn so white and tremble so much when they said it." He loosened his grip, not quite letting go, but pulling ever so slightly away. "Are you sure you're all right?"

"Yes. I'm fine. Sorry if I was a bit of a drama queen there."

"Drama isn't bad. It's what makes books come alive. It's why readers buy them."

"Okay and no, I didn't hear you coming down the hall. I was kind of lost in thought."

"Good thoughts?"

Dru nodded.

"Care to share?"

"Um, no, not right now. Maybe later. I warmed up some quiche for breakfast. Have you eaten?"

At her question, Justin looked decidedly uncomfortable. "Uh no, not yet. I'm not hungry. Maybe later."

"Okay. So well, here we are."

"So we are." He grinned and it made him even more devastatingly handsome.

"Well, um . . ."

. . . He took her lips in a kiss. A gentle kiss, testing, tasting, sensing just how much more she wanted.

She parted her lips for him, sampling the flavor of his tongue. Without thought she wrapped her arms around his shoulders, pulling him closer. He slid his arms around her waist and began to back her toward the couch. A few steps and he rubbed his growing hard on against her hips, causing a thrill of desire to shoot through her. From his shoulders she ran her hands up into his hair and tugged, showing him how much more she wanted from him. He groaned as they reached the couch. Suddenly, his hands were on the buttons of her blouse and he parted the sides without even a glance. It wasn't until he laid her down that . . .

"Dru? Are you sure you're all right?"

She blinked. "Wha . . ." Oh damn, had she said anything? Did he know what she'd been thinking? Even worse, had she said something or made a move on him? *Oh crap.*

"You kind of zoned out there for a moment. Maybe you should go upstairs and lie down for a while or even take the night off. You've been working hard the past few weeks and with the changes in your life you might need a little break."

Reluctantly she took a step back and rubbed her arms. It was feeling just way too good to be near him and Dru had no doubt those moments in his arms had triggered her fantasies to venture to a more intense level. "No, I'm fine. Really. Honest. I just got a little focused on work, that's all."

He studied her, looking into her eyes as if he could see the truth hidden in their depths. "Sure?"

Or, was trying to mesmerize her so he could bite her and she wouldn't remember. "Positive."

"Okay, but if you need to take a break or want to call it quits early, no worries, okay?"

"You got it."

Man, I've got a boatload to talk to Haley about.

CHAPTER TWENTY-FIVE

Saturday morning Dru woke before the alarm, ate a quick breakfast and without even a thought about the creaks, groans and locked away rooms of the house, took off for Marin. Taking a break the night before, she'd made a list of the things she needed to check, wanted to pack and had to do to make sure the closing of the house in Marin were taken care of. It never occurred to her that the attorney would have had the locks changed and kept her from her own home. After all, she had two weeks to decide what she was going to do, right?

So there she stood, trying her key over and over when she knew it wasn't going to work after the first time.

"What's up?" Haley asked her when she pulled up.

Hands on hips, Dru answered, "It appears the lawyer locked up my house and didn't bother to tell me."

"Well that sucks. Did you try the back door?"

"Yeah. Locked."

"How about the windows?"

"You mean, break in?"

"It's not exactly like breaking in since it's your house and your stuff is in there. Besides, it's not like we haven't climbed in your bedroom window before." Haley leaned over and tried the door handle herself.

"No. But we were doing that in the middle of the night after sneaking out."

"So now we're sneaking in in the middle of the day. Come on."

With a glance up and down the street, the pair headed to

the back of the house. Fortunately tall bushes covered up the lower half of the windows. For as thorough as the attorney had been, he apparently hadn't checked to see if the windows were locked. Talk about a lucky break. Haley and Dru shimmied into the bedroom. In the dim light caused by the trees, bushes and the angle of the sun, they turned to each other and laughed.

It felt good, just so good to laugh. Dru felt like it had been years since she had a deep down-to-the-core laugh. For as difficult as her mother made things, Haley was beside her through all her little life dramas. And they had laughs. Oh yeah, they'd had some absolutely deep down, pee-in-your-pants, cry-your-eyes-out, can't-catch-your-breath laughs. It took them a few minutes to catch their breath and look around the room.

"Well it looks like he left my room alone." Dru poked around her drawers and closets. "Let's see what the rest of the house looks like."

Together they walked down the short hallway, past her mother's room. They stuck their heads in to see a number of boxes with numbers on them sitting against one wall. Dru shook her head and they started into the living room. There too, as well as the dining room, were boxes with numbers on them. Some of the objects in the living room had already been packed and put in a box labeled with the name of the last church her mother had gone to. The kitchen had already been picked bare.

"Wow," Haley whispered, stunned. "They didn't waste any time, did they?"

"Apparently not. And if I'm not mistaken, he used some of the moving boxes *I* bought. Asshole." Dru's stomach hurt. "I can't believe she'd do that. She was mean-spirited and controlling but I can't believe she'd do something like this."

"What are you going to do?"

Dru wandered back into the living room and then paced into the dining room. "I guess I need to call the lawyer and ask him what's going on. I thought I had two weeks to decide. This makes it look like he's been at it since I moved into Gabrielle's. It's like he was watching me . . . just like Martha did . . . and as soon as I left for work with my suitcase that night he started moving things. I can't believe it. I just can't believe it."

"So what do we do?"

Dru walked back into the living room and sat on the sheet-covered couch. "I guess I need to pack up what I can tonight, the things I really want and try to move as much as I can now. The problem is, where do I go with it? The storage places close at 5 so I've only got maybe two hours to move anything. I don't have enough boxes, at least I don't think I do unless I unpack some of the stuff he put in the boxes I bought. And then, how do I move things?"

"Well." Haley looked around the room. "We've got his as well as yours boxes."

"Yeah."

"But the things in them aren't the lawyer's, they're yours, or some of the things are yours. We pack things up and leave him a note saying thanks for them or, I guess you could tell him you'll pay him back."

"Okay."

Referring to her boyfriend, Haley told her, "I'll call Ricky and see if he can come by with a few of his friends and his truck, and we'll start moving things."

Dru rose and went to hug her friend. "Haley, what would I do without you?"

"Probably nothing illegal or sneaky."

Together they laughed.

"Thank you. I can't imagine life without you there to help me. Yes, please, call Ricky and I'll see if the storage place in town has a unit available. At least I can get what means the most to me out."

The storage company had room and took her credit card number over the phone. The owner, one of her regular customers at the bank, assured her he'd wait for her to come with at least one truck load before closing up for the night. Being nice and going out of her way to help customers at the bank was simply Dru's way, but it sure paid off now.

Ricky arrived with two of his friends a short time later and starting with Dru's room, they began to pack her things. She loaded the clothing into her car and figured she could leave it in there until she had time to explain to Justin.

Justin. What would he think? Would he fire her because she had such a screwed up life before she met him? Or would he make more of those notes of his that were somehow ending up in what appeared to be a book. And with all this she hadn't had a chance to even begin to tell Haley what was going on at the painted lady in the city.

Then again, maybe going back to work at the bank and forgetting all this was the better route. If she did she'd need to give notice. Gabrielle's latest book was two weeks away from the publishing deadline and there was more work to do. She owed the author that much. If in fact the author even knew what was going on . . . if she was alive.

Well of course she was alive. She couldn't be living with a . . . a . . .

Well, she owed whoever gave her the job and was paying her so well time to find a new assistant and go back to her bank job.

And say goodbye to Justin.

That would be the hard part because despite the fact they had a strictly business arrangement and he may be engaged in something not quite right, he sure made for great fantasies. She used to imagine the hero of her latest read lying beside her in bed at night doing all kinds of wonderful things with her body. Since she met Justin he'd filled that role. She just hoped she didn't suddenly start talking in her sleep. Not that it would matter if she was sleeping in the cottage but if she fell asleep at her desk yet another night . . .

Well she might not exactly talk but calling out his name the throes of passion filled dreams . . . could he hear goings on in the cottage from the house? With a mental head shake, she told herself what she really needed to be doing was focusing on packing up her stuff and not doing all kinds of erotic things with Justin.

Ricky and his friends made short work of moving out a good portion of Dru's belongings. At least they got the things that meant the most to her to the storage facility.

After everyone enjoyed being treated to pizza and beer and left, Dru sank down on the front steps and stared out at the street for a few minutes. Clearly, this part of her life was over. There was no going back. She was so deep in thought she didn't her Haley approach from the side.

"Hey."

"Haley." Dru couldn't help the squeak in her voice.

"Didn't mean to scare you."

"Not really scared, just kinda startled."

Haley sat down beside her and joined Dru in gazing out at the street. "You doing okay?"

Dru took a long, slow breath. "I think so. I'm just . . . I shouldn't be, but I'm still stunned at what my mother did. Haley, what kind of mother treats her child the way Martha treated me? What kind of mother tries to control from the grave? Did she really hate me that much?"

"I don't think she hated you . . ."

"No? Did I tell you about the time she told me if I hadn't been born that her beloved Grayson would have come back and rescued her from her marriage to my father?"

"Wow, no. Really?"

Dru nodded.

"And she said she didn't buy into romance. Man. That is . . . I just don't comprehend someone like that. She was sick, Dru. I can see now she was mentally ill."

"Mentally ill? If that's so then every person who ever tried to manipulate someone else is mentally ill. She just got way too much pleasure hurting me."

"Sadism like that is mental illness. I think she had a weird kind of Munchausen by proxy."

Dru snorted. "Well if she was mentally ill, I'm sure I'm not far behind."

"Because of how she treated you?"

"No. Because of what I think is going on."

"You mean the house?"

"No. Wanna get a coffee and I'll tell you about it? Maybe you have some ideas."

"Sure. You know me, I'm always up for something strange."

A short time later, settled into a favorite coffee shop, Dru held the cup in her hands as if they were cold.

"So what's going on?" Haley reached a hand across the table toward Dru.

"Justin."

"The hottie assistant?"

"The very same."

"And? I feel like I'm pulling teeth here." She lifted her hand and wiggled her fingers at Dru.

"He's . . . well he's . . ."

"Sexy. Hot. Every woman's wet dream. Oh . . . he's . . ."

"No. At least I don't think he is. Haley, this is going to sound reeeeaaallly strange so stick with me here."

Haley took a swallow of her coffee. "I'm all ears."

"I think he's a vampire."

Chapter Twenty-six

Haley quickly swallowed to keep from spitting her coffee all over the table. "He's a *what*?"

"Vampire," Dru whispered.

This time, Haley swallowed her coffee before speaking. "You're right, you have lost it. I know you've hinted about it with his not eating and drinking and the weird stuff that happens in the house, but vampire? Dru . . . everyone knows vampires aren't real. They're fiction. Plain and simple. Authors, other than your favorite, Gabrielle George, write incredibly spicy, shockingly, indecently sexy alpha males who happen to suck blood to get their mojo going. They live forever, are great in bed, despite not having the blood flow to get themselves a hard on, kiss like it's their last meal—only it's yours, and have bodies women just want to crawl over. That's unless they're pasty white, bald nasty guys like Nosferetu and then the hero is the sigh-with-pleasure-gorgeous guy you want to get into bed. But other than that, they aren't real."

"I'm not sure about that."

"I am. But I'm willing to listen."

"Okay, but you can't tell anyone. Seriously. Not a soul. I'll deny I said it and you'll look nuts."

Haley quickly looked around the room and then leaned in close to whisper, "I'm not going to say anything. Spill. Why, aside from the fact he likes to work nights, is your boss a vampire?"

"His wanting to work nights makes sense. He explained that when I interviewed—with Gabrielle's schedule and her traveling and all, it is just easier. And she's totally reclusive . . . if she's even alive."

"You haven't met her yet?"

"No. And that's another reason he may have like another life. He said she's been traveling but she never calls when I'm there. Not even the past week when I've been there during the day. The phone never rings. Justin sometimes calls her agent or publisher in New York, but Gabrielle never calls. Sometimes I think she may be dead or just a prisoner that he keeps alive sucking her blood so she can keep writing, and he can continue to live in the lifestyle being her assistant has afforded him."

"Uh huh. Anything else?"

"You mean besides the fact that my employer may or may not know I work for her if she's even still alive?" This time it was Dru who took a quick look around while she spoke.

"Slow down. Are you sure she's not alive? You said Justin lives in her house, right? Maybe he has a separate phone line in his room that she calls or he talks to her away from you so they can discuss business you don't need to know about. That happened at the bank, right? Sometimes Millan would need to talk to the higher ups and she did it away from the rest of the staff, right?"

"Sure. Maybe. But Hale, he doesn't eat. Ever. And there are no mirrors on the first and second floors. Well actually there are a few, but he never stands so you can see him in them."

"Maybe he's not into looking at himself."

"It's Gabrielle's house!"

"Maybe she doesn't like to look at *her*self."

"She's not even there. Seriously, the house is almost completely gothic. They use candles instead of lights."

"Maybe they're saving money by not using electricity."

Dru shot her friend a look before continuing, "and the house is creepy."

"Creepy?"

"There are strange sounds all the time. Well not all the time, but for no reason, other times it creaks, like the stairs will sound like someone is walking up them but no one is there. And things fall down. A few times I thought it was Vincent, the cat. But when a figurine falls off a table across the room and Vincent is sitting right next to me . . . well there's no other explanation."

"So you're saying the house is haunted?"

Dru snapped her fingers. "Could be. But would ghosts hang out with a vampire?"

"I don't know. You'd need to ask the experts or people who believe in those kinds of things."

"Experts?"

"Yeah, like the authors who write about them. Wouldn't they research vampires and what they do?"

"I thought you said you didn't think they were real."

"*I* don't think they are, but *you* do and a bunch of other people must. There's all this lore about them, so some people think they're real. I'd ask them . . . or not. Not if you want to lose your job, which brings me to my point. If you think he's so creepy, why don't you quit? Why go through all this, losing your house. Just go back to work at the bank, move back into your house and wait till, I don't know, something else comes along or you decide to like the bank."

"Quit? I love my job! And *he's* not creepy, the house is. I mean, aside from the vampire thing, but that's not creepy. It's kind of . . . romantic."

Haley shook her head. "Then go back to the bank until you find one where the guy isn't into draining blood and works days. And really, sucking blood is not romantic. At least not to me."

Dru started to laugh. "I knew you'd make me feel better. I do sound nuts. The poor guy probably has reasons why he never goes out in the daytime, there's no garlic in the kitchen and sometimes he sits there staring at me."

"He stares at you? Like in a creepy way or a 'I wanna get in your pants' kind of way?"

Dru thought about that. "You know, I'm not sure."

"Are you happy there?"

Dru nodded. "I am. For the first time in my life I feel like I'm alive and doing what I want most with my life."

"Then there's no question. Stay and enjoy every minute of it and your hottie vampire."

"You mean until he bites me and drains my blood?"

"Dru, I told you . . . vampires aren't real. He's not going to bite you, but if you let him know you think he is, he might fire you."

"Good point. I feel better talking to you about it. So you don't think the house is haunted?"

Chapter Twenty-seven

Justin was awake and at the computer when Dru returned. Flames from the stocky white candles illuminated the room, in their own way obliterating the fog outside the house. He sat, oblivious to Dru returning, his head bent in concentration.

"I'm sorry. I'm late." She stammered.

Dark eyes met hers, stopping her in her tracks, mesmerizing her. His hair hung loose about his shoulders and Dru had the urge to step over to him and run her fingers through the strands she had no doubt were silky smooth.

Justin's pale green cotton shirt hung open — only a few buttons at the bottom done up, exposing his chest and the fine dark hairs that covered the smooth, well-defined muscles. Her imagination turned fertile as she visualized undoing the button of his jeans then slowly sliding the zipper down exposing his penis.

"Late?"

"Yes. I'm late." She glanced around the room.

He glanced around the room trying to see what she was looking for and seeming confused. Justin's life ran by his body clock, not man-made constraints.

Finally he murmured, "It's Saturday, Dru. We don't work on Saturday."

"Then what are you doing at the computer?" She held up her hand. "Wait. No. I don't mean that. It's none of my business what you do in your own home."

"You have every right, Drusilla. This is your home too." He

stood but didn't move beyond that.

Her breath caught because she had to fight her growing desire for this man. What she wanted to do was walk up to him, rub against his body, run her fingers in his hair and draw his head down for a kiss. A part of her mind wandered with images of him lowering her to the floor, pulling down her jeans and sliding into her. Images of grasping his butt while he pounded into her, his breathing harsh and needy with desire for her danced in her mind, making her panties dampen.

She took an unconscious step back, ready to run rather than make a bigger fool of herself than she already was. Dru knew she wasn't making sense. Of course they didn't work on Saturdays. Still, she plodded on making a bigger fool of herself. "No. No. You see, that's where it's wrong. You're wrong. I, I . . ."

Justin started toward her and she froze, locked in the heat of his gaze. "Dru, you're shaking like a leaf. Come. Sit down."

He guided her to one of the overstuffed chairs near the fireplace. The flames rose as she sat as if they were a living thing, and breathed a sigh of relief that she hadn't quite alienated him.

"You are white as a ghost, Dru. Can I get you water? Tea? Something stronger?"

"I'm okay. Really."

"Are you sure? You're shivering. Do you feel ill?"

"No. I . . . I'm just tired. It's been a long week."

He knelt before her and chaffed her hands. Worry settled in his gaze. "Are you sure you're all right?"

"Yes. Honest, it's just been a long week with a lot going on."

Justin nodded. The glow from the flames in the fireplace cast luminous highlights in his hair. She really had to fight the urge to keep from sliding her hands up to his shoulders and then into his hair to pull him close for a kiss and then some.

He was gorgeous, just so gorgeous.

"I can only imagine. I owe you an apology."

"For what?"

"I should have realized you probably needed some time to kick back and adjust to what's going on."

"Oh no. Keeping busy was the best thing for me. I just needed to know when to slow down and take some time to let it all settle. Going up north today was good."

Justin nodded. "So you went back to your place?"

"Not so much my place anymore. I thought I had two weeks to get my things out, but apparently the attorney already changed the locks and started to see about disposing things."

"He did?" Justin sounded stunned.

"He sure did. I got there and he used all the boxes I'd bought for myself to move, had boxes brought in, the locks changed and some notes about what was going where. I don't blame him for all of it. Pretty much everything he's done was at my mother's instruction."

"It is stunning how she has tried to control you from beyond the grave." He shook his head in disbelief.

Dru smiled to herself at his phraseology . . . from beyond the grave. "Yes, well that's what my mother was about. At least I knew how to get in, and my friend Haley called some friends of hers and they helped me move quite a bit to a storage facility. I need to go back up tomorrow to finish picking up a few things."

"Would you like me to go with you?'

That stopped her in her tracks. Was Justin offering to head up to Marin with her? "Would you mind? We'd need to go in the daylight because the storage facility closes at 5."

"Sure, why not?"

"Um, well it would be in the day time."

He looked perplexed. "Right. You said that. We need to go

in daylight. Is that a problem?"

"No. Not for me. I just wasn't sure about you, you know, with your . . ." she twirled her hand in the air while she searched for the right word. "You know."

Justin looked even more confused. "No, but that's all right."

Well, if he didn't want to talk to her about going out in daylight or why he could, she wasn't going to pry. Justin would know better than she why he didn't go out when the sun was up.

"There's a couple of restaurants up in Marin I've wanted to try. Maybe we could check one of them out after."

Dinner? He was going to eat dinner? Dinner and out in the daylight? Maybe he was just a normal guy with a reclusive streak. "That sounds great. Yes, I'd like that."

"Great, let's plan on it then. Well, if you're feeling all right, I've got a little work to do."

"I'm good. Well then, I think though I'm going to head out to the cottage and unpack some of what I brought back with me."

"Sounds good." He rose and headed back to his desk and as if their whole conversation hadn't taken place, he sat and started typing.

Dru watched him for a few moments before rising and heading out the door. "Uh . . ."

Justin looked up at her as if he'd never seen her before then smiled. "Yes?"

"I could help with mail or whatever if you need me to."

"Ah, no. It's the weekend. You should take the time for yourself."

"Okay then. I'll see you in the morning."

"We should head up to Marin relatively early so you can do whatever you need to before the storage facility closes, and we can load up whatever you want to bring back while it's light out."

"You got it. Night."

"Night."

Vincent rose from where he'd been lounging on the couch and headed out of the room behind her. She stopped in the kitchen to grab an apple and well, to check out if Justin had eaten anything. With how neat he was though he could have had an eight-course meal and no one would have any idea of what he'd had.

Apple in hand, she headed out to the cottage.

Tired as she was, sleep didn't come easily. Her thoughts ranged from losing her home to her mother's vindictiveness to the oddities she found in Gabrielle's house.

And then there was Justin. On the surface he seemed like your basic normal, educated, interesting guy. Okay there was that and the fact that he was drop dead gorgeous.

Could a man be drop dead gorgeous?

"Sure, why not?"

So why was a guy who looked like him with his smarts and interests single? Not that he shared many, if any of his, interests. If anything, he was all about the work. Beginning, middle and end, he was all about the work.

No women ever called him.

Nor did any men.

And he didn't seem to call anyone either. Especially Gabrielle.

She looked at Vincent. "Maybe he texts or emails them?"

The cat had no response. "So either you are protecting your human or you aren't much into conversation."

Vincent meowed in response.

"I see your point. You could meow me all kinds of things, but that wouldn't exactly tell me what you think or know now, would it?"

Once again the cat meowed and this time he rose,

stretched, and changed his position. With a twitch of his tail, he closed his eyes and appeared to doze.

Dru blew out a sigh. "So much for scintillating conversation, huh? Right." She gazed up at the ceiling trying to sort through her thoughts and figure Justin out. Granted, she'd only been in the job for three months, but if he had a girl-friend . . . or boyfriend . . . wouldn't they have shown up or at least called or there would have been some sign of one? Even if he'd had a recent break up, would he really be all about work?

Or was that one of Gabrielle's criteria for an assistant? That he be a candidate for hunk of the year but not have a social life outside work.

"So what if I want one? What if I start to date?" Not that she'd want a date coming to the house and being found lacking when he saw Justin.

Or Justin knowing she was out and about with another man.

Not that she had any other men. Anytime she'd met some-one and made the mistake of bringing them home or letting her mother know, Martha would do something obnoxious and find a way to end the relationship. So confident in her ability to control Dru's every move, Martha even told her once that she was never going to put herself in the position of either being alone or having to take care of someone.

So now she could date anyone she wanted . . . and what was she doing? Fantasizing about a man who, even if she could have him, wouldn't be the best choice since he was, in essence, her boss.

Dru rolled to her side and cuddled against her pillow, not for the first time, imagining she was snuggled up against Jus-tin. She nuzzled the pillow and pretended he was skin to skin with her and placing sensuously soft kisses against her lips. As her imagination carried her deeper into the fantasy, it turned decidedly erotic, making Dru's last thought before succumbing to sleep, "if only."

Justin watched as Drusilla walked out of the office. He smiled to himself when Vincent followed close behind. The cat stopped a moment at the threshold and looked back at Justin. "Go on." He smiled at the cat.

He shook his head when the cat left the room and padded down the hall behind Drusilla, thinking Vincent was one lucky cat. Vincent could curl up beside his employee in bed. He would most likely, now that Dru knew Vincent was just a cat who loved attention in any way, shape and form, be petted and cuddled. If only Justin could be a cat for a few short hours, he'd know what it was like to sleep beside Dru.

Sleep? It wasn't sleep he wanted with her. Oh no. What he wanted, craved at times, was to have her naked beside him, beneath him. He had no doubt her kisses would set him on fire and making love with her would be the most intense sex of his life. For as shy as she could be, as meek and retiring as the presented herself, Justin had no doubt that once she let go, she'd be amazing in bed.

But that was a line not to be crossed. She was his employee . . . well Gabrielle's employee. But given the times, these modern times, one step out of line and he could be accused of sexual harassment and the repercussions of that kind of lawsuit would put the famed author out of business. Readers would not take too kindly to their favorite author's assistant doing anything improper with the assistant's assistant.

Yes, that was one of the problems with the modern world. If they'd lived in the time Gabrielle wrote, the issue of an improper relationship wouldn't enter into the discussion at all. In fact, it would pretty much be a given that he, as lord of the manor — because that is what he definitely would be — could have any woman at his beck and call and if there was one thing he wanted, it was to beck Drusilla Montgomery.

He turned to the computer and typed in a quick phrase in a search engine. Smiling to himself, he opened up his . . . Gabrielle's . . . latest book and began to type about the hero "becking . . . beckoning" to his maid. Tonight Emma would be falling into bed with Gavin. Tonight Justin was more than ready to write what he was sure would be his most torrid love scene yet.

Chapter Twenty-eight

A shard of light shone into Dru's room. With a glare toward the door, Vincent rose, stretched and pawed at the covers until Dru rolled over. The movement was enough to wake her from an otherwise sound sleep. "Vincent . . ." she mumbled. The cat settled down and began to purr.

It was the light, pale though it was, that caused her to roll over and glance out the door. Sure she saw a shadow standing in the hallway, peering in, she called out, "Justin?"

Just like that the shadow faded back into the hallway.

"Justin?" she called again.

Vincent didn't move from his comfy nook on the bed.

Why would Justin be standing at the threshold of her room? Was there something wrong? Well it was too comfortable in the big bed with its plump feather pillows and down comforter to do more than wonder. After all, the cottage was securely locked and secreted behind the Victorian. Besides who would break into her little cottage in the middle of the night when the residents would clearly be home. Or was it a ghost?

A crash in the living room startled her to full wakefulness. "Shit!"

Dru jumped out of the bed, grabbed a candlestick and headed toward the door. A pale shard of light filtered down the hallway where a shadowy figure stood. Armed with her candlestick, Dru called out, "Justin?"

She stepped toward what she thought was the figure and her toe hit something on the ground, causing her to look down. By time she saw it was a table ornament from a nearby end table and glanced back up, the figure disappeared.

Vincent brushed along the bottom of her nightgown. When she looked down, the cat was looking up at her as if to say, "So what do you think? Does Justin sleep walk? Or is there a ghost living here? Or am I seriously going crazy?"

Vincent glanced at the door of the cottage and then back at Dru.

"I think, Vincent, we need to go find Justin. Either he was roaming around sleep-walking or this cottage is haunted."

Vincent gurgled a soft meow and although he padded behind her, had no problem following her out the door and toward the main house.

There was no sign of Justin downstairs nor was there a sound on the stairs to the second and third floors, and Dru knew from starting to work before Justin came in on some nights that at least three of those steps creaked when someone stepped on them. Given the age of the house, could it be haunted? There were those times when an object would fall for no reason at all. Maybe her mother was haunting her from the grave. Martha would do that. Without a doubt, the woman would do that.

Armed with her candlestick and a fur ball of courage beside her, using the dim light shining from outside, she made her way to the stairs. The stairwell was dark and completely devoid of any life-sized shadows.

Not a sound came from the other floors.

When Dru glanced toward the office, she noticed a dim glow coming from there. "Hmm, do you think it was Justin on his way downstairs and just sort of ended up out in the cottage?" Even though the noise seemed to be coming from the opposite end of the hallway, who knew how sound carried throughout the house. "What do you say, should we see if Justin's still up working?"

This time Vincent headed toward the office ahead of her but instead of going in, the cat abruptly turned and headed back to the kitchen. "Aren't you the sly one?" Dru asked him. "Were you the one messing around in the cottage trying to wake me so you could have a midnight snack?"

Vincent glanced over his shoulder and continued on to the kitchen. Dru followed him in and walked over to the cabinet where his food was kept. She reached for a bowl and poured some of his favorite crunchy food out. After placing it on the floor, she stood for a moment while Vincent applied himself to his midnight snack.

Satisfied that it was Vincent who had woken her and she only imagined the figure, Dru started back out to the cottage but stopped when she saw the office light. At a minimum she should see if Justin was still up and wanted something to eat or drink. Right?

Okay, that sounded reasonable even though she was hoping for a look at her employer. For as proper as he was, maybe when he sat there working alone, he undid a few buttons and she'd get a glimpse of something more than properly dressed male.

But Justin wasn't in the office. The light from his computer monitor beckoned to her though and unable to help herself, Dru walked over. When she slid the mouse across the screen, it lit up to reveal his . . . or rather Gabrielle's latest chapter in whatever book Justin was working on for her . . .

Gavin leaned over Emma where she slept. The pristine white canopy over the large and ornate bed cast soft shadows on her so perfect face. In sleep she looked like the angel he knew her to be. While in the waning light of day he watched myriad expressions, it was the shadows of night that revealed her true innocence. No coquette his intended lady. No. She played her part by day but by night, ensconced in her room, away from the demands of society her angelic true self shone through.

He inhaled her scent. Not the light, delicate attar women of her time scented themselves with, but that which was his beloved. The scent of her blood pulsing through her veins, calling to him, making him not just want but need her to the core of his being.

It was time. He couldn't wait another moment. Tonight she would be his.

His groin ached with need. For no other had his member hardened so steadily. Each time she entered a room . . . no . . . even just the thought of her and his balls would tighten and his manhood rise in need. Theirs would be a joining for the ages. Together they would rule the night.

He knelt by the side of her bed. Slowly, savoring the moment, he brought his finger to the shaft of hair that lay across her neck. As he pulled the strand aside and saw the gentle curve of her neck, he ached with need.

There was no need to rush. She was his. While he wanted, needed, desired her above all others, this was a moment to be savored. He would take his time. Indeed he would begin tonight . . . and rather than rush to their culmination he would take her bit by bit, night by night until she herself demanded to join him forever.

He lowered his lips to the smooth white neck and opened his mouth. His teeth slid out in anticipation of the delights that awaited him when her blood would be joined with his. A breath away, a sound echoed in the hallway.

Gavin lifted his head and sniffed. No! No! He'd been so careful, so stealthy when he entered her room.

Perhaps it was the wind. Or someone below stairs.

But no, the step sounded again!

Quickly he rose and backed away from the bed. Back, back he moved, into the shadows.

"Emma? Emma?"

Her elder sister Marta entered the room. Always the faithful watch bitch, Marta. Would she never leave Emma to her own devices? Would there never be a time for just the two of them, he and his beloved? Or would that bitch always stand between them?

Marta stopped half way into the room and looked around. Clearly, she sensed someone or something. Well if need be he'd make *an end to her. He was in need of a feeding. Despite being sure her taste would be stale, dry, bland, her blood would do.*

"Is anyone in here?" Marta called out.

Just as Gavin stepped to dispense with the older sister's interference once and for all, Emma moved in the bed. Slowly she sat up, the white lace cuffs of her nightgown trickling down her hand, almost covering it. The white a bright beacon in the otherwise still and silent night.

"Marta? What is wrong?" Emma asked her sister.

Marta made her way to the bed where Gavin had only a moment before knelt. Looking about watchfully she finally looked to her sister. "Nothing. I thought I heard you call out but obviously you were asleep."

"Yes," she chuckled. "Asleep and dreaming."

"Pleasant dreams I hope?"

"Oh yes, wonderful dreams."

"Do you want to tell me about them?" the older woman probed, demanding to be told by her tone.

Emma yawned. "Perhaps tomorrow. Right now I am sleepy, so sleepy. We shall walk tomorrow and I will tell you about the wonderful dream." With that she lay back down and snuggled into her covers.

Marta stood and watched a moment, an evil gleam in her eye. Clearly, the elder sister had no goodness to give to her sibling. There was no doubt she meant to use Emma for her own devices. Well, Gavin would have something to say about that.

Finally the woman left. With a last look into the room, looking for whatever she felt was there, she left.

Gavin waited a few moments before making his way to the hidden panel in the wall. Tomorrow would be soon enough to begin his life with his beloved.

A hidden panel? Now that might explain the figure or what she thought was a man standing in her room. Gabrielle's house was old, a classic Victorian, and the cottage had to have been built about the same time. Justin told her the house was built early on in the 1850s. Given the history of the city and how quickly it grew from the gold and silver kings, didn't most of the houses have hidden passageways? Some place to store their treasures and come and go without anyone knowing? It made perfect sense this house would have at least one hidden passage. So of course it made sense there was one in the cottage.

But if that were so, why would Justin spy on her that way? Why not knock on her door, wake her and ask her whatever he wanted to ask her? If he had a question that was. Or just tell her what he wanted her to know?

Once again, she looked at the chapter on the screen. A chill raced up her spine. Was Justin using her life to write his own book? Or was her life simply imitating his, or rather Gabrielle's art?

Dru huffed out a breath. Maybe she was just nuts. If she asked him, would he be offended or angry? That was the last thing she wanted to do given her own precarious situation—not at all unlike the heroine in a dark and brooding gothic.

She put the computer back into sleep mode and slowly made her way into the kitchen. She stopped when she was half way to the coffee canister and let her hand drop. This was one of those times when a hot chocolate was called for instead of a hit of caffeine. Not that the cocoa was caffeine free. More like it was the need for some kind of comfort food or drink. She rummaged in the beverage cabinet and found some cocoa powder. After pulling milk from the refrigerator and a pot from where they hung on the wall, she started making the hot cocoa. While the milk warmed, she looked in another cabinet and sure enough, there were some marshmallows.

As Dru stirred the milk and chocolate powder, she thought about the parallels between her life and that of a gothic heroine. Like those in her favorite books she came from a lower class . . . well not quite a lower class. Things like that didn't exist so much today. And she wasn't an orphan like the heroines, but her mother had acted like a truly wicked stepmother. And Ottila certainly fit the bill for the mean, prune-faced housekeeper. Even when she had her hair in braids, she still looked dour. Dru figured her finances were secure. At least they were until she stepped out on her own and sought out a life that would make her happy . . . just like a gothic heroine. And then there was the brooding, mysterious hero.

Well Justin didn't exactly brood. But he was secretive. Add that to his working hours, not eating, and the eerie creaks in the house. "I guess I am living a gothic novel."

"And is that a good thing or a bad thing?"

Dru let loose with a yelp and splashed some of the still warming milk out of the pan.

In three steps, Justin was beside her with a pot holder in one hand and his other arm going around her. "Didn't mean to startle you."

She put her hand to her chest and couldn't help but wish it was his hand on her chest, sliding over to her breast before pulling her into a hug and giving her a long, wet kiss. "No problem. It's just me being way too absorbed in my thoughts."

"And those thoughts are that you are living a gothic novel?"

She chuckled. It sounded nervous to her own ears but at the same time it was pretty funny. "Sometimes it feels like that."

Justin lowered the heat before turning to stir the cocoa. A slight smile curved on his lips. "Like what times?"

Dru rubbed her arms more for something to do than because of a chill in the air. Common sense told her to step away from the dark-haired man but her body told her to step closer and see what would happen. So she stood where she was and simply enjoyed the comfortable, yet undefined space between them. "Well, you have to admit, living in a Victorian, one of the originals, can certainly lead to feeling that way. Just stepping in the door makes me feel like I'm living in another time. Add in the contents and Ms. George's books and you can get carried away into thinking you've been transported to the distant past."

Justin smiled. One of those shy, sweet smiles that tended to make her girl parts clench with delight. "And that makes it a gothic?"

"Well, not just the house."

He turned the heat the rest of the way off and lifted the pot from the stove. Without asking, Dru pulled two mugs down from their hooks and Justin poured the hot chocolate. She was mildly surprised when he poured into both of them. Not that that meant he was going to drink any of it. Still, it was the first time he'd made any effort to share a meal or drink with her.

She snagged the bag of marshmallows and lifted it toward him in question. Dru felt like one of those marshmallows melting when he smiled and nodded in answer.

"So not just the house?"

"Hmm? No. My life in general. Don't get me wrong. I wasn't miserably destitute before taking this job. It just wasn't what I wanted for myself." The last thing she wanted was for him to know she'd been snooping around his desk. Well that was the second to last thing. The last thing she wanted Justin to know was how hot she found him. How she fantasized about him climbing into bed with her and making long, slow and sultry love to her even with his quirks.

Then again, hot and fast, totally out of control sex wouldn't be too bad either.

He raised his brows in question.

"Just my imagination. Don't you ever have that happen? You get so lost in what you're doing you start to feel now and again like you are living that life? Or that you want to?"

Justin nodded. "That's why I like my job so much. I can be anyone any time I want. And that is why you're such a great assistant. You know how to get into the characters' heads when you are proofreading."

Before she did something stupid, Dru figured it was time for her to be practical about things and end this discussion. "Speaking of which, I believe it's time for me to try to get some sleep so I'm awake for moving my things tomorrow."

CHAPTER TWENTY-NINE

She shouldn't have been surprised, but when Justin pulled up in the shiny black Lamborghini Aventador Convertible with the dark tinted windows, she gave herself one strong admonition not to drop her jaw, not to stare, not to say something so geeky he'd wonder why he hired her in the first place.

Of course he'd drive a Lamborghini, or a car in that same class. Not because he worked for a famous author. Nope, not because of that. In the past few weeks Dru had seen enough stats about how much authors made . . . or didn't make. Some came from money in the first place. Others worked their tails off writing six to eight full-length novels a year and they'd done it for years before they made their mark.

And how much did an assistant make?

It was probably Gabrielle's car.

Dru squinted her eyes in thought. Gabrielle's car? Would Gabrielle drive a Lamborghini? Nah, she was more the Cadillac or better yet the Mercedes type. One of the big Mercedes. It wouldn't be a sports car or a smaller version. Nope, it would be an S Class. Definitely not a sports car that went zero to sixty in five seconds.

A vampire now, *he* would drive a big, fast, black, tinted-windowed Lamborghini, specifically a Lamborghini Aventador Convertible.

But . . . it was daylight.

Okay, it was day *time*. They were in San Francisco and the fog was in and pretty thickly at that.

And the windows were tinted. Heavily tinted.

And as of right now, she had to stop thinking these really strange thoughts about the man sitting beside her.

"Penny for your thoughts." Justin startled her.

"Huh!"

"I said a penny for your thoughts. I asked you if your seat was warm enough."

"Oh, uh, yeah, it's perfect." Her little Honda had just plain ole seats. Great heater that worked pretty quickly, but no heated seats. Nor any of the other space agey looking gizmos in the . . . what did they call it? The cockpit?

That caused Dru to chuckle to herself. Cockpit and Justin. Justin in the cockpit . . . cock . . . pit. No, Dru in the cock . . . the cock in . . .

"What?" He turned and smiled her way.

"Just thinking about how, well, uh, just what the neighbors will think when we pull up in this car."

"Too much?"

"Not at all. I've never been in one but you can drive me anytime."

"Glad to hear that because there are a lot of places I'd like to drive with you."

Dru pondered that. Was Justin saying he wanted to get a bit more personal? Or was it that she was his tenant-room-mate and that maybe they'd do more than just work together in that capacity? Slow down, she told herself. Take it one step at a time and slow, baby steps. He could mean absolutely nothing by it.

In an effort to distract herself from her rather heated thoughts about Justin, Dru looked out the window as they crossed the Golden Gate. "You know, no matter how many times I cross this bridge it never ceases to take my breath away. I don't know which is more majestic, the bay side or the ocean side."

"I have to agree. I think the time of day has something to do with it too."

"Mmm."

"No?"

"Yes. Between whether the fog or sun is shining and if it's night or day, it's never the same twice. The night I came for my interview there was a full moon over the bay side. It looked huge. I guess we were at perigee from it. It looked like I could reach out my window and touch it. And white! It was one of those stark white moons, just hanging there. And on the ocean side the fog was rolling in, thick and fast. It reminded me of a big down comforter covering the ocean. And low to the water, so low you couldn't see the ocean. Even Mile Rocks was buried in it. I'll tell you, Justin, it was breathtaking. One of those once in a lifetime scenes."

Justin nodded. "I've seen nights like that. The fog blankets so low to the ground that it mutes out any sound. I do . . . well Gabrielle has said she does some of her best writing on those nights."

"I can see why." He smiled her way and winked. "That whole gothic feel to it."

"Exactly."

Justin was quiet a few moments as they entered the Waldo Tunnel. "You should write, Drusilla."

"Write? Me?" She chuckled.

"You have a great sense of language. Your words evoke a great visceral reaction. You don't just have a solid imagination, but your words evoke spectacular visuals. Seriously, in your off time you should give it a shot."

"Maybe I will."

By the time they reached San Rafael, it was late afternoon. Dru thought about asking Justin to lower the convertible top but even with the heated seats it would probably be too chilly. When the sun set, the cold would seep in. It was dusk when they pulled in front of Dru's house.

"Well here it is."

Justin looked out at the house Dru had grown up in. "It looks cozy, comfortable."

"I suppose it was. At least when my father was alive."

"Not so much when it was just your mother and you?"

"No, not so much. Uh, yesterday there was a bit of a problem."

Justin quirked a brow in question.

"The attorney changed the locks and Haley and I . . . well we climbed in the window."

"I take it you didn't leave the back door unlocked?"

"Didn't think it would be a smart thing to do. As safe as the neighborhood can be you never know. And, if Armstrong showed up, well I didn't want him to know we were in the house. At least not until I'm ready for him to know."

"That makes sense."

Together they walked to the back of the house and her bedroom window. Justin offered to climb in, but given his size Dru convinced him she'd fit more easily. Once inside, she hurried to the back door and let Justin in.

"Not very smart of him not checking the windows." Justin observed.

"Exactly. And no, I don't think he is all that bright. I met him a few times while my mother was alive and he struck me as one of those people who got where they are because they met some sort of quota. He definitely isn't the sharpest tool in the shed."

"Well lucky for us."

To avoid calling too much attention to their presence, despite the fact it was still, in a sense, Dru's house, they only turned on a few lights, the dimmest ones toward the back of the house. The neighbors wouldn't miss the flashy sports car sitting out at the curb, but they didn't need to know she was packing up her few remaining things. Inside the house, Justin looked around at the knickknacks that hadn't been packed away yet and started to wrap them and put them in a box. Dru headed to her bedroom to pack her remaining clothing and a few stuffed animals her father had given her.

"Dru?" Justin called to her from the living room.

She headed back down the hallway of the dimly lit house, standing at the threshold of the living room. "You rang?"

Justin turned and in the shadows he looked every bit the gothic hero. With his shoulder length dark hair, broad shoulders and gloom cast by the shadowy light filtering in, he looked otherworldly. In a novel he'd reach out a hand and she would step up to him and in a moment find herself in his arms while he bent his head down to kiss her.

However, this wasn't a romance novel. It was her life.

"I did." In the faint glow cast into the room from the light above the stove, Dru could make out his smile.

Dru stepped further into the room, almost to Justin's side. "What's up?"

"You don't have to give any of this up, you know. I can call my, our, attorney in the morning and have him take care of things. He can challenge the will. I'm certain we, you, could win."

She looked around the room and considered his offer. Finally, shaking her head, Dru told him, "No. Thank you, Justin, no."

"Not that you need to make up your mind right away, but are you sure?"

She walked over to the couch and sat down without removing the white covering that the attorney had draped over it. "I'm sure. Justin, this was my mother's house. Well my mother and father's, but it was mostly hers. Everything in this room are things she wanted. My father had very little say about anything. Even down to dinner or what he took for lunch. She liked to put on this whole Donna Reed image about preparing dinner and making his lunch, only it was all for show. My mother was all about the image. If my dad said he liked roast turkey for lunch, he got liverwurst. He's the one who taught me to ask her for the opposite of what I wanted in order to get what I really was after. Everything in this room and where it's placed is her choice. Well except for the bookcases. A few days after she died, I bought those. At the time it was my bid for independence and a chance to defy her. Taking the job with Gabrielle George was even more of that defiance even though my mother would never know about it."

She rose and paced around the couch. "And you know what? The past few months, after she died? I could have rearranged the furniture in here. I could have tossed her things out and bought things I liked or wanted and I didn't. Even if I did, it still wouldn't have been mine. The books and bookcases are really the only thing of me here in the house. The things I packed up and put in storage yesterday or brought back to your house with me? They are all things I bought. Things I chose for myself and most of them the past few months, since she died. So no, I don't want any of it."

"Not even the house?"

"I'm probably being really foolish here. No."

"Drusilla, the house is probably worth, oh, at least $500,000 easy. Let me call him. Let's see if we can challenge it."

Once again she shook her head. "We'd have to prove she was mentally unstable to do that, wouldn't we?"

"Maybe, maybe not. Some of your father's money went into the mortgage, didn't it?"

"Yes. But this is California, community property . . ."

"Let me see what I can do to at least get you some of the money."

"Why?"

"Because you deserve it, Drusilla. Because you deserve it."

CHAPTER THIRTY

"I'll think about it. Right now though, I think I'm done here." She looked around surveying the room. Not seeing anything else she wanted, she shrugged and turned to Justin.

"All right then. Let's lock up and get going."

They loaded up the boxes that would fit in Justin's car and headed to the storage. As Justin pulled out of the driveway, Dru stared back at the house. "Thanks, Justin."

"No problem."

"Still, I appreciate it. You didn't have to come up here today, help me pack and give me some much-needed moral support. I'm not used to people doing that for me."

He turned to look at her. "Not even your friend Haley?"

Dru watched the other cars pulling on to the freeway as they headed back toward the city. If she hadn't been so lost in thought about being with Justin and his question, she would have found the looks on peoples' faces as they passed the Lamborghini or rather as the Lamborghini passed them, amusing. "No. Not even Haley. Even she was kind of intimidated by my mother. Well, I don't know if intimidated is the right word, but no one ever liked to rebut anything Martha said. Haley'd stand by me, support me, but always with caution about my mother's reaction. College was different to a point . . . at least until my mother showed up one day and totally embarrassed me. At the bank though? She ruled the roost."

"Haley was there for you yesterday. Those were her friends who helped you move your things yesterday, right?"

"Yes. She and her boyfriend Ricky and his friends were. I would have been lost if it weren't for her and her asking them to help. Still, your offer to help me with the business side of things . . . seriously, I don't know anyone else who would do that or even know anyone who knows how to go about doing it."

"Well that's what friends are for." He turned his attention to navigating among the other cars on the road that seemed to have suddenly lost their forward momentum. Heads swiveled to look at the sleek black car, at times almost crossing out of their lanes.

Friends? Dru wondered. Were she and Justin friends? That would be nice. He'd be an awesome friend . . . he already offered to let her live in his house, listening to her problems. Hopefully if he ever needed someone to lean on, it would be her.

"So, do you like fish?"

"Hmm? Sorry, I was kind of lost in thought." Dru looked out the window and realized they were pulling into Sausalito's main street.

"Do you like fish? Seafood?"

"Love it. There's not much I don't eat but I do love good seafood."

"Me too. I like Ondine's on the water."

She smiled. "Did you know that's my favorite place? Haley and I usually go when we have something to celebrate."

"Would you rather not?" Justin glanced over at her while he slowed the car for a stop sign.

"Oh no, not at all. Like I said, it's my favorite. And we do have something to celebrate, right? I got some of my things out of the house without having to deal with Armstrong. It's kind of a victory, you know?"

"I can see that."

When he pulled into the parking lot, the valets vied for the chance to park the car and help Dru out. Dressed in jeans she felt a bit underdressed, but no one seemed to notice. Then again, how much would she notice with a car like Justin's sitting there?

At Justin's request they were seated in a window seat overlooking the estuary leading out to the bay. Dru couldn't help but notice how many female heads turned to look at him as they were escorted to their seats. Perusing the menu rather than focus on what looked good to her, she wondered more what Justin would eat. And if she ordered something substantial, would it bother him?

"What looks good to you?" His question interrupted her thoughts.

"Hmm. Everything?"

He chuckled and bent his head to look down at his silverware.

She couldn't help herself and twisted her head just enough to see if maybe he had a reflection in the shiny silverware. As they walked to their table, she'd made note of any mirrors in the room and didn't spot any to see if he had a reflection. Nor did she see any paintings or photographs that may have shown someone's reflection. That, however, seemed to be a moot point given he *had* been out in the daylight today.

Well, sort of.

It was foggy in the city and by the time they arrived at her house it was a bit overcast.

Justin continued to look over the menu and finally looked up and smiled at her. "So?"

"I'm thinking the Cesar salad with prawns looks pretty tempting. Although the swordfish with white bean ragout, sundried tomato, broccoli, and portabella mushrooms seems to have my name on it as well. What looks good to you?"

"I was thinking of the seafood soup shots and maybe the oyster shots."

Well that answered that, sort of. He could drink soup and the oysters would just slide down his throat. Although she would have thought he might have gone for a rare . . . make that a very rare steak. But that would require chewing, not sipping and swallowing. Was that what a vampire did? Just swallowed liquid?

Dru hadn't considered that before. Well, considering vampires and paranormal books weren't really her thing there'd been no reason to consider it.

And . . . she'd never met a guy who she thought just might be a vampire and had to think about what and how he'd ingest.

And why was she even thinking like this? Dru shook her head at herself.

"Something wrong?" Justin asked her.

"Wrong? No. Why?"

"You were shaking your head."

"Oh. Was I? Just the menu. There's so much to choose from."

"I know. Every time I come here I tell myself I need to try something different but always end up with the soup and oyster shots."

"Do you come here often?"

"Often enough. Mostly for business."

"So do you like chicken and steak and that?"

"Mmm hmm. Although for steak I like Ruth's Chris or House of Prime Rib on Van Ness. You ever been to either of them?" he asked.

Dru shook her head. "Before I started to work for Ms. George, I didn't come into the City very much. There wasn't a whole lot of reason to. You know how it can be in a small town . . . you work there, live there and your social life revolves around everything there."

"Well then, I'll have to take you to both restaurants. At

House of Prime Rib we'll have to have the Yorkshire pudding, of course."

"Real Yorkshire pudding?"

"As real as you can get here in the states."

"Have you had it in England? Well I guess the first question should be have you been to England?"

Justin nodded. "And yes, I had it there."

"Well maybe someday I'll get to travel there too. There are so many places I want to see, things I want to do."

"I can tell you this, working for Gabrielle you will definitely have opportunities to travel. Being she's an internationally known author, well sometimes the job necessitates travel. You wouldn't have to do. It's just something that happens sometimes, like when we . . . she has a new release."

"Oh, I'm all over traveling. Trust me. When you've lived your life in a small town as much as your world revolves around that town, you'll take whatever comes your way in terms of seeing new things."

"Then we'll have to plan on it."

The waitress appeared a moment later and Dru went with the swordfish. Justin ordered the soup and oyster shots. While they waited for their meals, the couple gazed out the windows and watched a few boats motor by in the glow of the rising moon.

"I love the moon over the water," Dru softly told him.

"It is beautiful. What do you like most about it?"

Dru absentmindedly ran her finger along her fork while gazing out the window and drew in a long, slow breath. "I think . . . I guess . . . well the mystery of it. The sun shining on the water is pretty. It can look like there are little diamonds just dancing around on top of it. But the moon, especially when it's full like tonight . . . that pale, almost blue stream of light sliding along the top of the water. You get the same impression of little diamonds floating there, but it's something more. When I look out over it, I almost expect a merman or other mystical creature to rise up out of the water and kind of float over it. It can look so peaceful, so alluring, it calls to you, makes you want to walk out into the water and join with it. What?"

Justin shook his head. "I like the way you describe it. Many women would just say it's pretty. You make it seem, as you said mystical. You give it a magical allure. I've told you before, Drusilla, like I said, you should write. You should give it a shot."

"Maybe someday. What about you? Do you see yourself published?"

Her question seemed to have caught him off guard and he looked almost relieved when the waitress brought their salads. With the tiny shrimp dotting a bed of baby lettuce and avocado, Dru suddenly realized how hungry she was. Breakfast was many hours before and she hadn't stopped for lunch. Justin picked up his glass of wine and waited for Dru to do the same. They smiled over a silent toast before each took a swallow. The crisp white wine left a pleasant taste in her mouth that blended perfectly with the bite of avocado and shrimp she took. Dru closed her eyes in sheer pleasure at the flavors exploding on her tongue.

"Good?" Justin smiled at her.

"Fabulous. Here, have a bite." She held her fork out to him.

Justin continued to smile but shook his head. "I don't like to confuse the taste of the soup with other foods."

"Other foods are vegetables?"

He chuckled. "You outted me. Yeah, I'm one of those guys who isn't a huge fan of vegetables."

"Not into the four essential food groups, are you?"

"No, not quite."

"Well, it doesn't look like a non-veggie diet has affected your health."

"Nope. Don't think so." He spooned a mouthful of the clear soup into his mouth. "Mmm, this is the best. Want to try?"

Dru nodded and sipped a mouthful of the soup Justin held out to her. "Oh that is good. I'll have to try it myself sometime."

"We'll come back. I promise."

Dru decided it was time to learn a bit more about her employer than his taste in food and went with a safe question. "So did you grow up in the Bay Area?"

Justin ducked his head and swirled his spoon in the soup as if debating whether or not he would answer her. Finally, he raised his head and with a small smile, nodded.

When he said nothing further, in the awkward silence Dru finally said, "Yeah. Me too."

He surprised her when, after sipping a mouthful of the clear soup, he spoke, "Well I did and I didn't. My parents traveled quite a bit and many times I was left with my grandmother here in the City. I grew up . . . well, it was different growing up with my Nana. She indulged me in a lot of ways my parents wouldn't have."

Feeling brave and very curious about the kind of child Justin was, Dru pushed on, "What kind of ways?"

Justin shrugged. "Things we did. Things I was allowed to do."

Figuring he was speaking more about the limitations Martha had put on her than on his own history, Dru was ready let it go. Clearly, something about his childhood troubled him and she didn't want to ruin an otherwise nice day.

But Justin continued, "I wasn't spoiled or anything like that. More like she encouraged me to explore my own creativity." He spooned some more soup and gazed out the window, his look thoughtful. I'm . . . shy. I was even more so, withdrawn, as a child."

"Because your parents weren't around?"

"No. I just was. In many ways I still am. It's hard to talk about myself. That's why I'm not the best when it comes to dating. I don't usually want to talk about the normal things."

"What do you consider normal?"

"You know, sports, baseball, football. I'm more interested in museums, cultural things."

"Ah, I see." Dru became absorbed in her salad. He was interested in the things she was interested in. One of Dru's favorite ways to spend an afternoon was going to the various museum exhibits the county offered. On rare, very rare occasions, she'd manage to drag Haley into the city to one of the museums there.

"A lot of women I've dated only seem to want . . . well . . ."

Dru looked at him expectantly.

"Well you don't seem that way."

"I don't?"

"No."

"Um, Justin. What way?"

CHAPTER THIRTY-ONE

He laid down his spoon and returned his gaze out the window. "You see me as a person. You talk to me as a person. And even though you're living essentially in the same house as me, you treat me the same way you did before. Like a person, not an object."

"I think I see." She smiled. "Justin, are you telling me that most of the women you know treat you like a sex object?"

He laughed. "I guess that makes me seem kind of arrogant."

Dru shrugged. "I don't know. You're a good-looking man. Seriously good looking and I can see how some women would think about hunky guys as sex objects and not much else. Look at how many men think that because a woman is pretty that she's an airhead. In this day and age it stands to reason it could happen to a guy too."

"Well, thanks for that. I think too, given my job, women expect me to be all about the sex and there is so much more to romance writing than just the sex."

"Obviously they don't read too many romance novels from start to finish and seem to only read the so-called good scenes."

Justin laughed. "Is that what you call them?"

"Not me, but friends of mine, well actually a couple of the guys, the few that worked at my old work would occasionally pick up a romance novel and they had this ability to go right to the sex scene. Every time, unerringly, they'd turn right to it and then insist that's what the book was about. They didn't want to hear about the historical aspects of it or sub-plots or characterization. They'd see what they wanted and end of story, in their mind that was that."

"But the sex scenes, they can be the good part, can't they?"

He looked so earnest when he asked she couldn't help but agree.

Finished with their meal, they had coffees and Justin convinced her to split a decadent chocolate dessert with him, but Dru noticed he only ran his fork through his portion. Only once, he seemed to nibble at a bit of the rich chocolate frosting. Obviously feeling awkward talking about sex outside the realm of a book, Justin moved the conversation to looking at the boats that sat at the pier and the glimmer of lights popping up across the estuary in Tiburon and Belvedere. That suited Dru just fine as well. The last thing she wanted was him knowing that there had been a few times she'd wondered what he'd be like in bed . . . or on the couch or rug in front of the fireplace or kitchen table or . . .

"Sorry, I was kind of lost in thought," Dru answered when she became aware that Justin had asked her something.

"Did you want to head on home or are you up for a little walk along the waterfront?"

"Oh, I'd love to walk. Even though I live, lived in Marin, I didn't come down this way often. A walk sounds perfect."

They walked a bit down Bridgeway alternating between looking out at the water and peering into shop windows. At the little park on the edge of the shopping section of town, Justin slowed and suddenly Dru found her hand in his. He briefly glanced down at her before continuing up the street, holding her hand.

His grasp was firm but gentle. His hand was comfortably warm. A block or so later he asked if she was warm enough and all Dru could do was nod. If she spoke she knew she'd be talking to him like the women he'd confided looked to him as a sex object and not a person. At the edge of the shops, Justin guided her across the street and back toward the restaurant on the other side. Even though most of the stores were closed, they took the time to peer in the windows at the merchandise on display on the darkened floors. It wasn't till later she realized that she could have been looking to see if he had a reflection in the darkened shop windows.

When they were across the street from the restaurant, Justin slipped his arm around Dru's shoulders and when she didn't shift away from him, he pulled her a bit closer. It felt so right to be snuggled in his arm. Neither spoke on the way home, each content in their own thoughts.

Dru stood off to the side of the garage while Justin locked up the car inside. She was pleased when they started toward her cottage, each carrying some of the boxes she'd packed at the house. They left their bundles on the porch while they walked back to the garage and picked up the rest. When everything was unloaded, it was Justin who stuck the key in the lock. With a smile, he turned to her.

The full moon cast its bright glow over the small yard illuminating the area almost as bright at day. His face shadowed, his cheeks caressed by hollows created from the shadows of the moon's glow. He was so handsome. He really did look like the heroes in her romance novels.

Slowly, ever so slowly, he lowered his lips to hers and brushed her mouth with a light kiss. So tentative in his touch, she wondered if in fact he'd really kissed her.

Dru sighed. Just that slight, almost there touch, felt incredible. In fact it rocked her to her toes because it was so sensual.

Responding to her soft sigh, Justin pulled her closer in his arms and kissed her again. At least in her mind. For a moment she gave into her fantasy, imagining that he moved his lips along her jaw and murmured her name. She leaned into him, wanting to rub against him and soak up the warmth of his body. Instead she held herself at an acceptable distance while at the same time sliding her arms up over his shoulders to embrace him back. With the fingers of one hand, she toyed with his hair where it caressed his collar. In response, he deepened the kiss. The lingering taste of coffee made her think of how his lips looked on the cup—the sensual curve of his lips on the rim came to mind. No wonder women thought of him as a sex object. She wasn't so far from that idea herself.

It took her a moment to realize her tongue had mated with his in a primal dance. The man sure could kiss. For the first time in her life, she knew what the writers talked about when they said the heroine's toes curled in response to the hero's kiss. Toes curled and a whole lot more happened in her body from tiny electric shocks coursing down her spine to a dampening in her panties. If she wasn't careful she'd come from the man's kisses alone, at least in her imagination.

Stopping the kiss was the last thing Dru wanted but common sense said they needed to. They really needed to. She was still, after all, his co-worker if not employee.

"Despite the reason we had to go to Marin, I had a good time today, Drusilla."

"I did too. It was nice getting to know you a bit."

Justin nodded and opened the door. She hung her jacket in the closet while he pulled his off and left it on the bench that sat in the entryway. Dru went to the thermostat to turn up the heat a bit while Justin brought some of the boxes into her room and others into the living room.

"Would you like a coffee or nightcap? I don't have much but did pick up a nice little sherry the other day."

"Not tonight. I have a few things I need to take care of before the week starts. I've got conference calls with the publicist tomorrow, Gabrielle's editor on Tuesday and some other marketing things to deal with during the week."

"No problem. Need me to start early tomorrow?"

"No, regular time is fine. Let me know if you want me to have our attorney take a look at the will for your house. I really do think you deserve something from it."

"I will and Justin, thank you again for today."

"My pleasure. We'll do it again soon. Well not the part about packing up your house, but going to dinner. If you want, that is."

"I'd like that. You did promise me a meal at the House of Prime Rib." And she added privately to herself, she'd also like a real kiss at the end of the evening. She didn't want to be one of *those* girls, but if the man wanted to kiss her again, she was up front and ready to go. "Well, I'll see you in the morning . . . or early afternoon. Night, Justin."

"Goodnight, Drusilla. Sleep well." He stopped at the door and closed his eyes for a brief moment. Then, much to her surprise, he leaned over and gave her a light kiss on the cheek. His head lowered, he hurried out the door.

She closed the door after him and watched through the side window as he made his way to the main house. They were friends. That was all. Friends and that kiss . . . that little peck on the cheek, melted her like a puddle of chocolate fondue. She'd definitely go up in flames if he kissed her for real.

From the back door of the Victorian, Justin looked back at Dru's cottage and smiled to himself. The woman made him happy. Plain and simple she made him happy. And content. For the first time he could remember, he felt content with a woman. Being in her company was restful and felt so natural. There were times it felt like he'd known her forever instead of a few months.

With a smile, he turned, headed into the office and booted up his computer. As he watched the little circle spin while it loaded up, his mind wandered to Dru . . . Drusilla. She made him smile. She was smart and cute and creative and had a can-do attitude. She understood confidentiality and the creative process. He'd seen she was good with money, organized and she fired his imagination. It was harder than he thought to stop at a mere peck of a kiss on her cheek when what he really wanted to do was follow her into the bedroom and make love to her till the sun rose.

The question was, could he trust her with his secret? What would she do if she knew? How would she handle it? If she told anyone, what would they do? If the secret were out, what would happen to him? His life? Gabrielle's?

Absentmindedly, he picked up one of the silver Cross pens that lay on his desk and twisted it end over end in his hand. Was it a mistake to ask her to live with him?

Live with him? He looked over at her desk. Living together implied sharing more than living space, didn't it? For all his research, his world traveling, the people he came in contact with, he'd never had a steady girlfriend.

No, that wasn't true. He'd dated different women for periods of time. Sex with them had run the gamut from a quick and tidy release to a trip to the stars. But the relationships took place out of his home. He went to their houses, their apartments. He courted them where they worked, took them where they wanted to go, did what they wanted to do and kept his own home off limits. Justin never trusted one of them to come into his home. To see the secrets here. Until Drusilla.

Hiring her as his assistant, as Gabrielle's assistant, had been a huge leap. Savvy, man of the world, Justin Hunt was debonair, worldly and knew how to show a lady a good time be it a trip to the theatre — after a ride in a private jet to New York and back again to California, or the sexual time of her life in bed . . . her bed. Or a hotel bed or the back of his car or any number of places that weren't his home.

He rose and walked over to the bay window fronting the

street. A few cars went by, their lights bouncing off the wrought iron fence, the occupants not even turning to look back at the stately Victorians they passed. It seemed they took the quaint neighborhood for granted. Justin didn't. He loved this house, the home he grew up in, where he explored his inner talents, where he could be himself . . . his true self.

Dru . . . could she accept who he really was? What he really was?

For the first time he thought about why he'd hired her in the first place. For years he knew he . . . they . . . needed an assistant. Someone to handle the mundane side of Gabrielle George's writing career. More than once he placed ads to hire someone, only to pull them down again in minutes, long before the first call could be made.

And then three months ago, things just got out of hand. There was too much to do with too many books due, edits to turn in, publicity to be done and letters to answer. That was one thing Gabrielle always insisted on—personal responses to every letter or email. That would never change. It was part of her signature image and part of what made her loved by fans the world over.

So he bit the bullet so to speak and placed an ad. The moment he saw Drusilla's resume, he knew she was the one. Not just from what was written on the page, but a feeling in his gut. When he met her, when she walked into the house for her interview, despite the dowdy outfit she wore—that dull gray suit with the skirt that fell below her knees, the blouse buttoned up to her chin, plain beige hose and flat, practical shoes, he knew there was spirit and fire in her.

Oh she worked hard to keep it under wraps. Unconsciously, as he thought about that inner fire she worked so hard to keep hidden, he walked over to the fireplace and contemplated an early morning fire. Shaking his head he looked at the ashes that hadn't been cleaned from the night before.

He needed to get to bed soon. It had been a long day, one that tired him by being out in public for so long.

Not that he was shy. Not by any means. It was the balancing act of trying to be a neutral observer and friend to Drusilla while at the same time wondering what would happen if he suggested they be more than friends and co-workers.

His head swam with ideas for the scene where Gavin and Emma would share their first kiss. Justin smiled to himself. Emma and Gavin's first kiss would be a lot like the one he'd wanted to share with Dru only instead of a staid goodnight, they'd end up in bed and they would make love for hours and hours until exhausted and sated, he would confide *his* secret to her. She would, of course, accept him for what he was. That was in part why readers devoured romance novels, especially Gabrielle's, like it was their last meal. There was a happy ending where the hero and heroine took each other at face value and their love was true and abiding, enduring no matter what happened.

Of course that was after their dark moment and after Gavin and Emma shared their kiss, he'd have to decide what their dark moment would be.

Of course if he told Dru and she turned on him, he's have that black time, the moment that drove his hero to despair where he would no longer want to live.

Maybe it was time to let someone into his life. Maybe Drusilla would understand his secret and willingly keep it.

And maybe once she knew, there would be no dark moment for them.

Chapter Thirty-two

The next evening, Dru crossed the yard and entered the house to find Justin already at work. "Hey, how goes it?"

He blinked as he looked up, and she felt a jolt of sheer desire taking in his tousled dark hair and how his eyes widened at seeing her. Any other woman would have kept him from leaving last night. Correction, any other woman would probably have gotten him into bed weeks ago. But she wasn't any other woman. She was Drusilla Montgomery and was just figuring out who that person really was. "It goes well. How are you?"

"Great! I slept like the dead last night and tonight I feel more than energized. Can't wait to dig in." Probably not the best way to phrase how she slept given who or what her boss might be.

"Slept like the dead?" He lifted a brow. "And how do the dead sleep?"

She put that thought away and sauntered half way into the room and considered his question. "Deep with only the best dreams."

"And did you dream last night?" He splayed his fingers on the desk.

"A little, but I don't remember much. Just that they were good dreams."

"Then I'm glad to hear it."

"Me too. I'm going to make some coffee. Can I get you one?"

"No . . . Dru . . . do you have a minute?"

Oh no, here it comes. She didn't put out, didn't drag him up to bed with her . . . either that or he was turned off by her kisses or worse felt like she'd forced him into it and now she was going to lose her job and her home. She gingerly walked further into the room and sat down at one of the desk chairs facing him. "Sure. What's up?"

Justin studied his fingers for several beats and finally glanced up at her. His cheeks reddened in either embarrassment or anger. "Drusilla. About. About last night."

"Yes?" Oh damn, it was about the kiss. That simple peck on the cheek. She'd blown it. She'd totally blown it.

"I wanted to apologize."

"Apologize?"

"Yes." He drew in a breath and slowly released it as if he needed the space to gather his thoughts. "It was . . . wrong of me. I shouldn't have kissed you."

"Why?" She blurted the question out, cutting off whatever else he may have had to say.

"I . . . it could be construed as me having taken unfair advantage of you."

"But you didn't."

"Drusilla, I want you to know," he rose and paced to the window and back, "I would never take advantage of you. I would never intentionally put you in a position that was untenable or uncomfortable. Last night, well I wasn't doing a very good job of controlling myself."

"You weren't?" She hated how her voice suddenly squeaked out the word.

"It won't happen again."

"Okay." Did that mean she still had her job? And her home? Or was he warming up to tell her to leave?

"Do you understand why?"

She squirmed in her chair. "No, not really. I mean, it wasn't a . . . well it didn't feel uncomfortable. It was a nice ending to a nice day. Well except for the part about losing my house. I enjoyed our time together yesterday. It was nice getting to know you outside work."

"Lot of nices in there." He chuckled.

Dru laughed as well. "And it wasn't a major kiss, you know? It was like from one friend to another."

Justin nodded. "I don't want you to feel uncomfortable."

"I don't. So are we good? You don't want me to move out because you feel uncomfortable about things?"

"Move out? No. I have to admit it's nice having someone else here. Vincent enjoys your company too. If you're good, I'm good."

"I am. Seriously, Justin. This is the best job I've ever had and I love the cottage. It's exactly the kind of place I'd design if someone asked."

"Good. I'm glad. I don't want you to feel that your home, a second home, is being threatened or that your job depends on sexual favors. I want you to feel that this is your home and your job is secure as long as you want it."

"I do. I do feel that this is my home. I know I've only been here a few weeks but it feels like I've lived here forever and that I've worked for Miss George for years. Justin, this is the best living and working situation I've ever had or could imagine."

"I'm glad because you're the best assistant I . . . or Gabrielle . . . could ever want."

"Well then. Life is good all around, huh?"

CHAPTER THIRTY-THREE

Way too early the next day the ringing of Dru's phone jarred her awake. "Lo." She mumbled.

"Ms. Montgomery, this is Mr. Armstrong."

She struggled to a sitting position in the bed. Somehow it felt way too creepy to talk to the attorney while lying in bed. In fact it felt unsettling to be talking to him in the bedroom at all. She cleared her throat in an attempt to clear out the sleep from her voice. "What can I do for you Mr. Armstrong?"

"Someone was in your mother's house over the weekend."

He was direct and to the point, she'd give him that. "My mother's . . . Mr. Armstrong, she's dead. I believe it's my house."

"As I explained Ms. Montgomery, in a week from now it will not be your home unless you return to your position at the bank. That said, I wanted you to know things were removed from the premises. In particular, things from what was your room."

She blew out a breath. Like it was his business. "You can put aside your concerns. That was me. I took some of my things."

"You had no right."

She had no right? Seriously? She had no right? "As I understand it, last week and during the coming week, it is still my house. Martha may have told you to sell it out from under me, but I paid for the things I took and I have the right to get the remainder of my things."

"Let me be very clear here, Ms. Montgomery. If you should

set foot in the house again without my permission and some-one of my choosing there to oversee things, I will call the po-lice and have you arrested for trespassing. Do I make myself clear?"

"Mr. Armstrong. Go to hell." Shaking with anger she hung up on him. At least she'd gotten the things that meant the most to her out of the house. Justin had promised to go back with her and arrange to move her new bookcases and a few other heavier objects out. Bringing both hands to her head to push her hair back, she blew out a long, slow breath. What to do now? She looked at the clock and laid back down, staring at the ceiling. Vincent scooted closer to her and started to purr. At least he wasn't disrupted by the morning phone call.

And then it occurred to her . . . the way he'd acted . . . threatening her with the police? Telling her what she could and couldn't do? Was he a contingency recipient of her mother's . . . correct that . . . her house?

"What am I going to do, Vincent? It's not like I'm leaving behind anything of value. It's the principal of the thing, you know?"

The cat looked up at her, blinked and put his head back down to go back to sleep.

"Well, I guess I'll call Haley later. I'm too tired to get into it now. Vincent, I am tired of all this. Why couldn't she just let me live my life?"

The cat had no answer for her. No one was more surprised than Dru when the alarm woke her several hours later. She'd been sure she wouldn't be able to fall back asleep. Fortu-nately, it was a deep and dreamless sleep — the kind she needed after the past few days.

She rose, showered, gave Vincent some crunchy cat food and started a coffee for herself. While the pot brewed, she gazed out the cottage window and studied the yard and main house beyond. Come spring there would be a profusion of roses, tulips and zinnias if she knew her plants correctly. A gazebo with evidence of some sort of blooming vines sat caddy corner to the cottage. It would be restful to sit out in the yard reading come the warmer weather. Now that would be something . . . warmer weather to sit in the yard in San Francisco.

Well, it wasn't unheard of.

The last of the coffee burbled into the pot and she turned to the counter and poured her first cup of the day. Debating whether or not to eat or wait till later, Dru reached for the phone and dialed Haley.

"Hey, girlfriend! How you feeling after moving all that stuff Saturday?"

"Good. Justin went back up with me yesterday, and I moved some more things."

"Vampire Justin?"

"Yeah."

"So how'd he manage that? Being out in the daylight and all."

"It was kind of foggy when we left and his car . . . Haley he drives a Lamborghini . . . has major tinted windows. Maybe he can go out in daylight if it's not bright and sunny."

"Or he's not a vampire." Haley chuckled.

"There is that."

"So did you ask him to go with you or . . ."

"He offered. Saturday night when I got in, he offered and I wasn't about to say no. He was very sweet—even offered to be the one to climb in the window, but I did. He also offered to see about breaking the will so I didn't lose the house."

"Are you going to?"

Dru took a swallow of coffee and thought a moment. "I don't know. Armstrong called this morning."

"That asshole. What did he want?"

"To tell me someone broke in and then when I told him it

was me, he got all pissy and told me if I went back in again he'd have me arrested for trespassing."

"Can he do that?"

"I don't know. I don't know if he could even lock me out of my house."

"So what are you going to do?"

Dru sighed. "I don't know. I just don't know. You have any ideas?"

"I wish I did. I wish we'd known before your mother died what she was up to. Maybe we could . . . you could . . . have talked to her. Made her see that you were entitled to live your own life."

"You know she wouldn't have listened. She would have given us that stunned look and told us . . . me . . . that I had no idea what I was talking about."

"Are you going to tell Justin?"

"I don't know. He says my job is secure. I mean, I told him about my mother's will and he saw the house. When we got back he kissed me and . . ."

"Whoa! Slow down, back up. He *kissed* you? The hottie boss *kissed* you? And you didn't lead with that? What did you do? Was it all hot passion and grabbing each other? Did he rip your clothes off you?"

Dru laughed and it felt good. "No. It wasn't that kind of kiss. He just pecked me on the cheek. Like a friend. But it was nice."

"Oh." Haley was clearly deflated by that revelation. "When you said kissed . . ."

"Sorry. No, it was a friendly kind of kiss. He assured me that these changes going on in my life don't impact my job. That's secure at least, and he said I don't have to worry about losing my home either."

"Well that's a relief. Isn't it?"

"Yeah, it is. So, I need to get ready to get to work. Since it doesn't look like I can remove anything else from the house for now, want to come over to the city this weekend and see my cottage? Maybe meet Justin?"

"Love to. We'll find some fabulous place to eat maybe go to a club and have a great time."

"Sounds like a plan. I'll talk to you in a day or so and let you know if I figure anything out."

Chapter Thirty-four

Midway through the work night, Dru wandered over to Justin's desk. There were only a few days left before the time ran out for her to either go back to the bank or lose her house and she'd moved into the cottage. Justin's offer about the will kept running through her mind. "Got a minute?"

He quickly minimized the document he was working on and smiled. "For you, anytime. What's up?"

"I've been thinking about what you said about fighting my mother's will."

He leaned forward, "And?"

"Do you know how much it would cost?"

"Hmmm, no idea. But I can ask our attorney to give me a ballpark figure if you like."

Dru nodded and absentmindedly rolled one of the pens on Justin's desk in very much like the manner he toyed with pens and pencils. "I would. Do you have any idea what it would entail?"

"No. I've never done anything like that and any research we have from Gabrielle's books would be Regency period or historical. Then you're dealing with familial rights and as you know, a good number of her stories take place in England, so a whole other set of laws. But we'll find out. What changed your mind?"

"Armstrong."

"The so-called attorney?"

"That would be him. He called me Monday morning first to tell me that someone broke into the house and when I said

I'd been there over the weekend picking up some of my things, he said if I did it again he's have me arrested for breaking and entering."

"We'll ask about that too. I'm not so sure about quite a few of the things he's said, but I'm not an attorney. I'll give him a call tomorrow and see what we can find out."

"Justin, thank you. I appreciate it. This is all new to me. Not just the legal issues but a lot of what's gone on since my mother died. I led a pretty sheltered life—mostly her doing. She controlled by omission rather than commission. She'd tell me, or anyone, the barest minimum and always, always kept something back. She'd always hold on to a crucial piece of information that might help you to make a better decision. I didn't realize it until I was an adult and then, well it was just easier to let her do what she wanted. The battles, the drama, if she didn't get her way were unbelievable."

"I mentioned this before and you may not want to hear it, but she sounds very abusive."

Dru nodded. "I think in some ways she was. I know some of the reasons she was that way, but it's still no excuse."

He looked distracted when he reached for her hand and gently held it. "Did you ever try to stand up to her?"

"Once or twice. Maybe more. If I made a decision to do something . . . like when I applied to college . . . she said, 'If you really think that's the right thing, of course.' But her tone implied that it was probably the stupidest thing I could ever come up with. Martha, my mother, did that with every decision I ever made."

"And did you go to college?"

"Yes. For a semester. Then she showed up and made a huge scene when she discovered I was studying lighting design. What was worse though was she called the student loan people and told them I'd falsified my application. Justin, she never saw the application. I kept all the paperwork at Haley's and I know Haley never told her or gave any of it to her. So she wouldn't know if anything in it was true or not. It was just her need to control and since she worked at the bank and called from there, they believed her and recalled my loan. She . . . graciously . . . interceded for me, so she said, and got them to drop any charges or convinced them not to file any."

"She sounds pretty awful."

"Like I've said before, she was. Justin, this is going to sound really awful, but in some ways her death was a blessing for me. I finally got to start living my own life. If I had applied for this job and she was alive, trust me, she would have found a way to sabotage it. At a minimum she would have called you and told you I was incompetent or couldn't be trusted. At the worst she would have followed me here and demanded to talk to you and tell you all kinds of half-truths about me. I probably shouldn't tell you that because you might think I have something to hide."

Justin squeezed her hand. "I know you don't have anything to hide. You probably don't want to hear this, but you're kind of an open book. Your emotions are clearly on your face and you're probably the most honest person I've ever met."

Dru considered his words. If only he knew she thought he was a vampire or that he'd done something suspect to Gabrielle George. Of course if she really thought he had, she'd be a total nutcase to stay here working. Unless he was a psychopath on top of being a vampire, Justin wasn't capable of harming someone, especially his employer. "Thanks, Justin. That means a lot. I really appreciate everything you've done for me."

"Not a problem. You do good work and I hope to have you doing good work for us for a long time to come."

"Well, now that we've solved my problems, I've been reading and rereading Sophie and Xavier's story and . . . well . . . do you mind if I make a small criticism?"

"No, not at all. That's one of the great things about a beta reader who's on top of things. We want to find those issues before it goes to print. What's up?"

Dru walked back over to her desk and picked up the pages she'd been proofreading. "Unless Gabrielle deals with this later on in the story, there's a gap here. I was thinking about it this morning when I called Haley and invited her to come by this weekend. Um, that's all right isn't it? She can come by on Saturday and see the cottage?"

"Of course. It's your home, Drusilla. Please feel free to have your friends come by anytime, and I'm looking forward to meeting Haley."

"Great, thanks. Anyway, Sophie's friend, Nicole, hovers in the background. They go for a few carriage rides, but don't talk about much. In that time period, would Sophie ask Nicole to go with her to the club to see what Xavier is up to? Unless, like I said, it happens later."

Justin snapped his fingers. "No! You're right! I knew something was off. That's it. They need to start investigating, together, earlier in the story. Nicole's story is the second book in the series and readers need to see something of her quirks now to entice them to find out more about her. Good catch."

"So you think Gabrielle will like that?"

"Gabrielle? She'll love it. She will totally love it."

CHAPTER THIRTY-FIVE

"I love it!" Haley exclaimed when she first laid eyes on the quaint cottage Dru had moved in to. "Oh Dru, when you said it was the cutest little cottage, I knew it would be pretty but I didn't expect this. It's perfect. And you even have a cat."

"Well, Vincent is Justin's cat, but he seems to like to stay here with me."

"They say cats choose their owners. Looks like he chose you, huh?"

Vincent eyed Haley and slowly blinked before turning to go back to his nap.

"So it seems. He scared the patooti out of me the night I came to interview but since then he's become great company. Haley, everything about my job has been the best. Soooo want a coffee while we plan where to eat tonight?"

"Sounds good."

They walked into the cottage's kitchen and Haley immediately noticed the espresso maker. "Wow, you went all out stocking this place."

"The coffeemaker? That was a house warming gift from Justin."

Haley laughed. "Your mom's Mr. Coffee wasn't doing it for you anymore?"

"Actually it worked fine. The problem was the way my mother made coffee, not the machine. Once I bought some good beans and made it nice and strong, it worked great. I left it at the house though because Justin has a machine like this at the main house and I was making my lattes there. When he offered me the cottage, he went out and bought me this one to, as he put it, welcome me."

"He knows you pretty well if he got you a coffee maker — no one in their right mind would ever get between you and your caffeine."

"That's for sure."

The women turned at a knock on the cottage's door.

"It's Justin," Dru quietly told Haley. "Justin, hi, come on in and meet my best friend, Haley. Haley, this is Justin, my boss."

"Nice to meet you, Haley. And please, I'm Dru's co-worker, not her boss."

"I've heard a lot of about you, Justin, so it's nice to finally put a face with the name."

"At least some good I hope."

"All good. And she deserves it."

Justin smiled and stroked his jaw. "Yes, she does. Well I just wanted to say hello. Drusilla told me you were coming by and when I saw your car, I thought I'd stop and do just that."

"We were just going to have some coffee. Do you have time to stay for some?"

Justin glanced at the pot. "Not right now, but I wouldn't mind some company if that's okay."

"Sure." Dru glanced at Haley to see if she caught the fact that Justin declined the coffee. Not so much the coffee, but drinking it.

Haley gave her a small smile. "If you tell me where you stashed your cups I'll get them while you get going on those lattes."

A short time later the threesome sat at the table, Dru and Haley sipping their drinks, Justin leaning back in the chair, a contented look on his face.

"I had a hard time imagining Dru moving to the city and actually living here. We grew up together, a few doors apart and we've never gone more than a few days without seeing each other. I can see why she was so happy to move here. It's not only really pretty but peaceful too."

"You sound more like an older sister than a friend." Justin observed.

Haley shrugged. "Maybe. We take turns though being the big sister, don't we?"

"We do. I think it's partly why we've been such good friends for so long. We don't have any secrets, at least not ones that stay quiet for long."

"Oh?" Justin quirked a brow.

Dru answered, "Birthday surprise parties, Christmas gifts, things like that. Nothing major."

"I see. Well then, Haley, I'm glad you approve of Drusilla's new home."

"It's perfect." Haley nodded.

"I guess it's okay to tell you . . . Justin's attorney went over my mother's will yesterday and he says there are anomalies in it. Things that can't be enforced. He said at first glance Armstrong engaged in some hanky panky with the provisions. It looks like he was trying to do my mother's bidding without paying attention to what the law actually says."

"So you don't lose the house?"

Justin answered for Dru, "Apparently not. It will take a little time, but my attorney is fairly certain the will can be broken. Then it's Drusilla's choice what to do about the house. For now my attorney has put a restraining order on any movement selling the house. Meeting you, Haley, was one reason I came by and the other was to let Drusilla know that my attorney has had the locks changed on the house. He'll messenger over the new keys Monday."

"Super. Oh, Justin, thank you." She fought the urge to jump up and hug him.

He shrugged. "It's what friends do for each other. So what

do you have planned the rest of the day?"

Dru glanced out the window. The moon was cresting the tops of the trees in the yard. "Haley and I were going to find some really fun place to go for dinner."

"Ah. I see. Would you like a few suggestions?"

"Yeah, I'm still getting used to the city so that would be great."

"What do you like? Anything you're in the mood for?"

"Anything!" Haley said.

"There's a few good places near here depending on what you're in the mood for, depending on if you want to walk or drive."

"Either's good." Dru looked at Haley and the two shared an unspoken conversation. "Justin, if you aren't busy, why not come with us?"

He looked at his hands a moment before looking between the two. "If I wouldn't be intruding, I'd love to."

"Not at all," Haley answered. "Gives me a chance to get to know Dru's co-worker and more about writers. Until Dru started working for Gabrielle George, I know I didn't know the first thing about writing. Course if you don't want to talk business, that's cool too."

"Let's see where the conversation takes us. When did you want to leave?"

"Soon, I'm hungry," Haley told then.

"Then let me get my coat while you decide if you want to walk or drive."

Dru saw the glimmer in Haley's eyes. "I told Haley about the Lamborghini, but since it has only seats two, how about we walk?"

"Sounds good to me. I'll be back in a few."

CHAPTER THIRTY-SIX

"Night, Haley. Drive safe," Dru told her friend as Haley climbed in her car.

"I'll call you when I get in. It was great to finally meet you, Justin."

"You too, Haley. Hope we see you again soon."

Justin and Dru stood side by side and watched until Haley's car was out of sight. Dru smiled to herself wondering if Justin knew he'd realized he referred to them as "we." Once again at dinner, he had clear soup and then picked at the chicken dish he'd ordered. Unless someone was watching, they wouldn't have known he hadn't eaten any of it. Well, that was his business . . . unless he bit her. She chuckled low thinking about whether or not he had any vampire friends who might be interested in Haley.

"What?" Justin looked down at her, his face in shadows.

"Nothing. Just thinking about some of Haley and mine's history. Things we've done."

"Ah."

Justin walked her back to the cottage and stood at the door. After a moment's debate, Dru invited him in.

"I'd like that," He told her.

"I'm not taking you away from anything?"

"No. It was going to be just another Saturday night home alone."

That was one of the things about Justin that didn't add up for her. Why was a guy who looked like him, acted like him, alone on a Saturday night? Did he have a broken heart? Was he one of those vampires who had lost the great love of his life and now, rather than get close to someone else who would die, did he choose isolation?

"Well come on in. I'll put on some coffee . . ."

"None for me, thanks, I'm full from dinner."

"Sure. You don't mind if I have one?"

"It's your home. Do whatever makes you comfortable."

Unable to keep her curiosity at bay, while measuring out her beans, Dru asked Justin, "So do you often get together with your friends? Or are you so buried in work there just isn't time?"

Justin continued to study his hands.

Well that answered that, Dru thought. He was probably torn away from the great love of his life, his soul mate and rather than live for eternity without her by his side chose isolation.

"To be honest," he began, "I kind of let my job take over. I guess in some ways I've bought into Gabrielle's reclusive persona and kind of hide away in the house. The hours aren't really conducive for keeping in touch with friends."

"I guess not. I know Haley's really the only one I talk to these days. Not that I'm complaining. With the changes and things I've needed to deal with since my mother's death, before taking this job, there wasn't time for much else. And lately, I've been focused on learning as much as I can to do my job right so I can see where it can take you over. I guess it's hard on the love life too."

Justin looked directly into her eyes. "That too. There hasn't been much time to go out and meet someone since . . . well the past couple of years. I have to admit I haven't had much inclination."

"Would it be intrusive to ask why?"

"No, not at all. The last woman I dated was a mistake for me. She was all about image. My car? The Lamborghini? I bought it because she wanted it."

"But you kept it after?"

"Yeah. I have to admit it grew on me. You have to admit, it's a nice car." He chuckled.

"It is at that." And a classic vampire car . . . was the old girlfriend a vamp?

"She . . . the woman . . . tried to move in with me almost as soon as we started dating. There were times I felt like she'd done some research on me, but then, since I'm only an assistant, there isn't much to find. I suppose you could say she saw money where there wasn't any. Not really. I mean, I do all right. There are some valuable antiques in the main house. I'm sure you noticed them."

Dru nodded and took a swallow of her coffee. Maybe not a vampire, but definitely graspy.

"She started suggesting I sell them and buy a big house in Marin, in Tiburon or over on Belvedere. She even went so far as to plan a trip to Europe, flying first class of course and staying in five star hotels, without mentioning it to me until it was time to pay for the tickets."

"Wow. I can't imagine even a husband or wife doing something like that unless it was for a special anniversary or something. That is beyond nervy."

"Yes, it was. I broke it off with her the day she showed up with the invoice for the trip. I have to admit she completely caught me off guard. I thought things like that happened . . ." He smiled, "in books."

"Well I can see why you'd choose to hang out here at home. I can't understand some people. They really shock me at times."

"That's one of the things I like about you, Drusilla. You take people at face value and really try to be fair and impartial. And, you're easy to talk to. Do you know I've never told anyone, not even my grand . . . Gabrielle, about what happened with Michaela. That was her name, Michaela. She wondered, of course. Gabrielle did, but never asked. She knows I do value my privacy."

"And I invaded it by asking. I'm sorry."

"No, not at all, Drusilla. I'm glad you asked. I like to think we're becoming friends, maybe more than friends. It's been a long time since I've felt this comfortable with someone. I have since the night you came to interview."

"I'm glad, Justin. We haven't done a whole lot together, but I enjoy doing things with you too."

Justin looked at her for a long moment and then blinked as if recalling himself. "Well, it's late and I have a few things I need to take care of."

They rose and Dru went with him to the door. He opened it and once again his gaze fixed on her eyes. For a moment Dru wondered if this was how a vampire hypnotized his victims and then it didn't matter. Vampire or not she was really starting to want this man. Seriously want to be with him as more than a friend or employer. If he wanted to bite her, so be it.

His gaze traveled to her lips, her neck and rested lightly on her chest before his lips drew into a small smile and he looked again into her eyes. He lowered his head and gently bussed her cheek. He barely lifted his head before he sighed and then brushed a light kiss on her lips. It was over so fast Dru barely knew it happened. So fast she couldn't begin to return the tender touch. So fast she wondered if she'd imagined it.

"Goodnight, Drusilla. Maybe I'll see you tomorrow."

Chapter Thirty-seven

Through the small clear glass window of the cottage's door, Dru watched Justin make his way across the darkened yard. Unerringly, despite the dark, moonless night, he made it to the main house. He didn't look back or deviate his path in any way. Just one step in front of the other, he walked down the garden path. When he reached the steps to the back-door of the main house, he stopped almost as if hesitating to make his way into the house. Almost as if he knew she watched and waited.

But waited for what?

Dru realized her fingers rested on her lips, as if holding his kiss, making it more than a memory.

He called them friends.

Friends kissed. But not on the lips. Right?

Was he feeling for her what she felt for him?

"And what do I feel for you Justin Hunt?"

That was indeed the question.

She was attracted to him. No mistaking that. She tried to keep that attraction hidden. He was her boss.

Okay, so Gabrielle George was her boss, but Justin was the one she dealt with. He gave Dru her paycheck each week, gave her the assignments he wanted done. It was as if Gabrielle didn't exist. So he was in charge and given how proper he was about everything, like a character out of one of Gabrielle's books, he wouldn't push her into a relationship. He wasn't the type.

Dru turned away from the door and made her way into the

kitchen. She rinsed out her coffee cup and set the pot ready to brew the next morning. With a last look at the doorway, she turned out the light and walked the short hall to the bedroom. Vincent was already curled up on the bed. Clearly, he wasn't concerned or puzzled by what the humans in his life were about.

She peeled off her clothes and walked into the bathroom to wash her face before bed. While brushing her teeth, she glanced one way and then the other in the mirror. *When am I going to get a grip and stop looking for bite marks?*

In bed she snuggled under the covers and relived both kisses. Neither was sexual. Both were friendly, gentle. Only in her imagination did Justin and she share passion.

A short while later, unable to sleep Dru rose and padded back out to the living room. She stopped in the middle of the room thinking to pick up the latest manuscript and work on it. Instead she walked to the window and peered out at the yard.

A glow in a lone second window illuminated a strip of the yard. She wasn't entirely sure but it appeared a shadow hovered in that window. Was Justin up there, looking out, thinking of her? The light flickered. Clearly, he'd lit a candle. That was so very Justin. Why use an electric light when a thick candle would do as well.

Did it recreate the time he came from?

Or was he just a romantic that liked to fashion his life to be as much like a long ago time as possible?

For the longest while she stood and gazed out the window until she knew she could sleep.

Justin shook his head at himself as he stood at the window looking out across the yard. With a sigh, he turned and paced to a large heavily cushioned chair near the bedroom fireplace. There was a time, not all that long ago, Vincent would have lain on the bed admonishing him to blow out the candles and come to bed. Oddly for a cat, Vincent preferred sleeping in the dark of night.

He sat a moment before reaching for the tumbler sitting on the table beside him. The dark red liquid picked up tiny shards of the candle's light. Justin took a swallow and closed his eyes. What was he going to do about Drusilla? Could she handle his secret? Would she be willing to keep it?

Was she even interested in more than a co-worker relationship? More than just being a friend?

He watched when her friend Haley pulled up today. He couldn't help but smile as the two friends hugged in greeting as if they hadn't seen each other in years instead of a week. In a way he envied their close friendship. How long since he'd had a friend, a buddy, to share stories with?

Since he began working for Gabrielle.

Not that he minded. With a gym in the basement and more than competent weekly housekeepers, life was pretty good.

Michaela almost changed all that. Model gorgeous . . . and man did she know it. The woman was all about looks and image. She was all about acquisition . . . a house, cars . . . him. That was when he'd lost touch with his friends. Not when he went to work for Gabrielle, but when he met Michaela. And he fell hook, line and sinker. He would have done and did do anything for her and bit-by-bit she came between he and his friends. Not that he had that many. But the few he had were good buddies. In winter they went skiing, spring fishing, summer hiking and fall football and baseball games. They picked up girls, screwed around and partied most of every weekend.

When he met Michaela she said she liked skiing, fished as a kid and hiking was great fun. She even said she watched the different ball games on TV because none of her friends ever wanted to go to a game.

Turned out they didn't like to go because the friends were pretty much non-existent. The few he met were just like her, dollar signs in their eyes. Acquisition in their hearts.

"So what am I doing with Drusilla?" Justin took another swallow from the crystal glass. "What am I doing with her and what do I want to do?"

He put the glass down, stood and walked to the window facing the yard. "What I want to do is climb into your bed and make love to you until the sun rises and sets seven times seven and then some."

He blew out a breath. Like that would happen. It was bad enough he'd kissed her twice. And not very satisfying kisses at that. A couple of simple pecks on her cheek and lips tonight didn't amount to more than a friendly little kiss. Not when he wanted something much, much more.

Justin walked back to the bed and sat on the edge. He picked up the pages he'd been working on earlier in the day and flipped through them. "If I were Gavin I'd have already wedded and bedded her now, wouldn't I? So do I risk losing a great employee for the chance at love, or do I put my feelings aside, bury them and keep things business only?"

CHAPTER THIRTY-EIGHT

"So, what do you think?" Dru lay against the pillows in bed late the next morning while talking to Haley.

"He's cute."

"Cute? That's all?"

"You meant Vincent, right?"

Dru giggled. "No and you know it."

"It was all I could do to keep my mouth shut and not drool when I saw him. Justin is hotter than hot. He's gorgeous and girlfriend, he *likes* you. He seriously likes you."

"We're co-workers, of course he likes me."

"Nu-uh, *likes* you. He could barely keep his eyes off you and he hung on your every word."

"And I was saying the most scintillating things, wasn't I?"

"I'm not sure the conversation called for scintillating. Seriously, you guys were totally on the same page with just about everything. I noticed, even if you didn't, that a few times you finished each other's sentences."

"Hmm, I didn't. He kissed me again."

"*What*? You wait to tell me that? I thought we were best friends . . . best friends don't wait for ten minutes into a conversation to say the hottest guy on the planet kissed them . . . when?"

"After you left. We had some coffee . . . well actually I had a coffee and he sat with me and we visited for a bit. I asked him about his friends, you know, thinking maybe he had one who I'd approve of for you."

"I noticed he had soup last night, but didn't really eat."

"You saw that?"

"If you hadn't told me he has these eating quirks, I wouldn't have noticed, but yeah, he was pushing his food around. Maybe his stomach was upset."

"Maybe."

"But the kiss. Give!"

"Well it wasn't a kiss, kiss. Not a hold me in his arms and make me senseless with desire kind of kiss. It was just a peck, but it *was* on the lips."

"That's progress, right? The other night it was a little peck on the cheek. Last night on the lips. Next thing, you'll be doing the tonsil tango."

"I don't think so."

"Why not?"

Dru squiggled around in the bed adjusting her position. "Because we work together. He's not going to mess that up and neither am I."

"Well if I had a choice between Justin Hunt as a boyfriend or my boss, I'd definitely take boyfriend."

"That doesn't pay the bills."

"Speaking of paying the bills, who is going to pay his attorney?"

"I'm not sure. I need to follow up with him about that. I plan to pay for the research, I just hope the attorney takes a payment plan."

"I'll cross my fingers for you."

"So, Hales . . . after meeting Justin, what do you think about him and Gabrielle?"

"What do you mean?"

"Do you think he could hurt her or is she really traveling around Europe?"

"He seemed really nice."

"So did Ted Bundy."

"Eeeuuu. Unless you've seen something creepy in the

house I'd believe him she's traveling around Europe. Seriously, Dru, don't buy trouble."

"I won't. To be honest I don't think there's any problem with her. Like he said, she's reclusive and if she's traveling and happy with my work, it doesn't matter if I hear from her."

"Right. So what are you doing today?"

Dru stretched and looked up at the ceiling. "I figured I'd walk up to the park and hike around here. It looks like a pretty day here in the city and it's good weather for walking. Not too hot, not too cold."

"No Mr. Hottie?"

"I don't think so. It's the weekend and I'm sure he's got things to do. What are you doing?"

"Oh I've got thrilling plans for the day."

"Do tell."

"Laundry."

"Oh wow, Hales, I envy you." Dru chuckled.

"I know you wish you could too."

"I do. I totally do. Well I'll let you get to it. Talk to you later . . . think about something fun to do next weekend."

"You sure you don't want to wait and see what Justin has in mind?"

"No . . . well . . . let's touch base later this week."

A short time later, Dru headed out of the cottage and debated passing through the house to see if Justin was around or heading to the park on her own. She picked up the latest book she'd bought and headed out to the park. She was barely at the end of the walk before she heard Justin call out to her.

"Drusilla! Where are you going?"

"Hi, Justin. Just to the park for a while. Did you need me to do something?"

"The park?" He glanced up the street. "Are you meeting anyone?"

"No. Just me and my book."

"Oh."

"You sure you don't need something?"

"No. I'm good. If you want later, if you aren't too tired, stop in for a coffee or something."

"Okay." She walked a few steps and turned. "Justin?"

"Drusilla?"

"Would you like to come with me? I'm not planning any-thing exciting . . . just hanging out and maybe read."

He smiled, that panty-dampening smile of his. "Let me grab my coat and a book myself." He turned, hurried back into the house and emerged a few minutes later with said coat and book.

Together they walked to the park, stopping along the way to pick up some lattes from an outdoor cart. Dru was sur-prised when Justin ordered the coffee and even more so when he took a swallow.

At least it looked like he drank some of it.

Not far inside the park they found a secluded area and sat down, leaning against one of the trees. For a few minutes Dru sat and simply enjoyed the nature around them. A few birds chirped, a squirrel ran by, stopping for a moment to gaze at them. Pigeons flocked until they realized there was no food to be had.

"This is nice," Dru told him.

"It is. You know, for as long as I've lived near the park I can't remember the last time I came here just to sit and relax."

"If you'd like my professional opinion as the assistant to an assistant, you work too hard. Way too hard."

"Maybe."

"You do. I know I've only worked for you about three months but seriously, every night I show up for work you're already at your desk typing away."

"Every night?"

"Okay, some nights I do get there before you, but I suspect you've been on the phone to New York or to Gabrielle where ever she is doing business. I see those faxes that come in after hours and I have no doubt you've already talked to the senders before they arrived. And I know a lot of nights you're at your desk after I've logged off."

"Hmmm. I never really thought about it."

"I suppose that happens when you really like your job. I know there's a lot of nights I lose track of time. But I take weekends off and I know you're in there a lot of Saturdays, at least, and working."

"That comes from being passionate about your work."

"This is really the first job I've had that I get to feeling that way — that I can go non-stop and lose track of time."

"If I remember your resume correctly, you've had one job?"

"Well, yeah . . . the bank. But for all the years I was there — I did start working part-time in the summers when I was in high school — I never felt like it was the be all and end all of jobs. I'd get in in the morning and immediately start counting down till morning break, then lunch, then the afternoon. I couldn't wait to leave at night."

"I haven't had that many jobs either — I started working for Gabrielle in high school — like you starting at the bank. I did some table waiting while in college but then it was right back to Gabrielle's."

"Did you always know you wanted to be in publishing?"

Justin considered her question. "I don't know if it was knowing I wanted to be in publishing or if it just felt right. I fell into working for Gabrielle. I was at odds what to do one summer and she offered me the chance to do some things for her. Mainly it was photocopying and transcribing some written notes. It grew from there."

"We had similar starts working, except I knew I didn't

want to work at the bank. I don't think it was just because my mother thought it was so great. To me . . . well I wanted something more creative. That's why I was attracted to theatre. It was a way to create, even if I was working behind the scenes. Actually that's why I liked doing the lighting. I could be completely behind the scenes and creating beautiful or dramatic impressions. Set design didn't appeal to me because it was structured, like costuming. You could design dresses and such, but they had to be true to period. With lighting it was like you could create a palette of your own choosing. You subtly set the mood by your choice of colors and intensity."

"So why publishing? Writers are like your costume and set designers, at least your historical ones are, but the strictures of the time."

"Yeeesss. But what I'm doing with you, for Gabrielle, that's all behind the scenes. It's making sure that the imagery is there, right? Well when I proofread anyway. And when I write the thank you notes or blog responses, I'm creating an illusion by pretending to be Gabrielle, right?"

"Is that what you do? Pretend to be Gabrielle?"

"Yeah . . . to a point. Is that wrong?"

Justin smiled, "No, not at all. You have a pretty solid grip in just who she is and what she would say. All that reading of her books has paid off in that respect. Now a question for you. Since you're reading Paula Gladstone there, are you looking for your next prospect?"

"No." She double-checked his grin. "Oh you. You know I'm not going to be looking for another job."

"Just checking."

"Uh huh. And you're reading Matt Meyers's latest thriller if I'm not mistaken. What does that say about your future prospects?"

"Just checking out the competition."

"Competition? What does a suspense thriller have to

compete with a historical romance?"

"Hmm, well, some of Gabrielle's heroes are secret agent types . . ."

"Right. Competition." She twisted the book to get a better look at the cover. "Is it good?"

"Yeah, it is. I've read all of his books. A guy can read just so much romance."

"I suppose." She tried to suppress a shiver and reached for her jacket.

"Are you getting cold?"

"Just a little. Actually I'm ready to head back any time you are."

"I'm ready."

Neither spoke walking back to the house. When Justin walked to the yard with her, Dru expected him to simply go in the back door. Instead, he walked her to the cottage. "Would you like to come in for a bit?"

Justin only nodded.

CHAPTER THIRTY-NINE

"Can I get you something to eat or drink?" Dru called from the kitchen. When she looked up Justin had followed her into the room.

"I always thought this kitchen was cozy. I like the one in the main house well enough, but there's something about this one, you know?"

"I have to agree. However, your housewarming gift *did* give it a bit of that modern touch and it's a modern touch I'll always been grateful for. It didn't take you long to get to know what I appreciate most."

"Your coffee? No." Justin sat, still not answering her about anything to drink. "You're pretty easy to get to know, Drusilla."

"Thanks . . . I think."

"It's definitely a compliment. I like it when I meet someone who what you see is what you get. And you're pretty easy to please too."

"Because of my lattes?" She chuckled.

"That. And just how you are. At the risk of sounding pushy, sometimes I feel like I've known you a long, long time."

And wasn't that the kind of statement a vampire would make?

Either a vampire or a romantic. Dru decided she'd take the romantic over the vampire any day.

Of course a romantic vampire . . . well in modern romance

novels, weren't they all?

Dru finished making her own drink and sat down at the table with Justin. "So answer me something if you would."

Justin momentarily looked concerned and then nodded. "Anything."

"Drusilla. Why do you call me Drusilla?"

"It's your name, right?"

"Yeah. No one has ever called me that. I can't think of anyone who has ever used my full name."

"Does it bother you?"

Dru considered his question before answering. "No, not really. It's just different, kind of old-fashioned."

Justin smiled, "I'm an old-fashioned kind of guy."

"That you are."

"And does that bother you?"

This time she didn't need to think about her answer, "Not at all. It's nice being around someone with manners and who is old-fashioned in some ways, ways that count. I kinda like that courtly side of you but I also like that you respect me as an intelligent woman who can make her own way."

"You are very intelligent and very good at what you do. We're very lucky to have found you. Or that you found us. I think placing that ad was the smartest move I've ever made."

"And pretty synchronistic that I picked that day to scan the jobs on that online site."

"You didn't regularly?"

"No. Actually once I started working at the bank, it never occurred to me to look for another job. What my mother decreed we all had to live with. It took awhile after she died for me to realize I could finally start living my life the way I wanted."

"We're glad you did . . . Drusilla."

Now she laughed. "You got me."

She wasn't entirely sure, but it seemed like he glanced at

her neck. "I hope so. Well, I should go. Has Vincent worn his welcome out yet?"

"Nope. I like having him here. I always wanted a cat and even though he's yours, it's kind of like having one with him here with me."

"Good. Then I won't drag him home with me."

They stood and Dru put her hand on Justin's arm. "I'm not keeping him from you, am I? He is your cat so if you want him home . . ."

"Ah you see, cats do not have owners, they have staff. He's clearly decided *you* are his staff of choice. As long as he's happy and safe, he can stay where he wants."

Dru wondered if perhaps Vincent might be Justin's familiar and reported her actions back to him and then tossed the idea aside. Witches have familiars, not vampires. At least according to the books she read. "Then we'll leave it to him to decide."

At the door Justin once again looked into her eyes before turning his gaze to her neck. "I had a good time today. It was nice to just hang out and read. Of course the company was great."

"I had fun too."

"Then we'll do it again sometime I hope."

Before Dru could answer, Justin dipped his head and once again quickly kissed her on the lips. But instead of lifting his head after the kiss he hovered there, a breath away from her as if debating something in his mind. A moment later he leaned closer and kissed her again, this time letting his lips linger on hers long enough for her to sigh and bring her hands to his shoulders. Justin tensed at the movement and when he realized she held on rather than push him away, he too brought his hands to her shoulders and pulled her closer. Only then did he lift his lips from hers and then rested his chin on the top of her head.

"Goodnight, Drusilla. I'll see you tomorrow."

Watching Justin once again walk down the garden path to the main house, it occurred to Dru that maybe it was time to have a talk about her future working for Gabrielle. Her attraction for Justin grew by the day — but the last thing she wanted was to lose her job if an initiated relationship wasn't what he wanted.

"Intimate my ass." She said to the door. "I'd jump his bones in a heartbeat if I knew I wouldn't lose my home and job."

Vincent meandered around her legs and meowed up at her. "You're right. He's the one making the moves. Still, I think we need to have a talk before too long."

Chapter Forty

As usual when she arrived for work Monday night, Justin was already in the office talking on the phone. "Great, Madeline, that sounds fantastic. Glad you like what we're doing with the series . . . right. Yes, things are going well . . . in fact she just came in . . . I'll tell her. Thanks, Madeline have a good evening."

Dru placed her coffee up on her desk and turned to Justin. "Gabrielle's agent?"

"Yes indeed. She liked what you did with that marketing package we sent in last week."

"I'm glad. Glad and relieved. That's the first time I've done anything like that."

"Well you did it like a pro. Madeline was impressed."

"Good. So what's on the agenda tonight or should I just keep on with proofreading the *His Helpless Damsel* manuscript?"

"Hmm, proofreading for now. We're coming up on a deadline in about six weeks and I want . . . Gabrielle wants it ready to go before then."

"You got it."

"But first."

Dru noticed Justin suddenly looked decidedly uncomfortable. *Here it comes.* "Yes?"

"Our relationship."

"Our relationship?"

"Or the lack thereof."

"Lack thereof?" And why was she repeating everything he

said only making his statements a question?

"I like you, Drusilla."

"I like you too, Justin."

"As more than . . . well I know we haven't known each other long. We haven't worked together that long and we've only socialized a few times but I think I can assess people pretty well. Even if I can't, I know what I like in a person. I know what I want in . . . well a friend. And I'm certainly babbling, aren't I?"

"Well, no. Not really. Okay. Yes, you are. I think there's something you want to tell me and you're kind of worried about how it's going to come out and how I'm going to take it."

"Oh, Drusilla, yes."

"Well let's start with something easy. Is my job in jeopardy?"

He looked totally stunned. "Absolutely not!"

"Good. And my home? Are you going to want me to move back to my house in Marin once we get that whole thing with the will settled?"

"No. Actually I'm hoping it goes the other way."

"What kind of other way?"

"Well I'm hoping that we can be more than friends. I'd like to be more than friends with you. If you'd like to be more than friends with me."

"You mean like dating?"

"That sounds bad, doesn't it? Man, I've just really screwed this up. I can write a great love scene, a first meeting between a hero and heroine but my own life I sure can mess it up."

"Um, I don't think you messed it up. If you're talking about how Gabrielle writes her heroes, well they're alpha males. They're in a different time period where things were done differently."

"Exactly."

"And back in those days, sure it was taboo for a governess to marry the master of the house, but that's what makes those romances so wonderful. Or at least part of what makes them so good to read. The everyday plain Jane type gets the prince, or at least the Marquis or Duke, right?"

"Right. And today we have to worry . . . I have to worry about sexual harassment and all that can entail. It's not that I don't meet women. Like I said the other day, I've done my fair share of dating, but I didn't really feel a connection with them. Not like . . . not like I feel with you."

"You feel a connection to me? A romantic connection?"

He ran his fingers through his hair and paced away from the desk. Turning, he answered, "Yeah. I feel like I've known you forever and that there is this romantic connection between us. Sounds crazy, huh?"

"No."

"No?"

Dru stood, walked over to him and reached for his hands. Holding them, she stepped closer and looked into his eyes. "I feel the same way and I've tried to hold back, way back because I don't want to mess up my job and lose it. Moving back into my house wouldn't be so bad. I love living in the cottage but if we started to date and you felt it wasn't such a good idea for me to live there, sure I'd move home. I really like you, Justin."

He blew out a relieved breath. "You know I've been trying to figure out how to have this conversation without ticking you off or making you feel uncomfortable the past month or so."

Dru chuckled. "No, actually I had no idea. I suppose that's because I was worried about the same thing. I didn't want you to think I was coming on to you and make things awkward."

Justin pulled her into his arms. "Oh man, Drusilla, you can come on to me anytime you want."

Before she could answer, he pulled her closer and lowered his lips to hers. This time instead of a chaste, brotherly kiss, his lips lingered a moment and then ever so tentatively stroked his tongue along the crease of hers. Dru sighed and parted her lips, sliding her tongue along the edge of his before welcoming him into her mouth.

To her surprise he tasted ever so slightly of coffee and mint. Maybe he did eat and drink . . . but it didn't matter. Nothing mattered but the incredible sensations running through her body. Her lips tingled, her heart raced, her knees felt weak and moisture rushed to the juncture between her legs. Being in his arms, kissing Justin, felt old and new, comfortable and exciting. It was everything she ever wanted and all she would ever need.

It felt right.

A long, torrid kiss later, Justin raised his head but didn't move his arms from around Dru's shoulders. He rested his forehead on hers and smiled. "That was nice."

"Nice?" Dru whispered back.

"Best I've ever had?"

She smiled. "I know it was for me."

"And you're okay with this?"

Dru leaned back. "You mean taking a kissing break in between work?"

"Well that and changing our relationship a bit. I'm not pushing you to do anything. It's all up to you. You set the pace but I would like us to be more than co-workers. I'm not saying we need to jump into bed or anything like that. I'd like us to, you know, date, do things together, share a good night kiss and then if, whenever, you want to move things to the next level . . . well you let me know. What are you smiling at?"

"You."

"Why?"

"Because now you really sound like one of the heroes in a

Gabrielle George historical romance. All proper and courteous. Don't get me wrong, I like it. You started out all nervous and then you let your emotions or at least your libido speak and . . . Justin, I do like kissing you."

"Glad you do. So should we give it a try?"

"You mean kissing or moving into a different kind of relationship?"

"Dating. I can promise you it won't change our working life. And if you ever feel uncomfortable, I promise you if you want to leave, I'll help you find another, even better job."

Dru's answer was to lean in and plant a light kiss on his lips. Her last thought before he took that kiss a step further was that maybe dreams do come true.

The world stopped spinning and at the same time Dru's turned into a kaleidoscope of color and emotion. From behind her closed lids, colors exploded into vivid blues, greens, pinks and purples. She forgot to breathe but she didn't need air. Oh no, she didn't need air, she needed this man. She needed Justin.

Beneath her fingers she stroked the softness of his hair where it crested his collar. It felt better than her imagination ever led her to believe. Her breasts rubbed against his own powerful chest. A thrill ran from the top of her head down to her toes when, in his own primal abandon, he rubbed his groin against hers. When Justin moaned in sheer need, she joined him with her own. Nothing had ever felt so good.

She cried out as if in pain when he raised his head and groaned low in her throat when his lips came to rest where her pulse beat in her neck.

Dru had kissed and been kissed by a few men. Mostly they were ones who took her out with Martha's approval. Mostly they were ones handpicked by her mother to date her. Every one of them practically put her to sleep. Not one kissed even half way as good as Justin. His kisses raised her temperature to a fever pitch and melted her with desire. From the gentle nips along her throat to the long lingering tasting of her neck, racing along her pulse points to the deep down heart stopping kisses they shared with tangling tongues, there was nothing in the world like kisses Justin Hunt.

She had to stop.

She couldn't stop.

They couldn't do this.

They couldn't not do this.

Every smile, every chuckle, every sigh at a particularly romantic scene in one of Gabrielle's books paled to what she felt in Justin's arms.

There was no life before him.

There was only now, here with him. Suddenly Justin was her world.

And how did that happen?

Easily enough—with each look, each smile, each moment spent with him.

Gradually, reluctantly, he raised his head but only to place his forehead against hers. "We need to stop," he whispered.

Of course they did. And now he'd tell her she couldn't work with him anymore and couldn't live in his home. "Okay."

Okay? Did she really just tell him it was okay to stop the earth moving beneath her feet, turning her world on end?

"If we don't, a few simple kisses won't be enough. At least not for me."

A few simple kisses? He thought the fireworks racing along her nerve endings were simple kisses? The man must have had some spectacular moments with other women. So why was he with her?

"I don't want to stop," Justin told her.

"We . . . that is . . ."

"I don't want to rush us. I think we have something

special."

"Oh, Justin, I do too."

"Then we need, I want, to keep it special. This isn't about sex. At least I don't feel what we have is about sex. We connect. I felt it the moment I met you. And now I sound like some junior high geek."

"No. Oh no, not at all. I feel the same way. I feel like we had a connection and that we . . . that is working with you . . . was meant to be."

He smiled, that smile that melted her heart. "Just working with me?"

Dru slid her hands up his arms, stopping just above his elbows, at the crest of his biceps. "Well, for starters."

Justin laughed. "I'm all for starters. But like I said, I don't want to rush things. I do, but I don't, know what I mean?"

"I think so. Your head says one step at a time but there's boy parts that like my girls parts, or they think they will."

"That sounds about right." With that, he pulled away from her only to take her hand and lead her over to the couch. That said, he turned to Dru and took her hands. "So how do we do this?"

"One day at a time?"

"Ah, I knew you were the perfect assistant."

"Why thank you. We can't let our dating get in the way of our work. So maybe we need to set some ground rules."

"I told Madeline you were the organized one." He kissed her quickly again. "Do we want to set them now?"

"I think that would be best. Or at least start to."

"Good. For starters I think we should keep this room, the office, for work. No hanky panky in here . . . but we can panky anywhere else in the house."

Dru giggled. "Maybe we should go into the kitchen to discuss the rest of those pankies?"

CHAPTER FORTY-ONE

While Dru brewed herself another coffee, Justin soberly asked her, "So what if I'm in the middle of a torrid love scene and need a little inspiration. Do I ask you to join me in the hall or kitchen or . . . bedroom . . . and I get inspired . . ."

She laughed. "Well, in that case, instead of losing your train of thought writing, we could do some hands on research. But wait a minute . . . what do you mean about writing love scenes?"

"Oh yeah, that." He didn't want to tell her. Not yet. He didn't want to mess things up just after they got straightened out. "Well sometimes I help out with writing the more intense scenes. You know, the modern um, things that are more open today that they didn't do back then but readers like reading today."

Dru poured her coffee into a cup and held the pot up to Justin who declined any. "That makes sense. Did I already know that?"

"Have you ever noticed a change in the voice, the writing in the manuscripts you've looked at? Or even the books the past few years?"

"No. Never. I guess you and Gabrielle have it down to a science."

Justin swallowed. "We try. So then, the only place we agree not to be . . . romantic . . . is in the office, right?"

"Right. Unless it's research."

"I think I might need a lot of research." Justin leaned over and planted another kiss on her lips.

"I'm all for good, solid, research."

"I can assure you it will be solid."

Dru giggled. "Bad boy."

"But a good bad boy, right?"

"Mmm hmm. Justin, you know I didn't set out to seduce you."

"I know. Trust me, I've had women blatantly throw themselves at me and that's not your style. I knew that from the moment we met. So we take it one step at a time, right?"

"Right. Justin, what about Gabrielle?"

"What do you mean?"

"Will she . . . mind about us?"

"Mind? Oh, no. She'll be happy for us. Trust me. She'll think it's awesome that her employees have made a connection."

"Good. That's good."

"Right." He studied their hands for a moment and then looked up at her. "One more kiss and then to work. Okay?"

Half way through the night, or their workday, Dru stood and stretched. "I need some more coffee, how about you?"

Justin looked up and smiled. "I'm good."

"Want anything to eat?"

"Not right now. Maybe later."

In the kitchen Dru pulled out the makings for her coffee and thought about their evening and what had happened earlier. From the moment they sat down to work after they agreed on the boundaries of their relationship, Justin had been focused on whatever he was doing on the computer. She'd gotten up and went over to the bookcase twice and he never even looked up. When she left to make another coffee for herself, he'd sat there, brow furrowed in concentration, completely absorbed in whatever was on his screen. Maybe someday she'd be that engrossed in something she was doing. If Justin was one thing, it was single-minded about his work.

So single-minded he never stopped to eat.

"And why am I so fixated on what the man does and doesn't eat?" she whispered to the coffee pot. "Great, now I'm talking to the coffee pot. And while I'm at it, he did eat at Ondine's and when he went to dinner with Haley and I. Well he slurped soup and some oysters. Well it doesn't matter, now does it? No. What matters is he's great to work with and he can kiss like no body's business."

Haley! She needed to tell Haley about this change in her relationship with Justin. But a part of her said no, it was new, new and special, and for now it was something to be kept near and dear.

Determined to put Justin's eating habits out of her mind, Dru walked back into the office and settled back down to the copy edits she'd been working on until the hall clock chimed five.

The sound seemed to startle Justin and sheepishly he looked over at her. "Sometimes I get so deep into what I'm doing, I kind of lose track of time and where I am."

"That's one of the things I like about you. Your focus. I wish I'd be that driven sometimes."

"As long as you don't feel neglected."

"No."

"Well the sun will be up soon. Time for me to hit the sack."

That was the first time he'd said anything so blatant about the sun and him needing to get to sleep. Maybe he was on the verge of opening up about that side of himself.

Dru turned back to her computer and with a sigh began to log off.

"You don't have to stop just because I am, you know?"

"I do. I'm at a good stopping point."

He glanced out the window and the slight lightening of the sky, "Me too." With a few hurried clicks, he booted down his computer and waited for Dru to join him at the doorway.

He walked her to the back door and Dru wondered if he would kiss her again. And if he did, would he then ask her to join him or go to the cottage or invite her upstairs? Or would he continue to play the part of the proper gentleman? He did say one step at a time but already she could see that wasn't going to be easy. At least not for her.

The hall clocked chimed the half hour. Quickly he bent his head and gave her a gentle kiss. "Till tonight. Sleep well."

With that, Justin whispered goodnight, turned and opened the door for Dru to leave. As she made her way to the cottage, she turned back to see him watching her, making sure she made it safely . . . not that there was anything to worry about in Gabrielle's yard. As much as she wanted to get up close and naked with Justin, it really was better to take it slow. At least that's what she told herself.

And wouldn't Martha have a fit knowing her plain and dull daughter was capable of such lascivious thoughts?

CHAPTER FORTY-TWO

Sleep did not come quickly or easily for Dru. Not that it was a bad thing with how she replayed every moment of that torrid kiss with Justin. It happened, didn't it? It really did happen and he did say they were going to be together, as a couple, right? And he kissed her goodnight. Just thinking about those kisses, even the staid and sober kiss goodnight at her door had her girl parts clenching and nipples tightening. When she'd read those phrases in her romance novels, it sounded farfetched. Having had it happen and then some . . . well those phrases didn't quite sum up just how good kissing Justin felt.

And how different from the men her mother approved of. Dru smiled to herself . . . what was his name? That really awful one Martha set her up with. "Gordon . . . Gross Gordon!"

It had been months since she thought about him. Not that he regularly went through her mind. Usually he'd pop up in there when something particularly wrong about Martha entered her mind. Martha and her human nature projects . . .

Okay so he wasn't really all that gross per say. He was nervous, nervous as a cat in a room full of rocking chairs and he was one of those men who when he got nervous perspired. Well actually, he sweat enough to fill a pond. He picked her up exactly on time and chatted up with her mother. They went to a movie. One of those mundane B movies with a tedious plot she promptly forgot. After he took her for a bite to eat and while he slurped a shake and scarfed up some potent garlic fries and a greasy burger, she had a fruit salad with cheese. She did her best to talk to him but he didn't seem to notice. In fact he droned on and on about his plans and work. Heaven knew where Martha had found him.

When he brought her home, she rushed out of the car. He tried to do the right thing and walk her to the door where she feigned a migraine and upset stomach. Gordon tried to kiss her and instead his lips landed on the wool hat she'd worn. Ducking her head, she hurried inside, called a quick goodnight to her mother and headed into her room.

Martha followed her, asking about her date. Feigning a sick headache, Dru assured her mother she just needed to get a good night's sleep and she'd be just fine.

As soon as her mother shut the door, Dru dove under the covers and with a flashlight under the blankets, lost herself in an escapist love story.

There'd be no hiding under the blankets to avoid Justin, that was for sure. And she certainly didn't need a book to capture her imagination when the real deal was but a few steps away.

With thoughts of Justin and their relationship moving to deeper levels, she fell asleep. No nocturnal or dawn awakenings as she dreamed of making love with Justin. When she woke, Dru found herself blushing at some of the things they'd done in her dreams.

That evening Justin greeted her at the back door with a smile and a kiss. He looked good enough to eat in his jeans and white fisherman's knit sweater. In the office he handed her some pages to read that left her blushing. He noticed her pinked cheeks from across the room as she read the pages and asked, "Is the sex in them a bit too much?"

"Did Ms. George send these?"

"Ms. George?" Justin's complexion paled for some reason. "Uh, no. Um . . ." He rose and walked over to her. He cleared his throat. "Remember when I told you that sometimes I, well, supplement her writing?"

"Yes."

"Those are mine. Did I go overboard?"

"No. I don't think so. I have to admit they're pretty hot. A lot hotter than anything I've seen in Gabrielle's books."

"Are you sure it isn't too much?"

"Well . . . like I said, it is more than I've seen in any of Gabrielle's books. I'm wondering though how would she feel if you wrote a book."

"Me?"

"Yes. This is good, Justin. I like it. Maybe that makes me sound kind of lascivious myself but a lot of my girlfriends eat this kind of story up. Oh, that's a bad analogy, isn't it?"

Justin laughed. "Actually it's pretty good. So tone it down for Gabrielle but if I were going to write, say under my own pen name, it's okay where it is?"

"I'd buy it. Man would I buy it. Yes. Justin, I think you should go for it."

"Maybe I will. On my own time, of course. If I do, would you be willing to be my beta reader?"

"And your research assistant?"

Over the next few weeks they fell into being a couple and by tacit agreement developed a comfortable pattern. They worked side by side, keeping things to business only in the office. Justin always arrived downstairs first and some nights Dru would hear him on the phone in the office either to New York or who she thought might be Gabrielle George. He'd join her in the kitchen while she made her coffee and pull her into an embrace and give her a delicious welcoming kiss. Justin would bring her up-to-date on whatever business transpired on the phone and then hand-in-hand they'd walk to the office.

Once inside the office they went to work. As usual, Dru

first tackled any snail or e-mail responses before digging in to proofreading the latest manuscript. Justin worked away at his computer. Working so close together, both of them on the same timetable, Dru didn't notice any more passages that sounded like her life. Whatever that had been about seemed to have ended. It was too bad in a way, she thought, because she wanted Emma, the character from the book, to have the same sort of happy ending Dru felt she was heading toward.

On weekends Justin would call at the cottage and they'd head off to the park or a museum. When he asked about getting together with Haley, Dru blushed and stammered, "I uh . . . she doesn't know."

"About us? You haven't told her?"

"No. Does that bother you?"

Justin shrugged. "No, should it?"

"No. I need to. I want to. I just don't want to hear anything negative or her to get all worried. She used to always be reminding me about what my mother would and wouldn't want but since Martha died, she's been better about it. And I didn't want you to feel pressured."

"I don't. I wouldn't. Maybe we should tell her together? Want to go up to Marin this weekend and hang out with her? We can check on your house and maybe talk about what you want to do about it now that my attorney has resolved the issue with the will."

"Hmm, I hadn't thought about that. Maybe. There's no rush to decide."

"Not at all. It's your house. I'm just glad he was able to resolve things so easily."

"I think he scared Armstrong. He was never the sharpest tool in the shed and since his first loyalty was to that church I think he messed up, bad, when it came to my mother's will. Yeah, I do need to check out the house. I'll call Haley and see when she's free. Maybe we can double with her and Ricky."

"I'd like that. Should be fun. Tell her to see what's going on, some music or something and where a good place to eat dinner would be."

"I will."

"Sure, that sounds great," Haley told Dru when she called to ask about a double date. "He seems to like you a lot."

"Yeah. I like him. A lot. Too."

"So you aren't worried about what happened to Gabrielle anymore? Or that he's a vampire?"

"N-n-no."

"You don't sound too sure."

"I am. Haley my life . . . I'm so happy. I didn't think it was possible for someone to be this happy. All because I answered an online ad for a job. I did kind of ask about Gabrielle and she's still in Europe and he goes out in daylight and eats . . . sort of. I think if he were, you know, a . . . you know, he would have taken a bite out of me by now."

"Well I'm glad you've put all that behind you. And I think you guys look cute together. It's time you had some happiness in your life. Real happiness."

"Thanks. So we'll see you Saturday about three at my old house?"

"Sounds good. See you then."

CHAPTER FORTY-THREE

"That was fun," Dru told Justin as they pulled away from her former house.

"It was. I haven't double dated in a long time."

"Me either." Dru chuckled. "I haven't either. My mother used to try to set me up with what she felt were acceptable guys, but I didn't view them as date, dates. Mostly I spent the evenings trying to figure out how I'd get away without having to touch them or worse, kiss them."

Justin looked over at her. The glow of oncoming headlights made him look mysterious in the darkly glowing interior of the Lamborghini. "Uh, you aren't much for kissing?"

"No, I wasn't much for kissing them. I like kissing you. A lot."

He blew out a breath with a smile. "That's good to hear because I like kissing you too."

Justin reached for her hand the same moment Dru reached for his. "It seems like we're almost always on the same page with each other."

"Great minds think alike."

Neither spoke the rest of the way home. Dru wondered if perhaps . . . hopefully . . . they were on the same page as to how their evening would end. A part of Dru told her it was too soon to move things to another level with Justin. Another part asked what did time have to do with happiness?

Justin held her hand walking her from the garage to the cottage. At the door he bent to give her a kiss. At first tentative when Dru moved deeper into his embrace, with a groan,

Justin deepened the kiss.

Dru slid her hands up his arms and rested them on his shoulders. Feeling his arousal against her belly, she slid her hips back and forth and was rewarded with Justin's groan of pleasure.

He pulled back and nipped at her lips.

Breathless Dru asked, "Do you want to come in?"

Justin rested his forehead against hers. "I do, but I'm not sure it's wise."

She slipped her hands from his shoulders, down his arms and around his back to cup his buttocks. "Am I being too forward?"

Justin gave her a light kiss. "No. I just don't want to rush you."

"You aren't rushing me. Am I rushing you?"

"I've wanted you since the night you interviewed."

"You have?"

Justin nodded.

"Well then I have to tell you, I've thought about getting up close and personal with you since then too . . . a lot."

"You're sure? Because once we share a bed, I don't think I'm going to want to sleep alone again."

"I hope we're going to do more than sleep."

Justin chuckled. "I'd like nothing better than for you to have your way with me."

Dru turned the door handle.

Justin pushed the door open.

Hand in hand with only the moonlight to guide them, they made their way to the bedroom. Eschewing a light, Dru picked up a box of matches and lit several of the candles sitting about the room.

As she lit the last one, Justin came and stood behind her, massaging her shoulders. "I've imagined making love to you by candlelight."

Dru blew out the match, set it down and turned in his arms. "I like your imagination."

Justin bent his head and kissed her. Without breaking the kiss, he stepped back and she followed to the bed. Dru reached up and unbuttoned his shirt.

He took the bottom of her sweater in his hands and raised it above her head.

She glanced up and gave him a tentative smile before leaning in and flicking her tongue against his nipple. His quick, indrawn breath encouraged her to explore further, so she traced a path to the other nipple before kissing and licking her way to his navel.

Justin tucked his hands into her hair and slid them through the silky strands. He reached for the button of her slacks and tugged them down her legs, while at the same time Dru did the same to him.

Dru chuckled softly. "I should have known you'd go commando."

"That please you?"

"It does." She reached around and squeezed his butt.

Justin reached over and pulled down the comforter lying on the bed. He backed Dru to the edge of the bed and she lay back, pulling him with her. Side by side, skin-to-skin they kissed each other while exploring the other with their hands.

Justin slid his hand between them and stroked her woman's folds. "You're so wet."

Dru kissed him and said, "I have a confession about that."

"What?"

"I'm always wet around you."

Justin groaned, shifted Dru to her back and with a pleasure-filled groan, slid inside her. Amidst the softly glowing candlelight they touched, kissed and let their bodies speak what words couldn't say.

As the last of the candles sputtered out, Dru shifted along

Justin's side. She studied him relaxed and in sleep. If he were a hero in one of Gabrielle's books, the heroine would see him as being unguarded in sleep. Unable to help herself, she traced the curve of his pec, her finger coming to rest on the tip of his nipple.

Justin turned his head and raised a lid. He smiled and shifted to give her better access to his chest. "That feels nice."

"It does. I like touching you."

"I'm glad because I like being touched by you." Justin gave her a quick kiss. "No regrets?"

"None at all."

"Good. I don't think I could have waited much longer."

Dru giggled softly. "Me either." She lifted her hand from his chest and momentarily covered her mouth. "I think I'm not supposed to admit that."

"I like that you admit it. Now we have to decide . . ."

"Decide?"

"Do we continue live apart or do you move into the main house with me?"

That was indeed a question to consider. If she moved into the house would she be tempted, too tempted, to poke around and see what she could find? What if she found a coffin or other objects that would lead to proving Justin was a vampire? And what if he was? Would it really make a difference? She already lived in his world.

Dru finally answered him with a non-answer, "Why don't we take it one day at a time and see where it leads us for now?"

"As ever, you are the wise one. But you're going to have to tell me if you want a night . . . day . . . home alone because I have a feeling I'm going to want to be with you as much as possible."

"But we still keep work at work. Right?"

Justin looked at her with a put upon, long-suffering look.

"I suppose I can do that."

Dru smiled. "You'll just have to soldier on."

"Mmm."

Monday night Justin greeted her with a long, lingering kiss when she arrived for work. Determined to be as professional as possible, the twosome went to their desks and set to their respective tasks. Dru seemed to sense whenever Justin was looking her way because every time she looked up, he was gazing in her direction. Either that or he hadn't been doing any work and had spent the evening studying her.

When the clock struck four, Justin immediately rose and went to her desk. His voice gruff with desire, he said, "Can I persuade you to spend the day here?"

"You could."

He took her hand and guided her to the door and up the stairs. Dru felt a thrill of anticipation at seeing the upper floors of the Victorian. Despite her imagining what lay above stairs, the reality was so much better.

The floors were a highly polished wood with colorful Oriental runners down the middle of the hallways. An occasional table dotted the side of the walls, each with flowers or a stout white candle in a heavy silver or pewter holder. A book, a collectible looking hardback sat on a few of the tables. It was, as she had said before, a very proper Victorian mansion—just without a lot of the clutter she'd seen in photographs.

Justin led her down the hall of the second floor. Dru caught only a glimpse of the third floor and a bit of the stairs leading to the garret of the fourth. He stopped at the doorway to his room. From the threshold, Dru took in the heavily masculine room.

The bureau, dresser and night tables were heavy dark woods. As with the rest of the house, candles sat on the night tables. One side had a stack of books and a clock. The other a pad, pen and antique looking phone.

Light switches were carefully hidden in intricate silver wall ornaments.

There was not a coffin to be scene.

Nor were there any mirrors in the room.

Justin pointed out the en suite bathroom . . . which did have a mirror over the sink. There were minimal objects on the counter — a toothbrush, comb, razor. Clearly a bachelor lived in this room.

Which pleased Dru to no end because it meant he hadn't been sharing the space with another woman . . . at least she thought that's what it meant.

But really, no women had called or come by since she'd started working for Gabrielle and none had shown up since she'd moved into the cottage. Now it remained to be seen if this was a one-night stand or if she'd be spending more nights in Justin's room.

Before Dru could say a word, Justin pulled her into his arms and lowered his head to kiss her. A long, slow, kiss later they made their way to the bed.

The next morning, Justin held her close. "Well, we've tried your bed and now we've tried mine. There's a room adjoining mine if you're inclined to moving in here."

"Separate rooms?"

Justin quirked a brow. "Nooo, yes, sort of. A room for you to hang your hat and we sleep where we happen to end up?"

"Mmm. So are we still taking things slow?"

"Maybe." He toyed with a stray thread on the black velvet comforter.

Dru kissed his shoulder.

"Slow isn't bad . . ."

"I'm sensing a but in there?"

"Are you now?"

"Mmm hmm."

"Do you want to take it slow . . . still?"

Dru blew out a breath. "I'm not looking for a sprint."

Justin shifted to face her. "Neither am I. We have crossed a line."

"That we have. Are you . . . are you okay with it?"

He smiled. "More than okay. Drusilla, you know the moment I saw you I knew I wanted to know you. I felt a connection."

She nodded.

"So . . . do we treat this as a one-time thing or do we take it to the next level?"

"You mean like moving in together?"

"Something like that."

Dru considered his words. Glad he sat quietly beside her, doing nothing more than toying with her fingers. A gust of wind rattled the windowpanes ever so slightly. A creak sounded in the hallway. Could she live in this house with all its strange events? The figurines falling for no reason at all? The creaks when no one walked by? Justin's habits?

A light rain, one not mentioned in the weather reports pattered against the windows. The metallic gray of the sky peeking through as day turned to night.

"Justin? I'm thinking for a bit maybe I should stay in the cottage and we can . . . visit?"

"Visit? Is that what we did last night?"

"Hmmm, I think so."

He shifted, so they lay side by side. "Then I'm thinking maybe I should visit you again right now."

"I like the way you visit." Dru giggled while she scooted down in the blankets and cuddled against Justin.

"Do you now?"

She nodded. "But I'm thinking we should be getting downstairs to work soon."

Justin looked toward the window and at the dark sky

beyond. The light rain had turned into a full-blown storm over the past few hours. "I think we deserve a night off."

"Gabrielle won't mind?"

"She'd think it was good romance."

"Well then, if the queen of romance says that it must be true."

Two nights later, Justin suggested she move in.

Dru demurred.

Justin promised her her own room.

A few hours later, Dru hung up the last of her dresses in the closet in the room she'd moved in to, musing on how much her life had changed in the past few months.

In the en suite bathroom she arranged her comb, brush and toiletries before taking a quick glance in the mirror. Musing while she turned her head side to side, making note that her neck was as smooth and unblemished as ever, she wondered again if she was being fanciful that Justin was a vampire or if perhaps now that she was living under the same room with him, if now he would bite her.

Or was her imagination just running wild?

With a shrug, she turned out the light and headed through the bedroom and down the stairs. So what if he was a creature of the night. Did it really matter? They were not all that different than some of Gabrielle's heroes and heroines — two people wildly attracted to each other but for at least the appearance of propriety, keeping separate rooms. Not that anyone would know or even care.

A few nights later after sitting and staring into space for a while, Justin stood and came over to Dru's desk. As was his habit when he'd venture over to her desk, he leaned a hip on the edge and toyed with a pen, collecting his thoughts.

Dru looked up at him expectantly.

He swallowed and finally asked, "Can I tell you a secret?"

"Of course." Whatever he had to say couldn't be that bad,

could it?

"I . . . I've been . . . well I've been trying my hand at writing myself."

"You have?" It wasn't quite what Dru expected him to say. But they were in work mode so what else would he want to talk about?

Justin nodded.

"That . . . that's wonderful. And this is it?"

He nodded again.

"I . . . wow . . . I . . ."

"I was wondering if you'd read it and let me know what you think. What you honestly think?"

"Oh, Justin. I'm happy to. Seriously? You want my opinion?"

"I do. If you don't mind."

"No, not at all. I look forward to it."

Dru settled in with the pages Justin had given her. Within minutes though, she began to feel decidedly uncomfortable. The few times she'd looked over what Justin had written—those times when she'd come across what she thought was Gabrielle's story on his computer, she had a strong sense of it being based, in part, on her life. This though . . . it felt like an invasion into her deepest, most private thoughts. Uneasily, she glanced up to see Justin frantically looking through papers on his desk. Methodically he pulled out each drawer and shuffled through the papers in one, before turning to the next. In between, he flipped through papers on his desk. He grabbed the computer mouse and after a few clicks, resumed looking through the drawers even though he'd already looked through each one.

Frustrated, he combed his fingers through his hair, completely oblivious to the woman sitting stunned and bordering on frightened across the room. This was more than thinking he might take a bite out of her or that he lived on another human's blood. This felt somehow sinister and frightening — and not good, gothic scary.

She swallowed and tried to keep her hands from shaking. She glanced at the door, trying to figure out if she could make it out the door, up to her room, get her car keys and get away from the man who seemed to be taking her life and making it into a story — a scary story.

Of course he'd be on her before she was out the door. And then where would she be? No, she needed to plot and plan and quietly make her escape.

A moment later, he turned and began to pull out files on the credenza behind him. Apparently not finding what he wanted, he finally looked over at Dru.

From the look on his face, she had no doubt her own fears and concerns showed so plainly on her face. He knew she knew. He knew she'd figured it out and now she was going to have to fight for her very existence. She started to rise but couldn't find the strength to move out of the chair.

Dru swallowed. She could be brave. She had survived worse than what was coming and really, would living pretty much forever with a guy like Justin be that bad? He might get tired of her or decide he wanted someone else, but then she might too. In the books his kind — vampires — were generally mated for life. Not that those authors who wrote about them knew for sure . . . or did they? Maybe many of those authors who wrote about vampires and other creatures knew the truth about them because they were vampires and hid that truth in the guise of fiction.

Justin rose and slowly made his way across the room to her desk. He stood before her and looked down at the pages that she still held in her hands.

"Drusilla, what you have . . . I gave you the wrong pages."

"Really?" Was that really her voice squeaking so badly?

"They . . . there was something else, another book . . ."

"Are you sure it wasn't a Freudian slip and you really wanted me to know? That this was your way of telling me?"

"Telling you what?"

"About you."

He looked confused. His gaze fixed on the papers, he began to reach for them and then pulled his hand back as if they would burn him. "Tell me you didn't read them."

"Justin, I read them. They are . . . good. It's um . . . interesting."

He drew in a breath and again ran his fingers through his hair. "It was a mistake. They weren't meant . . . Drusilla . . ."

Dru put the pages on the desk, on the far side from where Justin stood. Then stood and gently laid her hand on his arm. "Justin, I already knew. At least I suspected. It's okay, really, it's okay."

"Do you mean that?" He stopped and considered her words. "Dru, what did you suspect?"

"Why, about you. What you are. And it's okay."

"What I am?"

"Yes."

"What do you think I am?" He looked genuinely confused.

She smiled. "Do you need me to say the words?"

Confusion settled in his gaze. His brow furrowed. "That might be helpful."

"I know about why you work at night. Why you don't eat. And it's okay if you want to turn me."

"Turn you?"

"Yes, turn me. You know? If you want a forever kind of thing . . . turn me. If you don't, well that's okay. You don't have to worry I'll give away your secret or anything like that."

From the look on his face, he clearly thought she'd lost her mind. It occurred to Dru that maybe she should politely excuse herself and leave, permanently. Either that or cut to the chase. "The vampire thing."

"Vampire . . . Dru! You think I'm a vampire?"

"Aren't you?"

He chuckled, a deep rumble in his chest. Then entwined his fingers with hers and kissed the tips. "No. I'm not a vampire."

"Then why . . ."

He started to laugh and abruptly stopped when he saw how serious she was. "Oh, Drusilla, I'm sorry. I am so sorry. I meant it when I said I work better at night. While this is a pretty peaceful neighborhood, during the day, even with double pane windows, you can still hear cars going by and kids playing outside. There are still cars passing at night, but not like the daytime. When it's still, I can focus better. And, I . . . we write historical romance. The time periods I write in, they didn't have cars and busses and electricity and all the other modern accoutrements. It helps me to set the scenes I'm writing or rather working on for Gabrielle. To have them more or less existing around me."

"*You* write historical romance?"

"I . . ."

"You said 'I', several times. You said 'I write romance.'"

She tried to pull her hands from his but he held on tight. In a bid to get him to let go, she pulled a little harder and said, "Justin, you just said you write historical romance. Where is Gabrielle George? What about her? Is this all some sort of con you've been running? Or is she dead?"

Justin's eyes opened wide.

Dru shuddered and leaned away from him in her chair, realizing that if he had in fact killed Gabrielle it wouldn't be a stretch for him to kill her too.

"Gabrielle, well she . . ."

Before he could finish or explain about Gabrielle, wanting to keep him from focusing on the Gabrielle being dead part, she cut him off, "You don't eat."

"I do."

"No. You don't. I've never seen you eat. And, and the cottage . . . it's haunted. Or you used a secret passage to come in and . . . and . . ."

"I wear Invisiliners, you know, braces. They're a pain in the butt, but better than the metal braces. I eat, brush my teeth and put them in again. I didn't want to gross you out when I took them off, so I took my meals when you weren't around. And the cottage . . . this is an old house and that building is just as old. The sounds you hear? It's just the structure settling. There's no secret passage, I promise. When the wind picks up it can sound like an old haunted house, but it isn't."

"Invisiliners? Seriously?" She peered at his mouth.

Seeing she didn't believe him, Justin released her hands, turned slightly away from her. In the old television shows that's what the vampires did before they bit someone. Well they did it to put in the fake vampire teeth but maybe real ones did it too so that regular humans wouldn't see their fangs come out.

She watched as he raised his hands and turned while quickly rubbing his handkerchief over what he held in them. When he finished with the cloth, he held out his hand. "Invisiliners. They are like braces but don't show. You take them out to eat so they aren't as painful or invasive as braces."

"You wear braces." Dru sat down and shook her head. "Man, do I feel stupid. But what about Gabrielle George? Do I work for her? Is she real or did you make it up that you work for her?"

He glanced around the room as if making sure no one else was around. "I'll let you in on the secret. But you can't tell anyone. Not ever."

"I won't say a word." She had no idea what he was talking about but in that instant she knew she'd do anything for Justin. Even if he was crazy, she would stand by him. Even if he killed the famous author, something told her she'd still stand by her man.

"I'm Gabrielle George."

"You're . . . of course you are. Right." Yeah, she'd do anything for him but give into some bizarre fantasy. "Justin, vampires I can handle. But you thinking you are one of the most famous and well-loved romance writers? No how, no way. You're joking, right?"

"No joke. For real. I'm Gabrielle George. Well, not Gabrielle in the flesh. Gabrielle George is my grandmother. She lives up in Sonoma in a great board and care. She came to a point where she wanted to give up writing and just enjoy life. Sometimes she sends me story lines and I turn to her for help if I get stuck on a scene or need help with some research, but we talked about it a few years ago and I stepped into her shoes. Anything of hers you've read in the past four years is me. That's why we, our agent and editor, made such a big deal of the reclusive lifestyle. Readers have an image of Gabrielle George in their mind and to continue her voice, I write in her stead."

"Justin, no offense to your grandmother, but you definitely feed my imagination and not just in books."

"And you do mine. If I haven't said so before, my love scenes are increasingly electric since you've been in my life and my bed. My agent and editor are beyond thrilled at some of the scenes I've written. In fact, since you've moved in and we've . . . you know . . . my writing has gotten a lot hotter. My agent suggested we come up with a pen name so that I can write the steamier stuff while still preserving Gabrielle's aura." He placed a kiss on her forehead before resting his own on it.

"And when you tire of me?"

"Tire of you? Drusilla, I've waited a lifetime to find you. A dozen lifetimes would have to pass before my feelings for you could even begin to fade. I meant it when I knew the moment I saw you that you were the one I've been waiting for."

Chapter Forty-four

They married four months later — in broad daylight — beneath the arbor in the Victorian's backyard. Gabrielle came to the wedding, her pleasure at Justin's choice of bride evident in every look and word.

She laughed with sheer pleasure when Dru told her about her image in the window. In a quiet moment with her favorite author . . . well second favorite, now that she was married to her absolute favorite . . . Dru told her how, before she moved in, she would look up to try to see her every night when I came to work.

Gabrielle explained it was a cardboard cutout they'd used to advertise for her signings when she was younger. "It was one of the memories of my time gone by."

"Well I had fun looking up and thinking it was you. But not as much as meeting you in person."

"My grandson waited a long time for the right girl and I am so happy he finally found her."

"I hope so."

"I know so. When he you first started working for him, I had a feeling and here you are, my granddaughter!"

When the last of their guests left, Dru took a few minutes by herself to freshen up before joining Justin for their wedding night. She stood before the full-length mirror that sat in her room on the second floor and studied the woman she saw standing there. Gone was the mousy, timid bank teller who quaked at her mother's slightest word. She was free. Once and for all she was free because she had the one thing Martha never had—someone to love. Martha never opened her heart up to anyone. She came from such a place of lack and fright she was incapable of truly loving another person.

She saw Justin's reflection when he came to her room a short time later. Dru smiled to herself . . . Justin's reflection. He'd laughed when she first told him he never looked in a mirror. It was simple he told her. "This is going to sound overly vain, but I have enough people stop and take a second look at me that I figured I don't need to see what they're seeing. I just didn't need to be looking at myself all the time."

The days before their wedding he busied himself on the third floor. With her promise that she wouldn't look, he set about doing something special for her up there. Now he took her hand and led her up the stairs to the third floor.

"I wanted our wedding night to be special," he told her at the top of the stairs before leading her to the turret room.

Outside the door a trail of rose petals began and they led them to the large four-poster bed. The white lace canopy had flowers holding back the sheer white drapes and more petals adorned the bed. Candles illuminated the room. A shiny silver bucket stood on a tripod near the bed holding a bottle. Justin pulled her into his arms and gave her a light kiss. Then he held her, his chin resting on her head. With a contented sigh, he told her, "Drusilla, I love you. I love you more than I thought I could ever love another person."

Before she could speak, he leaned back so he could look down into her face. His gaze took in her eyes, her cheeks and then lingered a moment on her lips before bending to give her a kiss. This one was deep and filled with toe curling passion. He ended it only a moment so he could turn her so her back faced him and with tantalizing slowness, undid the satin covered buttons of her satin Victorian gown. He slid the dress off her shoulders and down her hips. To Dru's delight, he fumbled with the stays of the corset she'd worn as part of the period gown.

She turned back to him as the corset slid to the floor and began to work on the buttons of his shirt.

Suddenly impatient, he reached for the button of his trousers and when it slid open, he reached for the zipper. While Dru pealed his shirt down his arms, Justin shimmied out of his pants. She undid the garters of her stockings, while he pulled off his socks.

He reached for her and slowly backed her to the bed. "I love you, Drusilla Hunt."

"And I love you, Justin Hunt."

About the Author

From earliest childhood Regan was an avid reader and upon discovering Alexander Dumas and Charles Dickens she was hooked on books that carried the reader away to a different time and place. Preferring the quiet of her room and a good book to spending time with people she traveled far beyond those four walls.

It was while working as a police dispatcher, first for the California Highway Patrol and then her local police department, she began to write fiction, primarily time travels and romantic suspense. In the spring of 2009 she returned to the day job she always liked best, working as a legal secretary. Although, curled up in her bunny slippers with her furfaced children, Missy, Lulu and Ollie, while writing is one of her most favorite things to do.

www.ingramcontent.com/pod-product-compliance
Lightning Source LLC
Chambersburg PA
CBHW061547170626
46811CB00001B/117